A CONSPIRACY OF SILENCE

ANNA LEGAT

ACCENT

First published in 2020 by Headline Accent
An imprint of HEADLINE PUBLISHING GROUP

1

Cataloguing in Publication Data is available from the British Library

ISBN 978 1 7861 5976 2

Typeset in 10.5/13pt Bembo Std by Jouve (UK), Milton Keynes

Printed and bound in Great Britain by Clays Ltd, Elcograf S.p.A.

FSC
MIX
Paper from
responsible sources
FSC® C104740
www.fsc.org

HEADLINE PUBLISHING GROUP
An Hachette UK Company
Carmelite House
50 Victoria Embankment
London EC4Y 0DZ

www.headline.co.uk
www.hachette.co.uk

PART ONE

Ring–a–ring o' roses

PART ONE

Chapter One

Sarah Snyder was waiting in her car. She tapped her blue finger-nails in close proximity to the horn, but she held back from sounding it. To kill time, she checked her lipstick in the rear-view mirror and rubbed her front teeth to remove a red smudge. She turned on the radio only to hear the part of the news she wasn't interested in: sport, followed by the weather. She was restless but she was pleased: Rachel was taking her sweet time.

Rachel was chatting to her friends – Rhiannon and a couple of other girls. Only once did she steal a glance in the direction of her mother's car – just to check Sarah was there, waiting. Reassured, she turned back to her chums and whispered something into Rhiannon's ear. Whatever she said, it made Rhiannon laugh.

Rachel laughed too. It was an immeasurable relief to see her child happy, having a conversation with other people, and laugh-ing. She was laughing! Sarah was so relieved she wanted to cry.

Only three days ago the picture had been very different. Head down, eyes boring a hole in the ground, Rachel would clutch her bag to her chest and run for the car as if the hounds of hell were after her. She would slump in her seat and mutter under her breath, *Drive, Mum, just drive,* and not speak for the rest of the day. She would lock herself in her room and brood.

Sarah winced at the memory and pushed it out of her mind. She waited and counted her blessings, of which there were many. She decided she would cancel the GP appointment. There was nothing wrong with Rachel, just the usual growing pains of puberty.

At last Rachel parted company with her friends, waved to someone hidden inside the school, and headed for the car. Her face, still beaming and full of bounce, appeared in the wound-down window.

'Hi, Mum.'

'I take it you had a good day?' Sarah pulled her sunglasses to the tip of her nose and produced an expectant grin.

Rachel made a non-committal noise. She pecked her mother on the cheek and slid into the passenger seat. She was still smiling, addressing her smile to the windscreen and to the view of the tarmac in front of the car, but that was enough for her mother to flick her sunglasses up her nose and start the engine.

'That good!'

The front right wheel stumbled over the kerb while the rear one rubbed against it as the car lurched sharply across the road to join the line of traffic leaving the school. Were it not a big and sturdy four-wheel-drive, it would have been written off a long time ago. Sarah did not treat it well. She used it more like a bulldozer than a means of transportation.

Accustomed to her mother's driving antics, Rachel didn't as much as blink. She bent forward in her seat and began tampering with the radio in search of a music channel. She tuned into the charts – Ed Sheeran was at number six.

Sarah decided to talk over Ed Sheeran. 'We can go shopping if you like.'

'Are you feeling generous?' Rachel was saving every penny for the Jerusalem trip in the summer.

'I might be.'

'OK. If you insist.'

'Cheeky beggar!'

Rachel sat back and relaxed her shoulders. She rolled her head to the right and, again, she smiled, 'Thanks, Mum.'

'Retail therapy is what we both need.' Her mother peered at her in that heart-melting way of hers. She leaned forward to pat Rachel's knee. 'That's my girl . . .'

With her eyes on Rachel and only one hand on the steering wheel, she was all over the road. The car veered in and out of the oncoming traffic. A white van sounded its horn, emitting an angry warning shot.

'Mum, watch where you're going!'

Sarah swiftly recovered control of the car and neatly swerved back to her own side of the road. She glared in the rear-view mirror, shooting daggers in the direction of the white van driver. 'There should be fines for road rage, and three points on their licence.'

'It was entirely your fault.'

'Whose side are you on?' Sarah mimicked a hurt look. 'Anyway, let's not split hairs. I'm so glad to have you back.'

'Back? I haven't gone anywhere.'

'Oh, but you have! There was a time when I thought we'd lost you. Dad and I —' An anxious sigh trembled in her throat. 'It was as if this stranger had moved in with us. We didn't know what to make of you. It was that boy, wasn't it? Did the two of you —'

'Mum, stop prying.'

'So it was him?'

'I've no idea what you're talking about.'

'Well, whatever it was, I'm glad it's behind us.'

'It was nothing,' Rachel muttered.

'I guess it was. But you pushed us to the limit. We didn't know what to do. I mean, how do you deal with teenage angst?'

'I don't know.'

It was true. Whatever it was it had consumed Rachel. She hadn't known what to do either. A heavy and malignant weight had crushed her chest, preventing her from breathing. It had nearly killed her. But it was over now — she had put it behind her.

Her mother punched the horn and held her hand down, piercing the air with sharp decibels. 'Look where you're going, arsehole!' she screamed at the car that had zoomed from a side road and cut in front of them.

'Didn't you mention fines for road rage?' Rachel enquired with a wry smile.

'Idiot!' Sarah dispatched a final, curt bark to the offending driver in front.

'And three points on the licence?'

'I had every intention of letting him in. If only he'd waited his turn. All it takes is a bit of patience and common courtesy.'

All it had taken Rachel was a deep breath and the press of a button: DELETE. Three days ago, finally, Rachel had erased all her online profiles. And once they were gone, it had stopped. The weight had lifted from her chest. Give or take another few days and she would convince herself that it had never happened.

'I'm exhausted!' Sarah puffed out her cheeks to illustrate the extent of her exhaustion. 'Shopping does it to me. It's all about the choices I can never make . . . Give me hard labour any day.'

They were queuing at the counter in Costa.

'You didn't have to make any choices,' Rachel pointed out. She was the one laden with shopping bags.

'I was supervising your choices – that does it to me. I'm still unsure about those hot pants. I could see your bum cheeks when you bent down.'

'Josh'll like them –' Rachel spoke without thinking. She bit her tongue, but it was too late to stop her mother. She was going to have a field day with that nugget.

And she did. 'So you *are* still together?'

'On and off.'

'How can you be on-and-off serious about a boy?'

'I didn't say I was serious, did I?'

'You brought him home to meet us. That used to be considered serious when I was young. I didn't bring your dad home until after –' Sarah screwed up her face in comic dismay and waved her hand over her lips.

'After what?' Rachel twisted the knife in her mother's deeply compromised propriety.

Sarah was saved by the barista. 'What can I get you, ma'am?'

★

6

Her mother was lapping the cream off her skinny caramel latte deluxe. God alone knew why she would have it skinny while at the same time demanding all that extra cream and swirls of caramel. Not to mention the flapjack. That was apparently a healthy option, with its fibre-rich oats and dried fruits. According to the gospel of Mother. She swore by its benefits, though none of them were apparent to the naked eye because, in her own words, Sarah Snyder was *on the cuddly side*. Rachel had inherited her mother's curves, but had lost most of them in the last two months. She was now working on reinstating them by indulging in a Crunchie milkshake. Josh liked her with a bit of meat on the bone, which was a phrase Rachel had borrowed from her father. He liked her mother the same way.

Rachel hoovered the depths of her plastic cup with her straw and moved onto the chocolate brownie.

'So, like I was saying,' she carried on in reply to her mother's persistent calls for clarification, 'you can be a couple, and that's like permanent. For the time being, of course –'

'Isn't that an oxymoron?' Her mother licked the cream from her lips.

'What is?'

'Permanent for the time being.'

'Well, that's how it is. Do you want to know, or not?'

'Yes, yes . . . go on.'

'Then you can be on-and-off, like Josh and me.'

'Right . . .'

'And then there are different variants of non-committal –'

'As in casual sex?' Her mother's eyes became rounded with alarm. 'I hope you're using protection . . . And did you know that at fifteen you're technically a minor and having sex with a minor is technically rape . . .'

'I didn't say Josh and I were having sex – technically.'

'You didn't have to say it. I'm just watching out for you.'

'OK, whatever . . .' Rachel slouched back in her chair and folded her arms over her chest.

7

'So . . . are you?'

'I'm not answering that! And I'm almost sixteen!'

'Then I'll have to draw my own conclusions.' Sarah's gaze bored into Rachel, her curiosity defeating her gluttony: her flapjack remained untouched.

Rachel laughed. 'Then go ahead – knock yourself out with *your own conclusions!*'

'You'll drive me to an early grave, you know that?' Sarah sighed heavily, but it was too theatrical to be believed. It was just Mum – the clown, the drama queen, the spy extraordinaire.

'So?'

'So . . .' Rachel rolled her eyes, 'we're not sleeping together. At least, not in the conventional sense.'

'And that means what exactly?'

'It means that I'm not stupid, OK?'

'I wouldn't be so sure.'

Rachel's phone went off, its lively ringtone making her jump. Her first reaction was to ignore it. It was safer to pretend she had not heard it. She stubbornly looked out of the window. Her hands folded into fists in her lap.

'Aren't you going to answer that?'

'What?'

'Your phone. It bleeped.'

'It's just a text. Probably Rhiannon.'

'OK,' her mother nodded, looking unconvinced. 'Are you going to read it, then?'

'I suppose I'd better.'

She whipped the phone out of her pocket and checked the sender. 'Yeah, Rhiannon. We're doing this soil erosion project for geography. Rhiannon's keen!'

'Didn't you say she fancied Mr Hatson?'

'Don't ever say that to her face, Mum! She'd kill me if she knew I told you.'

'Who do you take me for? Discretion is my middle name.'

'Hardly!'

Rachel braced herself – of course, it was nothing: gossip or homework. She opened the text message. It contained three unequivocal letters *WTF*, followed by *U @it again,* a question-exclamation mark combo – and a link. She clicked on the link and her face turned ashen. She quickly pushed her phone deep in her pocket. Her mother gazed at her.

'Hurry up, Mum.' Rachel growled.

'Oh dear, aren't we in a mood! Teenage angst?'

Rachel's phone tinkled away in her pocket relentlessly, announcing a barrage of messages.

'What's going on?' Her mother's tone sobered. She sounded alarmed rather than just nosy. Her eyes narrowed and scrutinised her daughter's face as the girl bit her bottom lip and furrowed her forehead. 'Well?'

'It's Rhiannon. I told you, it's our geography homework. Let's go. Are you done?'

'What's the rush all of a sudden? I haven't finished my flapjack.'

'Best you don't. I'm doing you a favour.'

'What is that supposed to mean?'

'Nothing. I need to go. And get started on it, OK?'

'Right this very minute?'

Rachel glared at her mother. 'Yes. Right now.'

'Let me just –'

Another ping on Rachel's phone provided a welcome distraction. This time she pulled it out and read the message. It was from Josh.

It had been a while since she had a text from him. This morning he had brushed by her in the cafeteria. It could have been by accident, but somehow it felt deliberate. Her heart had skipped a beat. She had bought the frayed hot pants, hoping that –

She was such an idiot!

She gawped at the unopened text message with Josh's face next to it, looking back at her. It was a face one could easily fall in love with; with its soft contours and honest gaze, it seemed to be assuring her that he loved her back.

9

He may have not seen the Snapchat stream.

Rachel's finger hovered over the button briefly. She had eleven messages. She inhaled deeply like someone who was about to jump naked into freezing water. She clenched her teeth and opened the latest text to see a string of grinning emoticons and the words: *Am enjoying ur Snappy output.* Rachel's hands closed over the screen of her phone as she pushed it between her thighs to mute its sound. She shut her eyes.

'Are you all right, Rachel?' Her mother's voice was gripped with tight anxiety.

'It's Rhiannon. How many times must you ask!' she snapped.

'I didn't . . .'

'Please, Mum, stop asking me stupid questions.'

Sarah watched as her daughter dropped her shopping bags in the hallway and took off to her bedroom. She recoiled when the bedroom door was slammed. She tiptoed up the stairs, one at a time, not to make any noise, and put her ear to the door. A groan of the bed as Rachel collapsed on it interrupted the relentless pounding of Sarah's own heart. She could swear she heard Rachel whisper, 'Oh, God! No, please, no!'

There were more bleeps on her phone, then a crash and clank, followed by a muffled sob.

Sarah pressed her eye to the keyhole. Her daughter was rocking on her bed, her forefinger sliding across the screen of her iPad. Her cheeks were burning red. She looked ill. Perhaps Sarah should keep that GP's appointment after all.

'Rachel, are you all right in there?' Sarah spoke into the keyhole.

Rachel yanked her head up like a spooked horse. Hurriedly and guiltily, she wiped her eyes and held her hand to her mouth.

'Rachel?'

'I'm fine! Told you . . . Leave me alone! I'm fine!'

Sarah remained by the door, unconvinced. Slowly she forced herself away from the keyhole, and just listened with her heart in her throat. She was rubbing her chest, looking down at the floor, every inch of her body fixated on what was going on behind the door.

'I am fine, Mum,' Rachel repeated. She sounded more composed. 'I think it's my period, you know . . .'

Sarah exhaled: she could take that, could deal with that. There was a remedy at hand. 'Do you want a paracetamol?'

'No. I'll be fine.'

Talking through a closed door was tortuous. Once again, Sarah descended to her knees to peep through the keyhole. Rachel was bending down, picking up her mobile phone from the floor. She turned away to face the window. Sarah could not see her face, could not tell if tears were still there. But she could hear her breathless and urgent half-whisper: 'It's me. Call me. We've got to talk . . . Let me explain. Believe me, I've nothing to do with it . . . I don't know who's doing this.'

'Rachel, dinner's on the table!' Sarah shouted from the bottom of the stairs.

'Not now! I'm not hungry!'

'Rachel! Now!' Her father sounded fed up.

'I'm busy! Leave me alone!'

Sarah shook her head. She glared at her husband. 'Do something!'

Jonathan raised his shoulders and flung his arms in the air. 'I am! I'm telling her to get the hell down here and sit at the table with us. What else do you want me to do?'

'She's obviously not coming down, is she!'

'Obviously not. Obviously, she feels no need –'

'For God's sake, go and get her,' Sarah hissed.

Jonathan gritted his teeth and, red-faced with anger, stomped up the stairs and banged on Rachel's door. 'Rachel! You will come down now! We're waiting with the dinner!'

Rachel paused with her finger over the SEND button, wishing her father away.

'Now, Rachel! You don't want me to come in there!'

'I'm coming!' She pressed the button, and flung the door open.

Rachel and her dad stood eye-to-eye on the landing, both seething with emotion. He was taller than her only by a few inches. His mouth was compressed with white fury, his thick brows drawn together. His breath smelt of coffee. He was searching her face for an answer, or an apology. She should be sitting at the table, having her dinner with her parents, without the need for special invitations. This was his rule: the whole family sitting down to dinner together. One of his immovable benchmarks. He didn't have many of them, and this one wasn't too taxing. He was seething with sheer irritation. Not in a mood for girly tantrums.

Until he saw his daughter's face.

'You're crying? What in God's name is the matter with –'

Rachel felt her face. Her cheeks were wet. She hadn't realised. 'It's nothing.'

'It can't be nothing.'

'I'm not keeping up with things at school. It bugs me.'

'School stuff? You must learn to take it easy, Rach.' Her father's shoulders relaxed. He changed his tone. It became the sort of soft, deep murmur it used to be years ago when he would read her stories before bed. 'It's not the end of the world – I thought it was something like . . . I don't know what I was thinking. Who, in their right mind cares about homework? Blimey, I never did! Come down, have dinner with us. You can get back to it on a full stomach. That'll make a difference, believe me.'

'OK, I believe you.' Rachel attempted a smile.

'Now, downstairs. Don't make your mum wait.'

They were sitting at the table, discussing Jonathan's misadventures with the company auditor. 'He needs a holiday, I said that to him. "You need a break, Aaron. You've become a total arse," pardon my French.'

'He's just doing his job,' Sarah pointed out.

'That's what he said.'

12

Rachel was poking her food with her fork, distracted. Her elbow was propped against the table. She was holding her forehead in the cup of her hand. Jonathan and Sarah exchanged looks, Jonathan raising his eyebrows, Sarah shaking her head, *Don't ask* . . . He pushed his plate away, threw his napkin on top of his unfinished dinner and planted his hands on the table, palms down.

'What is the problem now? The chicken not to your liking?' He rounded on Rachel.

'I said I wasn't hungry.'

'And I said, sit down and eat. I'm sick and tired of your attitude!'

'Rachel, darling, just listen to yourself . . . I thought we'd put it behind us . . . I try, I really do! Please, Rachel –' There was a wisp of hair stuck to Sarah's cheek. She placed her hand on Rachel's shoulder, but Rachel pushed it away. Sarah got up from the table and started collecting the dishes. A small sniffle escaped her and she turned her head away to suppress it.

Jonathan ignored that. His attention was on Rachel. 'Are you dieting? Is that what it is? Because I'm not having it!'

'No. I'm just not hungry.'

'Is that why people cry? Because they aren't hungry?'

Rachel sat mute.

'Speak to me, for crying out loud!'

'I dare not ask her anything any more . . . She'll only snap at me,' Sarah called from the kitchen.

'She says she's not keeping up with her school work.'

'Do you really believe that's what it is?'

'That's what she says.'

They were talking about Rachel in front of her, asking each other questions only she could answer. They were trying to provoke her to respond, but she sat silent and sullen, avoiding her father's eyes as he attempted to look into hers. Her mother returned from the kitchen, pressing a dishcloth to her nose, like a handkerchief.

'What are we doing wrong, Jonathan?'

There was a moment when Rachel lifted her eyes, half-opened her mouth and inhaled deeply as if she wanted to tell them something at last, to confess something, to get it off her chest once and for all.

'Yes? Speak to me, Rach,' Father prompted her. Mother lowered herself into a chair next to Rachel, stiff with anxiety.

'I'm not hungry.' Rachel averted her eyes. 'And I've got a lot to do. Homework . . . May I be excused?'

She rose from the table before they realised what she'd said, and fled.

Her father's answer chased her up the stairs, 'Go! There's no point staying here with us. We'll only bore you to death.'

Chapter Two

The night was cloudless, the stars so high up that he could almost sense the distance of light years between here and there. With no clouds to offer shelter from the cold, he was shivering in his threadbare hoodie. His fingers were red and stiff. Although it was already March, the wind was blowing from the north, bound to bring with it the cold and the rain clouds.

It was an uneventful – and freezing – evening. There were only a few highlights which made it worthwhile for him to hang around. He watched her as she changed from her school uniform into her casual clothes: a virginal white T-shirt and a pair of black-and-white skinny jeans, or leggings. She didn't flash her breasts. Her shoulders were rounded protectively over her chest, which wasn't particularly adventurous of her. She was wearing a pair of sensible underpants, white and boring, the sort he believed were favoured by middle-aged women who no longer cared to look desirable for their men. He took a few photographs never-theless. Her voluptuous curves screamed for attention, whether she liked it or not.

She spent a bit of time on her tablet, her fingers moving fran-tically over the screen. She scowled, not liking what she saw, and reached for her phone. That, too, she did not like – she hurled her phone across the room.

'Wow, feisty . . .' he muttered under his breath.

She left her bedroom for fifteen, twenty minutes, and returned looking even more agitated than before she had left. Straight away, she went for her iPad, but then almost immediately tossed it away. She grabbed her mobile phone and pressed it against her forehead. She stayed in that pose for a couple of minutes, pondering something or other, and then eagle-dived on her double bed and spread her arms limply, still holding on to her phone.

He checked his phone. He had no messages.

He was disappointed. Sitting in the cold, waiting, increasingly convinced that nothing would happen after all, he was minded to pack up and go. It was getting late. Her room was dark but for the little pale green lights illuminating it from the ceiling. Those didn't offer enough light for any quality photography. She was still on her bed – probably asleep. He unscrewed the lens, resigned that the show was over. But then the phone in her hand lit up – an intense blue light bringing her back to life. She sat up, checked the phone and then, her iPad. She jumped to her feet and surveyed her room. She went mad: started pulling books from a bookcase, flinging them on the floor, peering behind them; precariously, she climbed the empty shelves and checked the top of the case. She threw herself on the floor and slid under her bed – came out, empty-handed – swooped on her desk and with one hand swiped the heap of cosmetics, pens, pencils and school equipment debris from her desktop. She pounced towards the window.

At last!

That was his adrenalin rush moment. He chuckled to himself and zoomed his camera on her face. She was a pretty girl: her features pleasingly symmetrical, her eyes dark and round, little buttons; her hair was swept back, but reluctant to stay out of her face, curling back on her forehead and around her soft, baby-girl cheeks. He had always thought her an innocent, fancied her because of that innocence.

She was staring right at him, but he was sure she couldn't see him up in the tree, on the low bough obscured from view by the fence. The light from the street lamp created a brilliant diversion: it made everything lying outside its boundary darker and more impenetrable. She couldn't see him, but to be on the safe side he climbed down and stood behind a thick hedge in the neighbouring property.

'Come on, Rachel,' he whispered. 'Come out to play.'

With one furious swipe of her arms she drew the curtains.

Seconds later, he saw her curtain twitch, or maybe it was just a trick of light in her bedroom. There was no point hanging around. It was time to go. He checked his phone again – no messages. He was fed up and cold, and tired. He had business to take care of before going home to crash out.

But the show wasn't over. She suddenly shot out of the front door, leaving it wide open behind her. For a split second, he was tempted to steal a peek inside – maybe a gadget or two worth nicking – but, on reflection, Rachel was a better catch. She had opened herself up to all sorts of possibilities. She was asking for attention. He couldn't say no. Wearing only a pair of jeans and a tight T-shirt, she was too good an opportunity to miss.

His interest restored, he whipped the camera out of his bag, readying himself to follow her. She wouldn't wait for him, dashing madly into the night, and almost disappearing from sight. The slipper-socks with pompoms she was wearing muffled her footsteps. He had to hurry to keep up with her. She was sure to catch her death of cold. Her bare white arms reflected the moonlight with a creepy tinge to them, as if they were translucent.

She was clutching something in her hands, pressing it hard against her boobs. Her shoulders were rounded and her head was cocooned between them. Doubled up, she cut a pathetic figure. He almost felt sorry for her, almost stepped out of the shadows to offer her his hoodie. But it wasn't his place, not now.

She looked frightened. He wondered what she was running away from. He glanced towards the wide open door and the dark windows of the house. There was nothing there. No one was following her. Only a short while ago she had been sprawled on her bed, those weird fluorescent lights glimmering softly over her head. Safe, warm – unlike him. And now she was running like the house was on fire.

17

Only it wasn't.

He hid in the hedge and flattened his back against its harsh, prickly wall as she passed by him. She was making squeaky, sniffling noises. The solitary street lamp caught her mid-flight. His camera clicked. Luckily, the flash was drowned in the light from the street lamp so she didn't realise she was being photographed. He was pleased with this series of images: the girl by the street lamp in the middle of the night. Fluffy pompoms. Skimpy top. One thing sprung to mind. He smirked. He took another photo, but this one was a dud. Only her back was lit as she crossed into the darkness on the other side of the road. That was where the road narrowed into a short pathway leading towards the river.

Momentarily, he lost sight of the girl. He broke into a jog. He mustn't lose her. Wherever she was going couldn't be the sort of place she would go in broad daylight. This would be well worth his trouble.

In case she realised she was followed and stopped to watch from the riverbank, he slunk after her cautiously like an alley cat, sticking to the wall of the hedge and giving the street lamp a wide berth. He plunged into the darkness beyond the street lights.

The footpath by the river would normally brim with dog walkers and joggers, but not at night. Now, a few narrowboats bobbed on the surface of the black, oily water and a fox cried in the distance. And a girl was running. His girl. Innocent little Rachel.

He had her trapped within the long lens of his camera. A series of frenzied clicks exploded as she climbed up onto the narrow pedestrian bridge, a shabby structure which might once have been quite pretty. But now its balustrade was rusty and unhealthy looking, with white paint peeling off like dry, grazed skin.

She stopped on the bridge and leaned over the balustrade. *Click. Click. Click.* She pulled herself back and pointed the iPad that she had been holding towards the river. She took a wide swing. The thing flew through the wind like a frisbee. *Click. Click. Click.* He was having a field day.

She stood for a while with her arms dangling by her side, as if she wasn't sure what to do next, where to go. She paced furiously along the length of the bridge, stopped in the middle and peered down at the black water. She stepped on the bottom rail of the balustrade. She was looking for something or, possibly, she was planning to climb over, and jump. He had his camera at the ready. *Click. Click. Click.* This was beginning to look like a video recording: his camera a machine gun emitting a relentless series of clicks.

She didn't jump.

She stared down, then she paced some more on the bridge, clutching her head and, again, looking down into the water. He was sure she must have thrown her tablet in the river, only why would anyone do such a thing? A decent iPad was worth a bit of cash. Then again, she had enough money not to care. His face twisted with resentment. How he loathed these rich brats!

She stomped off the bridge and headed towards him – he had to duck low so that his silhouette blended with the riverside bushes. There seemed to be purpose to her stride. She didn't stay on the pathway, but instead dived into the swampy shrubs under the bridge. They swallowed her, but before they did, he managed one photograph.

A message appeared that the memory card was full. He had a spare one in his bag and quickly made a switch. That was when he lost sight of her.

He heard a commotion, though he could not see what she was up to down there. He could hear a splash of water and pointed his camera in the general direction of that sound. *Click*, but there wasn't much hope that he had caught anything of interest.

A cry shot above the wind.

He stuck his head out above the reeds. He looked over his shoulder a couple of times and tuned into the sounds behind him. There was nothing at first but the cry of a distant fox. He shuddered. The cold was always worse by the water. It had penetrated him to the bone – the cold and an overwhelming sense of

19

foreboding. He rubbed his shoulders. A sudden movement in the shrubs startled him. A shadow stretched over the footpath. Soft padding of feet followed the shadow. He strained his eyes to look up the path. This was the quickest way home: a shortcut through the country park, with a stopover at the pavilion, their usual meeting place.

He was shivering from the cold and the consuming anxiety that he was feeling in his gut. He was going to put the price up. He was taking all the risks after all. And he needed money.

He gasped. Someone – or something – was slouched on the path in front of him. The shape unfurled and took off. A badger, or something: fat and furry. As it waddled away, it made the same soft padding sound he had heard before: splat, splat, splat.

He fumbled in his back pocket and took out his mobile. It lit his face with its eerie blue light. He checked the time: eight minutes past ten.

Another fox barked close by. That gave him another jolt and he dropped the phone.

'For fuck's sake!'

He crouched on the ground and felt around with his hands. Accidentally, he pushed the damned thing away and it slid off the path and into the thick, muddy riverside undergrowth. His fingers drowned in the muck. He raked through the mud, wondering how much dog shit must have got stuck to his skin. The thought made him shudder. It was disgusting. At last, his fingertips hit something harder. His mobile.

At the same time, he heard a faint sound of disturbed water, a plop and a squelch, the murmur of ripples. He peered through the undergrowth, and smiled at the sight before him. Forgetting the filth on his phone, he fingered the speed-dial and pressed the mobile to his lips. He would have to whisper not to spook the prey.

Chapter Three

In a last-ditch attempt to close the boot of his car, Charlie has placed his entire weight on it. Gillian raises her eyebrows, not too sure whether to applaud or bemoan his efforts. Sitting by her side, Corky looks equally bemused. It is plain that the car is called a Mini for a reason. Tara is sitting in the front seat with her arms folded over her knees and her head thrust forward. The luggage squashed behind her seat is pushing her towards the dashboard. The car wobbles under Charlie's weight but the obstinate suitcase in the boot won't budge. Neither will the backpack behind it. It doesn't take a genius to work it out, but Charlie seems to believe that he is a miracle worker and the universal principles of physics do not apply to him. He is kicking the suitcase. The suitcase puts up considerable resistance. Charlie mumbles curses under his breath. He and Gillian aren't yet at a stage of their acquaintance where either of them would feel comfortable swearing in front of the other, so he has to lower the volume.

Charlie wanders around the car to approach the offending suitcase from the other side. He limps in a more accentuated way than usual, thrusting his left foot out awkwardly as if he has little control over which way it may travel. His flaring temper may have something to do with his aggravated gait, but that isn't the only reason. After the train bombing, Charlie's crushed leg acquired several metal pins. Despite a course of intense physiotherapy, he is condemned to walk in the comical style of his namesake, Charlie Chaplin, for life. Only Charlie Outhwaite is tall and ginger, so it looks like he is taking the Mickey when he totters around the Mini with a scowl on his face and a broken spring in his step. Gillian stifles a smirk.

'Are you done yet?' Tara shouts from the passenger seat and sticks out her head.

Charlie's scowl deepens. 'What do you think?'

'Just tie the boot with string, or something like that, and let's go.'

Gillian can see from the expression on Charlie's face that the advice is not welcome. He compresses his lips into an angry grimace and holds himself back from unleashing a barrage of vituperation. Unsuspecting, Tara pops out of the car, joins Gillian and Corky on the kerb, and puts her hands on her hips. 'Have you tried pushing it in? It only needs a little push . . .'

'Why don't *you* try it, huh? I'm sure it'll bloody well shift if you ask it nicely!'

Gillian decides this is the moment where she has to step in before those two abandon the whole idea and move back in with her again. 'Let's put it in my car. The boot is much bigger.'

'Why didn't we think of this before?' Tara throws up her arms.

Charlie bites his lower lip.

'I'll bring my car over.' Gillian makes herself temporarily scarce. She watches from her driveway as Charlie drags the cursed suitcase out of the boot and tells Tara to stay the hell out of the way.

'I'm only trying to help, but fine – suit yourself!' Tara huffs and returns to her squatting position in the front seat. She slams the door with an ostentatious bang. Fritz scampers from under the car and disappears inside the house. He will remember this inconvenience for months to come. He may be a cat, but he has the memory of an elephant.

Gillian double-parks next to Charlie's Mini and together they shove the damned suitcase into the boot of her car. Not to be outdone by Tara in the tantrum-throwing department, Charlie slams the boot of his Mini and for some mysterious reason kicks the rear tyre. Gillian reckons this house move will either make them or break them. She smiles regardless of her doubts and says, 'I'll lock up and follow you.'

'Yeah, thanks, Gillian,' is his muttered response. He limps away to sag behind the wheel of his Mini, and takes off with screeching tyres.

Gillian locks the front door, tells Corky to jump onto the back seat, and then she follows Charlie.

It isn't a long trip. They're moving only a few miles away, to live with Gillian's parents in the village of Little Ogburn which lies on the outskirts of Sexton's Canning. Under any other circumstances, she would be delighted to see the back of Charlie and his random items of clothing scattered around her house, and she would be over the moon to have her home and the contents of her fridge to herself. But this is different.

Nine months ago, Gillian's mother suffered a stroke. It was unexpected: one minute she was pottering around the garden, pulling out weeds and unbeknown to anyone popping paracetamol for a 'touch of headache', and next minute she was dropping her cup of tea on the floor and losing her power of speech. All the while, Gillian's father was losing his grip on reality, paralysed with sheer panic. If it had not been for their lovely neighbour, Jenny Roux, who was at the time sitting on their sofa and companionably sipping her cup of tea, nobody would have had the presence of mind to call an ambulance.

Fast-forward six months and Gillian's mum was due to be released home, but she wasn't back to her old self. Despite several months of rehabilitation, she was only partially recovered. Her speech remained slurred. She dragged her right foot as if it were made of lead and had limited mobility in her right arm. Her muscle tissue had withered and her body needed to be re-trained on its basic functions. Teaching her left hand what her right hand used to do for the past seventy-six years was easier said than done. So there would be no more gardening, or cooking, or ironing, or any of the simple pleasures of cleaning, and she would have to rely on day carers. One of them would be her husband, but everyone agreed that at the ripe old age of eighty he would be hopeless at it. He would not know how to go about it. Teaching new tricks to an old dog was a non-starter. Dad was growing increasingly scared that he would make things worse: that accidentally and through inexperience he may break his wife somehow. He had no chance of coping with the demands of Mum's condition on his own.

Gillian knew it would come to this before Mum's release from hospital, so she came up with an offer of help: she would become the carer. She had been considering leaving the police force anyway, so why not? It was her turn to give something back to them. But her father wouldn't have it. And neither would her mother.

'You can't put your life on hold, dear. We'll manage, we have help, people who know what they're doing,' she'd stuttered.

'And I don't know?' Gillian was fuming. 'I am your daughter, in case you forgot.'

'Of course you are, but you're just not made to be a nurse. It's not you. God knows, you'd only make things worse,' her father hammered the final nail into the coffin of her devotion.

'She would, Ted, you're right,' her mother banged in another one, for good measure.

Following her failed attempt at making herself useful that day, Gillian drove home in a vile mood and threw a tantrum the moment her foot crossed the threshold. Tara and Charlie were watching football. Unceremoniously, Gillian picked up the remote and turned the TV off.

'Mum?!' Tara screeched. Charlie just looked deeply hurt. If only he could tell her what he thought of mindless arseholes who turn off the telly in the middle of a football match . . .

'I've had it with your grandparents!' Gillian flopped next to Tara onto the sofa, and hurled the remote onto the table. 'They won't be helped! They simply won't! Your granddad is not up to looking after your gran, he isn't! They just won't accept my help. I don't think there's a choice – they need to sell up and move into some retirement village where Gran can get proper medical care, round the clock.'

Tara sighed loudly. 'You know they won't sell up. They love their home.'

'Well, they'll have to love another one,' Gillian sighed louder and dropped her shoulders.

'That would just about kill them both. They've lived there for fifty-three years!'

'So what do you propose? Shall I just let them struggle through this and do nothing? The house is too big for them anyway. Four bedrooms and just the two of them rattling about, endlessly watering house plants and dusting furniture! Sooner or later . . . It's been coming to this for a while now . . .' As she was saying it, Gillian knew she would never be able to inflict this on her parents.

Charlie scratched his head, but clearly nothing useful came into it. He offered them a fresh cup of tea, which they refused.

'Not now, Charlie! Just stay out of it!' Gillian barked at him, and regretted it instantly. Charlie recoiled like a dog kicked in the head.

'Maybe we should move in with them,' Tara said, 'Charlie and me. They won't accept your help out of pride, but if I told them we needed *their* help . . . that we're finding it hard living with you –'

'Which they'd probably believe,' Charlie added, and was shot down with two fiery glares.

'Mum asked you to stay out of it!' Tara turned to Gillian, 'They'll want to help us rather than suspect that we're trying to help them. I could keep an eye on them, help with watering those plants, and the dusting, cook one square meal a day –'

'I only meant to say,' Charlie was intent on clearing his name, 'that they'd believe us as your school is in the village, only a walking distance from their house. It'd be convenient for you to stay with them, for the time being, until we find something of our own. It's a believable scenario . . . That's all I was saying – trying to say. Can I just finish a sentence here without being lynched?'

25

And so the plan was concocted and presented to Gillian's parents, who fell for it hook, line and sinker. They genuinely believed that they were doing their beloved granddaughter a favour . . .

Gillian smiles under her breath. She is relieved, and she is proud of Tara. Her child seems to have infinitely more wisdom than Gillian could ever hope for herself. She is also smiling because deep down, uncharitably, she is pleased to be shot of her house guests. It's been two years since her home and her life were hijacked by Tara and her boyfriend. Gillian needs to start living her own life before she is too old and too wrinkled for comfort. She is a woman of a certain age, but not quite over the hill. There are a few years left in her yet. She can't let them go to waste.

She parks behind Charlie's Mini on her parents' driveway and opens the boot. Charlie is at hand to remove the suitcase. He drags it into the house, following Tara who is carrying her backpack and, naturally, her handbag. Gillian grabs a couple of holdalls, full of what feels like shoes and more shoes. Her father has trundled out of the house and is picking up the last few carrier bags. Between them, they have managed to bundle all of Tara and Charlie's earthly possessions through the front door. Mother greets them from the living room. She is standing up, though not quite upright and not quite secure on her feet.

'Shall I put the kettle on?' she offers, her speech awkward. Gillian is still getting used to it.

'No. Sit down, Mum. I'll do it.' Gillian takes herself to the kitchen. Father follows and starts getting under her feet while suggesting a selection of biscuits from the tin. On top of that, there is a noise coming from the utility room: male voices speaking fast and furiously in a foreign language. The kettle begins to boil with a wheezy whistle.

'What's that?' Gillian pauses and listens, pointing up her finger to silence her father.

'The kettle's boiled,' Father informs her.

26

'Yes, I know that. What are those voices in the utility room? Do you realise there're some men there?'

'Oh, that!' Father's face brightens up. 'We've got Polish builders converting the utility room into a shower room, with a toilet. For your mum, to make it easier for her. She won't have to drag herself upstairs at all. We're moving our bedroom downstairs to the reception room at the back. It's nice and quiet there, plus we'll have the fireplace to keep us warm. Ophelia'll be very comfy, and so will I, come to think about it. Don't you think you should take the teabags out?' he points to the mugs. 'We don't like our tea too strong.'

'Yes, yes.' Gillian removes the bags and pours in milk.

'Not too much for me. Milk doesn't agree with me anymore. Gives me wind.'

'OK, Dad, thanks. That's too much information.' Gillian despairs. 'Never mind, I'll drink this tea and give you that one, with less milk.'

'But that's my mug. I always drink from my mug.'

Gillian grinds her teeth. 'Shall I make you a fresh cup?'

'If you don't mind.'

The kettle is empty though, so she puts it on again while the other teas are getting cold. So be it. Perhaps they are right: perhaps she isn't nurse material. Her fuse is too short.

Father babbles on, '. . . and that will make more room for Tara and Charlie, so that they can have some privacy upstairs.'

'Surely you aren't turning your life upside down for the two of them!' Gillian is exasperated. Their clever plan was bound to blow up in their faces, and so it has!

'Oh no, not at all. We don't need that space upstairs. Let the young ones be happy up there. We'll only be leaving the house to Tara, when we're both gone, so it's worked out well for all concerned in the end, hasn't it, dear?'

Gillian has to agree.

'Shall I show you where the biscuits are?'

'I know, Dad. In a tin, in the top cupboard above the fridge.'

Father's face crumples in a mysterious smile. 'You're wrong there, dear! We moved the tin to the cupboard next to the sink so we can both reach it with no trouble. How things change . . .'

Gillian decides to acquaint herself with the Polish builders and let them know that they aren't dealing with a couple of elderly misfits but with a competent young – well, middle-aged – woman who won't let them rip her parents off. She marches to the utility room and finds a pair of builder's cracks down on the floor. The two men are peering down a pipe. The toilet is already installed and the walls are tiled. The utility room is fully transformed. Two round, open faces lift and gaze at her.

'Hi, I'm Gillian. I am a . . .'

'Hello, Szczepan,' one of the builders gets up from his knees and shakes her hand. He's huge and his hand is in proportion to his frame. It absorbs Gillian's hand. The other man is small, skinny as a rat, and wrinkled. He also gets up and introduces himself with another unpronounceable name and a whiff of stale beer on his breath. His hand squeezes Gillian's like a vice.

'I'm Ted's daughter,' Gillian explains her intrusion and rubs her hand.

'Good,' says Szczepan. 'We finish today.'

'Oh? Great! It looks great. I'd like to settle the . . . money with you. Your bill?' She really wants to be useful to her parents in some way.

'No, no,' Szczepan waves his big arm like a windmill wing. 'We paid.'

'You did?'

'Yes, all paid.'

'Right,' she gets it at last. 'I'll leave you to it, then. Nice meeting you.'

'Good,' says Szczepan.

'Good,' echoes Gillian.

She is happy to be back home, on her own, thank you very much. First time in two years! She has put her feet up on the coffee table, on a pile of books for extra elevation. She is watching a cheap and trashy horror movie through her toes. When the gore gets tough, she pulls her feet together. A creature with bloody teeth (a severe case of scurvy?) is climbing a pipe in a dark, stained shaft. The creature is making squeaking sounds, like a sewer rat. Not that she has ever had the pleasure of listening to the cries of sewer rats, but she imagines that is what they sound like. The female protagonist – a fit, blue-eyed blonde in torn stockings and a strategically dishevelled blouse – is at the top of the shaft, swinging her leg over the ledge. The creature's dirt-encrusted nails are nearly touching the damsel's other leg.

Gillian draws her feet together to obscure the screen. She strokes Fritz, who has curled himself in her lap and is snoring softly, oblivious to the horrors on TV. Corky is sprawled on the rug, having temporarily given up on the huge bone Gillian got for him from the butcher's. It must be a cow's thigh bone: it's thick and long, and severely tarnished where Corky has taken the first bite, which is pretty much what the creature is going to do to the blonde bombshell's swinging leg if she doesn't stop pouting and posturing . . .

More creatures arrive at the scene. OK, the damsel is as good as dead. She is not a well-known actress so she is disposable and will soon join the ranks of casualties. It's time for another glass of wine. Gillian totters to the kitchen and fetches the whole bottle. There is little point in pretending that she won't finish it tonight, and even less point in yo-yoing between the lounge and the kitchen to refill her glass.

She slumps on the sofa. Should she be feeling guilty about allowing Tara to go and live with her grandparents, to be the one to take care of them? Isn't that *her* responsibility? Should she be even asking herself this question? She is a prodigal daughter, has always been. She's crap, really crap! She downs her wine.

Her phone rings. It's work.

'Erin? What's up?'

'A body's turned up in Ogburn Country Park – the end bordering the sports fields of Whalehurst School,' says DC Macfadyen.

'Is it the missing girl? Shouldn't you be calling Webber?' A fifteen-year old girl went missing on Friday night – or possibly Saturday morning. Webber has taken that case. It's his first independent one. Gillian wouldn't want to rain on his parade.

'No, it's not his missing girl. It's a male. I don't know more than that. I'm heading there now.'

'I'm on my way.' Gillian turns off the TV. The damsel in distress is probably dead by now, and frankly, Gillian doesn't care anymore. She gets dressed, puts her socks and shoes back on, and heads out of the door. Her self-mortification over her parents will have to wait. She jumps in her car. How lucky that she has only managed one glass of wine so far.

Chapter Four

Erin Macfadyen is on the scene, talking to the three pimply youths who found the body. They are local village boys who by day go to Sexton's Canning Comprehensive, and on Sunday afternoons climb the fence between the country park and Whalehurst school grounds for a game of football on the astro-turf pitch. No harm in that, surely? It's not like they're stealing anything. They aren't going to get into any trouble, are they? Because, if that's the case, they'll never come forward when they find another body. DC Macfadyen assures them they have done the right thing and that no one will punish them for breaking and entering.

'Cos we ain't got facilities, like, in Little Ogburn . . . not like the poncy lot here at Whalehurst,' one boy argues.

'It's not fair,' another boy concludes, and there is no arguing with that. Whalehurst School is an independent establishment of considerably high reputation which only the rich and famous can afford. A main employment – alas not education – provider to the local population, it sits in the heart of Little Ogburn which is a village of two halves: the leafy owner-occupied Upper Little Ogburn and the decrepit housing estate of the aptly named Lower Little Ogburn. The boys are from the estate.

Gillian ducks under the police tape and strides towards Erin and the trio of pubescent witnesses she is interviewing.

'Who do you have there, DC Macfadyen, potential suspects?' As usual, DI Marsh is political incorrectness personified. The youths glare at her, deeply offended.

'I said we should of kept our gobs shut, and walked away from this shite!' The shortest one of the lot nudges the tallest one, who looks just like him, only a few years older. 'Dad's gonna have our arses for this!'

'We done nuffin wrong!' the tall one shouts at Gillian, his voice breaking into poorly lubricated gear.

Erin steps in, pointing to the large boy, then to his smaller version, 'Alec and Barry Potter –'

'No relation to the wizard boy, and yeah, I've 'eard all them stupid jibes. You can save yer breath, yeah?' Barry Potter, the short one, makes an instant disclaimer, which forces a smile onto Gillian's face.

'And Ollie Quinten,' Erin goes on. 'These young gentlemen found the body.'

'Stumbled on it, more likely!' Barry Potter corrects her. 'We ain't been looking for it!'

Gillian's smile widens. She likes the feisty nipper.

'And they've even identified him as . . .' DC Macfadyen riffles through her notebook, 'as Bradley Watson.'

'That's Brad, all right,' Alec visibly shudders. 'And he's dead with a frigging arrow in his back!'

Erin nods in reply to Gillian's quizzical glance. 'That's right.'

'Like fuckin' *Hunger Games*, if you know what I mean!' Ollie Quinten adds.

Gillian doesn't know what he means – she has never watched one of those films from start to finish.

'It's them poncy arseholes what done it!' Barry Potter has apparently concluded the investigation all on his own. His face is contorted in anger as he looks intently in the vague direction of Whalehurst School. Gillian fears that if the other villagers agree with him the random finger-pointing may easily turn into riots.

'DC Macfadyen, get these young men to the station to take their statements. They may need some medical attention for shock. See to it that they get what they need, and get Uniform to inform their families as to where they are and that they aren't in any trouble. Uniform will have to give the parents a lift to the station to collect the boys, and drive them all back home. As little inconvenience as possible for the families, is that clear? These gentlemen,' Gillian nods pointedly towards the rascals who are feasting on her every word with widening grins, 'are our key witnesses, but they are minors. We play this by the book.'

'Told ya!' Alec Potter triumphs as he slaps his younger brother on the shoulder. 'We be taken home in style for our trouble.' The boys exchange a crossfire of shoves, punches, and pushes as they chuckle with delight, their shock and anger all but forgotten.

Gillian takes Erin to one side, out of the boys' earshot. 'Hold them at the station for the time being. Give me an hour or so. I want to talk to Bradley Watson's family first. I don't want them to find out about their son before we get to them. We have to handle this like it's our best china. This thing could get out of hand if we don't play it right.'

As Erin leads the juvenile witnesses away, Gillian approaches the tent to take a look at the victim and the crime scene. Dr Michael Almond and his moustache are there, examining the evidence. By now Gillian is used to Almond's enormous handlebars, but there was a time when the man would give her nightmares. In his prime, athletic and with deep soulful eyes, Almond would pass for a handsome man, but the moustache is his curse. It seems to hang over him, or rather off him, without any intention of disappearing anytime soon. Gillian often wonders, why the moustache, and why so huge, but she hasn't mustered the courage to ask him. The rumour around the station has it that the moustache is a result of a dare. If Almond had any sense he would now take on a challenge to shave off his facial hair for a half-decent charity; he would get out of that dare without losing face, so to speak.

'Cause of death?' Gillian tries to overlook the moustache and concentrate on the body. It appears to be a young male of slim build, residual acne scarring around his chin and neck. His lifeless eyes are staring into the fabric of the tent, and indeed, there is the sharp tip of an arrow sticking out of his twisted torso and a yellow-blue fletching protruding from his back.

'You tell me.' Dr Almond's gloved finger taps the sharp point of the arrowhead.

'So, he was killed by an arrow?'

'It appears so. It looks like it went straight through the heart, and this,' he taps the head again, 'doesn't look like a practice arrowhead. Whoever killed him was a damn clean shot.'

'Deserves a pat on the back!' Gillian squints at him. He peers at her quizzically, but goes on, unperturbed, 'I can't say any more at this stage. You'll have the post-mortem tomorrow lunchtime. I'm having the body taken to the mortuary.' He pushes the body by the shoulder and it flops, revealing more of the arrow shaft at the back. Almond asks the photographer to take a few shots, pointing to areas of interest, before he gets his team to bag it. He ignores Gillian. He is like that – poor communicator – but then, who is Gillian to judge him. She isn't much of a people person herself. She wanders off to talk to the Forensics lot. Bobby Hughes is leading the team. As usual he is wearing his overalls with the unflattering shower cap. They shake hands.

'Have you found the murder weapon?'

'Assuming it's a bow, no, we haven't.'

'Anything worth mentioning?'

'We found fragments of his clothing on the fence. It'll go for full forensic examination, but if it is his then it looks like he was climbing the fence when he was shot, fell down where he was, and never got up again. And that would imply he was shot by someone standing in the school field. Maybe he was chased, maybe he was doing the chasing, but he was in a hurry. I'll have my team examine the fields for footprints all the way to that building over there,' he points to what looks like a cricket pavilion. A number of forensics officers are hanging a *DO NOT CROSS POLICE* tape around the pitch.

'We informed the school?'

'Yes, Uniform are there, rounding up the students and staff. I don't want them trampling over my crime scene.'

'Good. I'll talk to them later. First, the victim's parents.'

'Always a pleasure, huh?' Hughes shakes his head and looks at her sympathetically, but his sympathy and the gist of his comment are lost on Gillian.

'No, not really,' she says and walks briskly to her car.

A man with a bloated belly and puffy face opens the door. Gillian searches for any similarities between him and the dead youth. She doesn't find any. She presents her ID and informs the man that the uniform police officer next to her is PC Miller. She asks if they can come in.

'What's this all about?' The man is defensive. He is instinctively blocking the entry to his house. He calls his wife.

'Is Bradley home, can you tell me, please?' Gillian does everything by the book. She must be sure, as sure as it is possible in these circumstances, that she is not dealing with a case of mistaken identity.

'Why do you want to know?'

'Just answer the question, please.'

'He's somewhere around,' is the evasive, mumbled response.

'Are they looking for Bradley?' a gentle female voice asks from behind the man's wide frame. A slim-built woman with a plaintive expression in her wide-set eyes peers at Gillian. There is a definite similarity between her and the dead young man. Gillian's stomach flips and sends a wave of nausea up to her throat.

'May we come in? It'd be best if we didn't have to talk on your doorstep.'

'Has Brad done something? Is he in trouble again?' The woman's voice quivers with apprehension. Gillian makes a mental note of the *again* qualifier. She will run checks on Bradley Watson when she gets back to the station.

'No, Mrs Watson, he isn't in trouble.'

'He ain't home either, so if you want to talk to him you'll 'ave to come another time.' Mr Watson changes his tune slightly but stands his ground. 'I tell 'im you came by when he gets back, all right?' As Gillian and PC Miller aren't shifting, he adds, 'Or else, you'll 'ave to talk to me.'

'We'll talk to you. Let's go inside.'

The flat is tidy and it smells clean and fresh. A pair of identical, mass-produced paintings hangs on the wall, behind a tired and threadbare three-seater. The theme of the paintings matches the pattern and the autumnal colour scheme of the curtains. Next to the three-seater stands a La-Z-Boy armchair, slightly reclined. Mr Watson sits in it, upright and tense, fighting off the invitation to lean back and relax. Mrs Watson takes a seat on the sofa. Mr Watson turns off the TV. A sudden bout of silence in the room sounds ominous.

'Well? Talk to me.'

'Do you know where Bradley is?'

'Out on the town in Sexton's with his mates, I suspect. It's Sunday night.'

'We don't keep tabs on him. Should we?' Mrs Watson's voice is still shaky.

'You're sure he's in Sexton's Canning?'

'To be honest with ya, no, we ain't. Now, get to the point. What's this about?'

'I'm just trying to establish that there's no mistake. Have you got a recent photo of Bradley?'

Mr Watson's face flushes red. 'You tell me first what the hell –'

'Here,' Mrs Watson hands to Gillian a photo of a schoolboy wearing Sexton's Canning Comprehensive's uniform. The boy may be fifteen. He has his mother's wide-set eyes and there is an angry outbreak of acne around his jaw. 'That's the most recent. He doesn't like photos taken of him. Not even selfies. Though he has got himself this big camera of late, hasn't he, Tom? He says it's not for selfies, that camera, it's for wildlife.' She is nervous and so she is warbling on to disarm the tension in the air.

Gillian examines the photo. In her mind, there's no doubt the dead man is Bradley Watson. She passes the photo to PC Miller. He was one of the first officers on the scene – saw the body. His face confirms what she is thinking. They exchange a brief, grim look.

'Does Bradley have any connections to Whalehurst School?'

'Sure he does! I'm the groundsman at Whalehurst. Brad works with me, 'as been workin' with me, learnin' the trade, like, what now?' Mr Watson looks to his wife for help, 'Goin' on for two years?'

'A year and a half, just over,' she says. 'It's been a year and a half since he got out . . .'

'Since he cleaned up 'is act,' Mr Watson confirms and falls into silence. They are both gazing at Gillian intently.

She realises they won't say another world. They want to know why she and Miller are here. She clears her throat. 'Mr and Mrs Watson, there is no other way to say it: I've bad news. The body of a young man was found on the periphery of Whalehurst School bordering the country park. We have reasons to believe it is Bradley . . . I'd like to ask you to come with us to identify –'

'Call Brad, Rose,' Mr Watson doesn't seem to be listening. 'I've just about 'ad it with them cops 'arassin' us. Tell 'im to come 'ome and stop playin' silly buggers!'

Mrs Watson looks at Gillian meekly as if requesting her permission to use the phone.

'By all means, do,' Gillian encourages her. 'We may be wrong.'

Mrs Bradley picks up the phone and presses a speed-dial button. She listens. They all listen, and they watch her face as it traverses from expectant to exasperated. 'He's not answering,' she whispers, her expression mortified.

'Try again! He can't 'ear it, I say! Is it ringin'?'

She nods and tries again, and again her face drops. Her husband has his own go at contacting their son, with the same outcome.

'We ain't seen Brad since Friday. Teatime,' he admits at last. There is guilt in his tone.

Gillian knows without a shred of doubt that Bradley Watson is lying dead in the morgue. His parents have run out of lifelines for him, but, as can be expected, they don't want to believe it.

They both decide to come with Gillian and PC Miller to the mortuary to, hopefully, prove her wrong.

Mrs Watson buries her face in her husband's wide chest. She is crying soundlessly. He puts his arms around her and rubs her back, mechanically and repeatedly. His face tugs away from the sight of his dead son. It goes into a convulsion of unimaginable pain.

'I'm very sorry for your loss,' Gillian says awkwardly. It is always awkward and so very pointless to offer bereaved families these routinely uttered words.

Mr Watson turns to her, with tears streaming down his face. 'Why?' he speaks with an effort as words seem to crack in his mouth, 'Why would anyone do that to 'im? He's cleaned up 'is act. He was doing all right . . . We was proud of 'im, ya know what I mean?'

Gillian nods. 'I'll find out who killed him, and I'll find out why. I know this much.' She guides them away from the body. 'PC Miller will take you home. I'm very sorry . . .'

At the station, Gillian rubs shoulders with the father of Alec and Barry Potter. A man in his forties, with a short crop of hair and a colourful tattoo adorning his entire right forearm, he indeed looks like the sort that will have his sons' arses for the inconvenience of having to pick them up. And he acts like it too. He gives Alec a clip over his head and hollers, 'What did I tell ya about sneaking into that bloody school at night!'

'We was in the park,' Alec protests weakly.

'My arse, you was! And 'ow many times did I tell ya about stayin' away from that good-for-nuffin Brad Watson? You tell me!'

'We only bumped into him cos he was dead!' Barry yells, but his father will have none of it. He shoves the boy out into the freezing cold of the night.

38

'And don't let me be pickin' your arses up again from the coppers!'

'What 'bout Ollie?' Barry looks back, anxious for his mate.

'What 'bout him?'

'Is he comin'?'

'Do I look like childcare on legs?'

'Thanks for the offer, Barry,' Gillian interjects, 'but a police constable's driving Ollie home.'

Mr Potter throws her a contemptuous look. 'Is what we pay taxes for!'

Gillian watches the trio disappear inside Mr Potter's battered old racer-boy's Subaru. The car takes off with a screech of tyres and a growl of the exhaust. She inhales deeply. The air feels crisp and fresh. A breath of fresh air never fails to clear her head. Invigorated, she dives back into the station.

She wants to check Bradley Watson's records. Erin is on her way out; she's had a long day and she is knackered. Gillian tells her to have a good rest and that she'll see her first thing in morning.

'I'll be fresh as a daisy!' Erin beams and pulls on her coat. She has taken to wearing a knee-length black coat with her collar up which, on top of her bob dyed black, makes her look like a character from *Pulp Fiction*. And that is a perfect match for Webber as these days, having lost some weight, grown sideburns, and groomed his hair into a sleek style, he is John Travolta personified. He is sitting at his desk, going through the evidence in the missing girl's case. The black circles under his eyes testify to the hours he has put into this case since the early hours of Saturday morning – since the girl's disappearance was reported by her parents. DS Webber has spent the whole Saturday waiting for a ransom demand while Uniform did door-to-door inquiries and mounted a search of the town and surrounding areas. A dead end on all accounts, Webber is now going through all the witness statements, looking for clues.

'I'd bet you my bottom dollar that she ran away if it wasn't for what she was wearing,' he seems to be speaking to himself. 'Not even a proper pair of shoes! And if it had been an abduction, we'd have a ransom demand by now, surely! So if this isn't a runaway case or a kidnapping, then what the hell is it? This is doing my head in. I must've missed something.'

Ignoring Mark's recriminations, Gillian is looking at the screen of her computer where Bradley Watson's information is displayed. Looking at his birth date, he would be turning twenty on 20 October. Two convictions for drugs: possession with intent to supply class A drugs at the tender age of fifteen; then again at sixteen, rewarded with a stint in a juvenile offenders' institution. He got out nearly two years ago, and hasn't been heard of since. He has become a good, law-abiding citizen, like his father says. Or has he?

Her phone rings. It's Bobby Hughes. 'You need to come back here, Gillian. The headmaster is jumping out of his skin. He's demanding to speak to the officer in charge. He won't let us get on with the job.'

'On my way,' she puts the phone down and throws her bomber jacket over her shoulders. She glances back at Webber. 'If I were you, I wouldn't try to label the disappearance as this or that – I'd just follow the trail of evidence and see where it takes me. You'll get there, Mark.'

DS Webber gazes at her, mortified.

Chapter Five

On Saturday evening, armed with the gentle touch of PC Sharon de Witt and a shedload of suspicions, DS Webber had gone to interview the parents. It wasn't an officially endorsed theory, but in most cases of teenage disappearance the parents, or other close relatives, carried the bulk of blame. The lack of leads so far lent weight to the credibility of this hypothesis. The example of his mentor and role model, DI Marsh herself, had reinforced Mark's resolve to bury political correctness and basic human empathy deep in his pocket, and go for the Snyders' jugular. Plus, he'd had to act quickly. The first forty-eight hours were absolutely crucial to solving a missing person's case; and this case was crucial to his career.

Jonathan Snyder accosted DS Webber on the doorstep. 'Do you have anything? What's the progress?'

'This is PC de Witt.' Mark remembered the mandatory introductions. Sharon nodded and smiled tentatively. She was a big-busted woman, short, motherly, and rotund.

Snyder hardly spared her a glance. 'You've news for us?'

'Can we talk inside?'

Snyder expelled a sigh and led them to the lounge. He didn't invite them to sit down. Webber took a seat nevertheless and de Witt remained standing.

'There are a few things we need to clarify with you. To help us with the –'

'Go on – ask away!'

Sarah Snyder walked in from the kitchen, still wearing the same dressing gown she'd had on when they reported the disappearance fourteen hours earlier. 'Have you found her?' Against all logic, she looked hopeful.

'No, not yet. We have a few questions that may help us – your answers may help us to re-enact the hours before Rachel's disappearance and her – her frame of mind.'

Sarah slumped on the sofa. Her dressing gown split open at her chest and she had the presence of mind to pull the lapels neatly together. She held her hand against her throat, her fingers curled in. 'Anything to help . . . Just hurry up, please, and find her.'

Webber shifted uncomfortably. 'We're doing everything we can . . .'

'Just ask us whatever you need, DS Webber,' said Jonathan Snyder.

'Can you take me through last night. Everything you can remember, no matter how unrelated it may seem to your daughter's . . .' He wished he could interview the parents separately, and that had been his original intent. That was why he had dragged de Witt with him. But he had quickly realised that it would send the wrong message. The parents would clam up; they would become suspicious. In the end, he wasn't and would never be as insensitive – nor perhaps as ruthlessly good at his job – as DI Marsh. But he was a father and he knew how he would feel if somebody even insinuated the possibility of him hurting his girls.

Jonathan groaned. 'We've been through last night over and over again in our minds. And in our minds, trust me, we're running in circles, wondering what we might've missed. Nothing! There's nothing we can add, and if we thought of something, I'd be the first one on the phone to let you know.'

'Yes . . . We spoke to her friends at school – Rhiannon and a few other girls. None of them has any clues as to what happened. The closest CCTV camera is on the T-junction with Claret Road. We checked that. No suspicious vehicles in the night. In fact, no vehicles at all. No pedestrians – not until six o'clock this morning when it was you who ran out into the road, all the way to the junction. It looked like you were calling out – but I don't have to tell you that . . . To be frank with you, we drew a blank. So if you could take me through last night –'

'Where do you want us to start?' Jonathan ground his teeth in exasperation. He gaped at his wife, taken by surprise as she suddenly broke down in tears. She let go of her lapels. One side of her gown slid off her shoulder.

'I don't know what to say! I can't remember . . . I'm sorry. I forget . . . I . . . I . . . I'm so sorry!' she sobbed.

'It's OK, Mrs Snyder, that's why we're here: in case you remembered something new. That's how it is, memories come and go. It's not a precise science.' Sharon de Witt sat down next to the woman and embraced her, pulling her gown over her shoulder and covering her chest. That may not have been the correct protocol, but it worked.

'Take your time,' Mark said, but his tone contradicted his words. He was doing his best to control his growing exasperation. 'Anything you can think of, anything at all. Anything out of the ordinary . . .'

Sarah Snyder nodded and seemed to have picked herself up again. 'Yes . . . She wasn't quite herself . . . It started when we were shopping.'

'What do you mean?'

'We were in Sexton's Mall, shopping and having tea, and everything was absolutely fine. She was happy, chattering away about things, boyfriends – the things girls talk about. And then she got a text message, and a number of texts followed, and just like that we were on our way home. I hadn't even finished my cake . . .'

'Wasn't that something about homework?' Jonathan asked. 'I thought she was upset about not keeping up with things at school . . . She said so, or you said it . . .'

'Yes, she did, but it was . . . well, it was sudden. We came

43

home and she just dropped everything on the floor and ran to her room. And shut her door. I mean, that *was* strange, wouldn't you say? We'd bought new clothes for her – normally, she'd be dying to try them on straight away. It was the phone, I'm sure of that. Whoever it was on that phone – She said it was Rhiannon. About the homework . . . Rachel is so serious about school – it didn't surprise me she was a bit ruffled when Rhiannon texted her, but then . . .'

'Have you checked her phone?' Snyder shot Mark a challenging look.

'We haven't found a phone . . . You didn't mention a phone. You said her iPad was missing but there was no mention of a phone.'

'Of course she has a phone. Every teenager has a mobile phone! They lead their lives on mobile phones!'

'We'll have that followed up.' DS Webber wrote down *missing mobile??* in his notebook.

'Rachel doesn't go anywhere without her mobile. She takes it with her to the bathroom.'

'They all do,' Sharon de Witt concurred with Snyder's earlier remarks. 'I've a daughter and a son, and both –'

'What is her number? We can put a trace on it.'

Frantically, Jonathan began searching for his daughter's number in his phone contacts, but Sarah knew it by heart. She quoted it to DS Webber who wrote it down next to *missing mobile??*

'It's a Pay-As-You-Go,' she added.

Webber scowled, disappointed. 'It'll take a long time to get a calls log from the service provider. I'll get the request paperwork in motion today. Still, we can try to trace it. If it's on and it is on her, we'll find her.'

Sarah inhaled with trepidation and cupped her hand over her mouth. 'Please, please do!'

'Do you think those text messages . . . it's what started it . . . I mean, she was acting up – I mean, she was . . . I thought it was your typical obnoxious teenage mood. I was bloody annoyed – told her off . . . I, at the dinner table, I . . .' Jonathan Snyder started a sentence, and paused, not quite able to articulate his thoughts. He looked at Webber for help. His face was white with panic.

'It's too early to comment, it really is. But something threw her off that night . . . There was a trigger of some kind. If you think about it: she hadn't prepared herself for this, there was no pre-meditation, she left the house as she stood – it was sudden. It was a spur of the moment decision.'

'But why! Why would she run away from us?' There was so much disbelief, so much hurt in the father's eyes that Webber knew: the man had nothing to do with his daughter's disappearance. And there went the theory of family involvement supported by police statistics. This family wasn't one of those statistics.

Webber stood up, 'If there's nothing else you can remember, we'll be on our way. Be assured that I'll keep you informed, day and night. And you can call me at any time. I'm a father, too – I've three little girls at home. I understand.'

Chapter Six

Gillian drives through the main entrance. Above it hangs a sign telling her that she is welcome to Whalehurst School, an independent day and boarding school for pupils 11-18 years old, a school that is consistently rated Outstanding by OFSTED, a school whose Principal is Dr Edwin Featherstone assisted by an impressive number of qualifications trailing behind his name. There is a school motto which states pretentiously in Latin *Primus Inter Pares*. In plain English this translates into *First Among Equals*. Transparently, the school has high aspiration for its pupils.

Dr Featherstone is waiting for her outside, alongside Bobby Hughes and his forensic team, and a few Uniforms. Apart from the headmaster, they all look paralysed with inaction. It seems like nothing has been done to further the collection of evidence since Gillian left the scene a couple of hours ago. She soon finds out why.

Even before he opens his mouth, Dr Featherstone radiates an air of pomposity. He is standing with his head proudly elevated, and to Gillian's amazement, he is wearing his headmaster's ceremonial gown. In the style of Napoleon Bonaparte, his left hand is tucked between the lapels of his outfit. He looks Gillian up and down with undisguised contempt, maybe even hostility. 'Are you the *senior* officer in charge?' There is a hint of doubt in his tone.

Gillian produces her ID card. 'DI Marsh.'

'Is there nobody of higher rank that I can speak to?'

'I am the SIO – the officer in charge of this investigation, sir. What seems to be the matter?'

He waves his arms dismissively towards the hapless assortment of officers. 'The matter is that those people have plainly and without authorisation invaded my school grounds. This goes against all and every safeguarding regulation and the privacy of our residents!'

'This is a murder investigation, Mr Featherstone –'

'*Dr* Featherstone, I'd prefer.'

'We are compelled to secure and thoroughly examine the scene of crime, sir.' Gillian refuses to play ball with his titles. 'You seem to be obstructing that process.'

'There are children on these premises, our residents whose safety is entrusted to me by their parents. I won't have strangers loitering here in the night. You will have to come back with a search warrant.'

'It doesn't work like that, sir. This is a crime scene. Murder was committed right on your doorstep –'

'That doesn't mean that you can –'

Gillian won't be interrupted. She has had it with this buffoon. 'Yes, it does. And yes, I can. We're going to secure the area. We will also need immediate access to that pavilion and all outbuildings in the field bordering the country park. I strongly suggest you hand over the keys to *Dr* Hughes,' now she has the pleasure of emphasising Bobby's title, 'or simply just open the buildings for his team to be able to enter and examine them. You may also be able to assist us with locating the likely murder weapon. Do you have any bows lying around?'

Featherstone's eyes bulge. 'Bows!'

'Yes – as in bows and arrows.'

'We have an archery club . . . Has someone been killed with our –'

'This is what we're trying to establish, Mr Featherstone, and you are obstructing us in this process . . . If you don't mind, we have to get on with it.' Gillian turns away from the man and faces the team. 'Secure the entire sports fields on the eastern side. No one is to enter the fields until we're done, understood? I want officers monitoring all exits.'

'This is outrageous!' Featherstone is shaking with fury. 'I'd like to speak to your superior!'

Gillian replies as she walks past him, without pausing to look him in the eye, 'Please return to your quarters and remain there until it is confirmed that our Forensics team is finished with gathering evidence. Detectives will be here tomorrow morning to interview any potential witnesses, including yourself, unless you prefer to come to the station with me right now?'

His lips quiver in sheer indignation, but he is unable to formulate another objection.

'And, sir? Consider yourself lucky that I don't have you arrested for wasting our time and obstructing us in our investigation.'

When Gillian finally gets home, the grandfather clock – her inheritance from her grandmother, paradoxically – strikes twice. There is no escaping the fact that it is two o'clock in the morning. Gillian is thirsty. The bottle of red, still open on the coffee table, is not a viable option. She will have to be up with the lark tomorrow – or rather, today. She drags herself to the kitchen and puts on the kettle. Both Corky and Fritz give her the evil eye for waking them from their slumber. Waiting for the kettle to boil, Gillian collapses on the couch and flicks on the TV. Bizarrely, the same film is on, or maybe it's a sequel. The damsel in distress obviously succeeded in hoisting herself up that ledge safely. Alas, the monster is also up and running, or rather leaping, behind her, hot on her (high) heels. She is as good as dead now, surely!

But Gillian will not find out because she herself is dead to the world. She doesn't even hear the kettle whistle cheerfully in the kitchen before it switches off automatically with a sulky ping.

The auditorium is large and plush. It is filled with teenagers, all dressed in their immaculate navy blue uniforms featuring ties with the school's crest. The teaching staff have congregated on the stage behind her. They, too, are in uniform, wearing robes as if they have just stepped out of a J.K. Rowling novel. Bizarrely, that congregation of lofty professors includes Gillian's daughter. Tara teaches modern foreign languages at Whalehurst. She started in September last year. Of course, Gillian always knew Tara taught at a public school, but it had never occurred to her that nowadays such an establishment would be as antiquated and pretentious as it was in the fifties. Tara doesn't belong here, yet it is not Gillian's place to tell her that. She would only get grief for her trouble.

Gillian arrived at eight o'clock sharp and demanded that she be allowed to address the whole school assembly before her officers started interviewing individual students and members of staff. Dr Featherstone nearly suffered a cardiac arrest and protested vehemently everybody's innocence. He didn't believe Gillian when she told him that she was seeking witnesses, not perpetrators. He advanced a heartfelt warning that he would not let this matter rest, and that he happened to know people in high places. A few of those respectable people sent their children to this school. They would not stand idly by when the school and its reputation were being dragged through the mud just because somewhere on the outskirts someone got killed. That had nothing to do with the school or its pupils.

Gillian wasted no breath trying to appeal to the headmaster's sense of civic duty and compassion. He probably doesn't remember what Bradley Watson, his groundsman's son and assistant, looked like. To him, such lowly employees were just manual labourers – they had no faces. She insisted everybody flocked into the auditorium, like it or not.

Her voice bounces off the walls and the high ceiling like a basketball. The blue-blood teenagers are a captive audience. They stare at her in sheer terror, their eyes hanging on her every word.

'Bradley Watson was just a few years older than you. Most of you know him: he's been working here, at the school, with his father, Mr Watson . . .'

A sea of bland oblivion to that name reminds her, these children don't mingle with the plebs. She shakes off the indignation that is slowly creeping up her spine.

'So, the body was found just outside your school grounds, on the eastern side of the pitch – that's where the cricket pavilion is. It may be that Bradley was running away from someone in the school, or that he was trying to get to the safety of the school from the country park. We don't know yet . . . If anyone of you saw or heard anything last night that may be relevant to our investigation, I and my officers will be here all day today, gathering information and listening to everything you have to say. No observation is too small or too insignificant. Feel free to come back here to the auditorium at any time during the day to talk to us. Perhaps you knew Bradley as a friend . . .' Again, a wall of indifference exposes that assumption as unlikely. 'Right . . . Well, thank you for your co-operation and your patience while we're carrying out our investigation. Any questions? Feel free to ask me anything – we all want to get to the bottom of it and find the killer as quickly as possible.'

A polite, but distinctly disengaged, silence answers her. This is going to be like getting blood from a stone. Gillian grinds her teeth with growing frustration.

Chapter Seven

Dr Featherstone seethed with fury. His turkey neck, all loose skin and no definition — the result of sudden weight loss seven years ago — was flushed livid crimson. Who was this little missy running circles around him and telling him what to do? And more to the point, who did she *think* she was! He wouldn't stand for it! He had a PhD in Philosophy *and* another one in Medieval History. He was a respected academic — he should be respected! He wouldn't be pushed around, certainly not on his own turf! It was scandalous!

He had not slept a wink all night, though God knows he tried. Before bed, he had poured himself a generous glass of single malt. His hands were shaking. The little missy had thoroughly unsettled him. He paced the length of his bedroom, from the door to the east-facing window overlooking the sports fields. He watched the intruders — Forensics and police officers — scratch for evidence, plunder his sheds and pavilion, carry bags, and take casts of foot imprints. Snooping around. He watched every step they took on his grounds. The artificial yellow light of their lamps and the droning of the generator they had brought with them irritated the living daylights out of him. It felt like a violation. It *was* a violation! They had no business doing that. That boy had been found in the park, not here, not on his soil. He would have never allowed that boy to get himself killed within the perimeter of his ancient and prestigious school. That boy's death would under no circumstances be linked to Whalehurst. He would do everything in his power to protect this place against slander and false accusations.

But had the little missy told him everything they had uncovered so far? She had told him about the arrow in the boy's back. Featherstone mulled that over for a bit. That was only one snippet of information. The one bit that might be proven to be related to his school. But how much had been held back from him? How much did they know that could drag him and his school through the mud? That was what disturbed him the most: the uncertainty. *How much did they know?*

He was driving himself mad with anxiety. A second glass of whisky was called for. He poured it with the same shaking hands as he had the first one. Even this prime single malt would not calm his nerves. He knew that once they started they wouldn't stop. They would dig deeper. They would prod and sniff until they lugged every last bit of dirt out into the open.

He downed the whisky in a single swig and twisted his lips. The liquid worked its way down to his gut, burning everything in its path. Armed with his Dutch courage, he made the decision to fight back. He had connections. He would stop the little missy in her tracks before she had a chance to cause any further damage. Dr Edwin Featherstone had not spent the last seven years rebuilding his good name to have it all destroyed in one surreal night. He would do all it took to protect his reputation and the reputation of his school. His home!

He waited until the decent hour of six in the morning before he descended to his office and searched for the phone number to call Ronald Sutherland QC. Sutherland was an alumnus and a benefactor of Whalehurst School; he sent his only daughter Joanna to board here. The school meant something to him. He cared for its good name. And he would know what to do. Featherstone reached for the phone and keyed in the number.

'Mr Sutherland?' A dazed grunt answered him, full of sleep and irritation. 'Mr Sutherland, I'm sorry to be calling you this early in the day . . . It's Dr Featherstone . . . um . . . the headmaster at Whalehurst –'

'Has something happened to Joanna?' The sleep fell off the

voice in a flash. 'What is it? Mary!' The voice swerved away from the receiver. 'It's Joanna's school! Something –'

'No, nothing happened! Not to Joanna, that is . . . But . . . how can I put it?' Featherstone regretted having had all that whisky. His tongue was tied in knots. 'It's the school, per se . . . I mean, I need your urgent advice. Legal advice.'

Sutherland was still talking away from the phone. 'False alarm! Go to bed, Mary. It's something to do with the school. God knows! I'll tell you later. Go back to bed.' He returned his attention to Featherstone. 'Isn't this a little bit early in the day?'

'Yes, I know. I realise, but it *is* rather urgent.'

'OK, I'm listening.'

'Thank you, much obliged.' Featherstone sighed with relief.

'Let's get to the point. I'd like to go back to bed. It's bloody six o'clock in the morning!'

'Yes . . . Well, this is quite out of the ordinary. The body of a young man was found on the perimeter of the school. In fact, it wasn't even the perimeter – it was outside, in Ogburn Park, the park bordering the school. The young man had been, apparently, shot dead with an arrow –'

'An arrow? That's an unusual choice of murder weapon.'

'Precisely! But that's what prompted the police to search for clues all over the school, the sports fields, the outbuildings, the . . . They're crawling everywhere! The school is swarming with people who have no business to be here! I fear for the . . . I . . . I don't know what to do! How to stop this! As you may imagine, I am concerned for my students, their safety and –'

'With the police there, I'd think, the pupils' safety is not compromised. Do they suspect that the perpetrator may be hiding on the premises?'

'Um . . .' Featherstone groaned. He didn't want to alarm this parent. Everything was turning to custard! 'Well, I thought . . . I was told they were securing evidence . . . They can't be possibly thinking there is a murderer in our midst here at Whalehurst. There are no murderers hiding on the premises, I assure you, sir.' He forced his voice an octave lower to sound calm and in control.

'OK, so they're looking for evidence. That's what the cops do. What is it that you want, Mr Featherstone?'

'*Dr* Featherstone . . .' He bit his tongue. This wasn't the time for correcting misconceptions about his academic status. 'I feel it's my duty to protect the students from the police intrusion and the potential fallout. Imagine if the media got wind of this . . . they'd be all over us like a rash! We are a respectable establishment. We have the children of diplomats and military personnel here. People rely on our absolute discretion. I must protect my patrons' privacy and the . . . Well, the detective in charge of this . . . this . . . *fiasco* is a woman going by the name of Marsh. She had her people enter the school grounds without a search warrant and despite my formal objection. There must be something I can do to stop her! I was hoping you can advise me. What steps can I take to ensure the school is kept out of this —'

'I can advise you, yes.'

'I knew I could rely on you, Mr Sutherland! Thank God for that! So, how shall I go about this?' He had a pen at the ready.

'You should offer the detective your full co-operation,' Sutherland told him and promptly rang off.

A couple of hours later, Featherstone was shaking with a mixture of anger and hopelessness. He clenched his teeth and his fists, ready for a final confrontation, as DI Marsh closed her speech in the hall and purposefully marched towards him.

'Mr Featherstone.' She still dared to ignore his proper title! 'I'd like to take a little tour of the school and the grounds, talk to the students and the staff. You know, a preliminary reconnaissance.'

'Reconnaissance?' Featherstone blinked. 'Haven't your *people* raked through everything already? They've been here all night with their lights flashing, and . . . keeping everyone awake . . .'

'It's not the same.' She didn't fool him with that fake smile! He was on highest alert. 'I like to examine the scene myself. I get a better feel for what may have happened, and how.'

'I don't think so, really . . . It didn't happen here, I can assure you. Why don't you scout Ogburn Park – that's where it happened.'

'Oh, I will, but one thing at a time. You can accompany me. It'd be useful if you could answer my questions –'

'I . . . I can't! I've got things to do!' He looked nervously about him, searching for allies. He wished he could control the surge of panic and the shaking hands, but that could only be achieved with the help of single malt.

The students were leaving the auditorium slowly and in an orderly fashion (of which he would be proud in other, less unsettling, circumstances). Monty Collingsworth caught his eye and nodded a brief greeting to him. He was his mainstay, the best prefect Whalehurst had ever had.

'Collingsworth!' he called out to the boy, who smiled helpfully, calmly, and walked towards him with an assured stride.

'Sir?' Monty had a steady, blue-eyed gaze and a smooth, high forehead with not a single ripple of anxiety crossing it. He was the epitome of self-composure. His athletic, sculpted body towered over Featherstone, and even more so over the little missy, who couldn't be taller than five foot two. There was strength in the boy's size that he found fortifying.

'Would you show DI Marsh around the school, answer her questions as best as you can.' He turned to the little missy. 'DI Marsh, this is Collingsworth, our Head Boy. He'll be your guide.'

With pleasantries exchanged, Featherstone hurried to his office, his robes trailing behind him. First things first: he unlocked the top drawer of his desk where he kept his hip flask. He took a drag and exhaled through his pursed lips. Then he turned on his computer and started deleting.

Chapter Eight

Mo stared at the police tape that had been wrapped over the rails fencing the track like parcel string. His feet were moving rhythmically: toe-heel, toe-heel; his elbows were sliding alongside his waist; his narrow chest jutted forward. He had done his stretching exercises. He was ready to go.

It was now less than half an hour before lessons were due to start and he hadn't as much as warmed his muscles. The races were in less than a month. He was obliged to intensify his training, aiming to peak at the right time. The Team GB scouts were coming to see him to be sure that they had the right athlete for the Games. This was not the time to drop standards.

Under his red and blue tracksuit, his body felt taut and ready to leap into action. He jumped on the spot, shot upwards like a rocket, and felt the crisp morning air wash over him. His muscles were cooling down. Mo was not used to this. He would be lost without running.

He wasn't feeling himself this morning. He clutched his head in his hands and massaged his temples in frantic circles. Then he threw his arms out and began circling them in the air. He was waving away his anxieties and his inferiorities – and everything and everyone who would try to stand in his way.

He saw Monty Collingsworth approach in the company of that detective who had already stolen the precious fifteen minutes of his time in the morning, talking about Brad. Mo's muscles tensed up as if someone had poured a bucket of cold water over him. The whole warm-up had been for nothing.

The discovery of Brad's body on the school's doorstep couldn't have come at a more inconvenient moment. It should have been dumped somewhere else – somewhere out of the way. Mo's way of thinking was that the body was just that – a body. It had no power to do anything else. It had no strength to fight back. It certainly did not have a personality, or feelings that could be hurt. Not that Brad had had any feelings to start with.

Mo tried to loosen up his muscles. He shook his fingers and rotated his shoulders. He rolled his head from side to side in an attempt to get back into the swing of his exercises. But it was pointless now that the track was out of bounds and the police were snooping around. If they had only given him until 9 a.m.! It would've made zero difference to Brad, seeing that he was dead and couldn't care less.

'Mo!' Collingsworth waved to him.

Mo came to an involuntary standstill and straightened his posture like a soldier saluting his superior, arms glued to his sides. It was an impulse in response to seeing Collingsworth, because the Head Boy was the Commander-in-Chief here at Whalehurst – everyone knew that. Even on those occasions when Collingsworth was nice to Mo, Mo wouldn't dream of taking him for granted. Being nice didn't mean fraternising with Mo – that would be the day! – but Collingsworth watched over him. He had his best interests at heart – for as long, of course, as Mo did well on the track and did Whalehurst proud. That was all that mattered to Collingsworth and it suited Mo to a T. It was part of the deal. Because Mo wanted to succeed and, to achieve success, he had to keep running. So he didn't mind so much when Monty would quip at him in that posh clipped accent of his, *Don't dangle your arms when you run, Abdikarim! You look like a bloody ape and I'm minded to stick a banana up your arse!* He meant to keep Mo on his toes, ready for the tournament. He meant well. And sometimes he would slap Mo on the back, and they would both laugh, making monkey grunts. It was all in jest, Mo had to remind himself of that from time to time.

'And this is Mo Abdikarim.' Collingsworth pointed to him, 'Not exactly Mo Farah, or should I say, *not yet*. He's the king of the track, tipped to represent the country in Birmingham, our secret weapon at the next Commonwealth Games. We have high hopes for Mo here at Whalehurst.' Collingsworth was smiling at Mo and Mo grinned back, flattered and relaxed.

'Hi, Mo.' The detective offered him her hand to shake. Now, that was awkward. That was something Mo wasn't used to and wasn't happy with. His hand went limp and clammy in hers. He couldn't look her in the eye. An irrational niggle troubled him that the detective could read his mind, what with the eyes being the windows to the soul. So he gazed at the sports field.

'When are you going to take off that tape? I need to train.'

The policewoman peered at him with narrowed eyes. 'When we're ready.' She spoke sharply. She was not as nice and chummy as she had tried to portray herself in the assembly. Mo had been right about her all along. She was suspicious of him, he could tell. A skinny black boy in a public school, asking stupid questions. It was a stupid question, wasn't it? About the tape . . . He had to keep reminding himself to keep his mouth shut.

Unnerved, he started jogging on the spot. 'Must go.'

'Have you seen anything out of the ordinary?' the policewoman drilled him with her narrowed eyes.

'Like what?'

'Anything that aroused your suspicions.'

'I go to bed early. No, I mean, I haven't seen anything.'

'Did you know Bradley Watson well?'

'Brad? No, not well. Not to talk to. I really must go. Lessons start soon.' His feet took him away from the woman and her questions. He was running across the courtyard. He shouldn't

58

be, he knew that, but he couldn't help it. He had to get away from her.

Collingsworth didn't shout after him to tell him off. He was putting on a performance for the policewoman's benefit. It seemed he too was out of his comfort zone.

Chapter Nine

They duck under the police tape and head across the sports pitches and towards the pavilion. Collingsworth is sharing with Gillian all sorts of superficial details one could easily find in the school prospectus. He is an obliging young man: articulate and well-mannered. There is an air of a cavalier about him: long blond locks bouncing in the breeze, assured stride, athleticism, and that spark of living dangerously in his eyes. All that is missing is a wide-brimmed hat with an ostrich feather and a rapier rattling against the side of a leather boot. He walks and talks like he owns the place, which in a way he probably does. That is the prerogative of being the Head Boy. Other pupils treat him with reverence, greater reverence than they offer to the headmaster who hasn't shown his face since the assembly and who struck Gillian as flaky and unhinged. It looks like the school is running all by itself. The students seem to carry on regardless.

'Does Dr Featherstone seem to you a tad too rattled, or is he always like that?' she interrupts Collingsworth's soliloquy about the school's sporting achievements.

'We haven't had so much excitement in all my seven years here,' Collingsworth replies evenly. 'That's as long as Dr Featherstone's been here. I guess we're all acting a little out of character. It's not every day that bodies are found hanging from the school fence.'

It is an answer worthy of a politician: it tells Gillian nothing. The boy is heading for a bright future in the Cabinet, and he knows it. Alas, Gillian is not interested in his bright future.

'So, would you say that, normally, the headmaster has a cool head on his shoulders and no alcohol on his morning breath?'

Collingsworth responds with a half-smile that quivers on his lips intermittently, and promptly flies away. That smile renders his answer non-committal, and partially contradicts the words that follow, 'Dr Featherstone is an exemplary headteacher. Relatively speaking.'

They enter the large pavilion situated at the far end of the field. From inside it is more like a gymnasium; it features all the space, apparatus and other trimmings of a sports hall many a comprehensive school's headmasters would kill for.

'This is impressive,' Gillian's voice echoes, lost between the walls and high ceilings.

'Yes, we take physical fitness extremely seriously at Whalehurst. Let me show you our archery range. It may be of some interest to you. I understand Bradley Watson was shot with an arrow?'

'We didn't share that information with the public.'

'Word travels fast in Little Ogburn.'

'I imagine it does.'

He leads her through a side door and along a narrow, suffocating corridor lit by flickering fluorescent lights. It smells of teenage sweat and something musky, probably due to the lack of air circulation. There isn't a single window here. He invites her into another large room with several target boards at the far end of it. An open cabinet displaying at least a dozen bows is fitted in one corner, with a collection of arrows and bracers beneath it.

Gillian is alarmed by the ease of access to these weapons. 'Is this pavilion locked at night?'

'Yes, but everyone knows where the key is.'

'Oh?'

'Mr Watson – our groundsman – he always hangs the key on the hook by the fire exit. I'll show you if you like.'

'By *everyone* do you mean everyone at school?'

'Everyone in the village, I'd say. If Bradley knew where the key was, all his mates would've known too.'

'That's brilliant.' Gillian rolls her eyes. 'It really narrows our field of suspects.'

Collingsworth picks up one of the bows and selects an arrow. He adopts an erect position, his fingers clawing the shaft of the arrow, his long muscular arms taut, his focus entirely on the target board. He expels the arrow and remains standing in the same statuesque position, following his arrow's trajectory with his eyes. It quivers through the air like a plucked guitar string. It hits the bullseye.

'Excellent aim,' says Gillian.

He puts the bow back on the stand, shrugs nonchalantly in response to the flattery. 'We're all pretty good at it. Archery is on the school's PE curriculum. As is fencing and a couple of other medieval martial arts. Everyone leaving this school is a competent horseman, for example. We all take horse riding lessons at Palmer's Stables, in Bishops Well. You see, Dr Featherstone is a great believer in our country's medieval heritage. Medieval martial arts is what he studied for his PhD. When he came here he set up The Medieval Martial Arts Society of Whalehurst. We call it *Mass*. Not just because it's a sort of acronym but also because it's almost a religion, at least for Dr Featherstone it is. Mass's code of honour is based on that of the Knights Templar. It's all very serious – we do take it seriously. It's what makes this school unique. If you're a sixth-former and you want to do well here, you're best advised to join us.'

'Us? Are you a member?'

'What do you think?'

'You seem to be living in a different era, a bit like children playing with plastic swords.' Gillian stifles the exclamation that is screaming at the back of her mind: *Oh, get over yourself, you pretentious twat!*

'We're very much in touch with reality.' Collingsworth throws back his head and peers at her down his nose. He clearly resents her comparison. 'We're well rooted in the past, but we have a very contemporary outlook.' He says it well, without the slightest undertone of irritation. The Head Boy is a model of political correctness.

'Do you have a first name, Collingsworth?' She has to break through his veneer of stiff politeness if she is ever to gain his confidence.

'Yes, I do. Don't we all, DI Marsh?' There is a hint of arrogance in his tone. He is beginning to lower his guard; he is toying with her. He has allowed himself a joke. Good.

'So what is it?'

'Monty, as in *Python*.' He doesn't laugh at his own joke, and neither does Gillian, but then again, she never laughs at jokes. He seems to appreciate her cool. He says, 'Do call me Collingsworth. I prefer that if it's all the same to you. Whalehurst is all about appearances, and about the pecking order. It takes one a while to climb to the top of the ladder. I quite like being here.'

This is where Gillian does smile. The boy is full of insecurities, as any eighteen–year–old should be. He is just good at glossing over them. 'OK, I'll pretend I've never heard of your Christian name, Collingsworth.'

'That'd be appreciated, DI Marsh.'

'So, seeing that you know the murder weapon, would you say that anybody from this school would be capable of handling a bow and arrow?'

'With proficiency! But not just anybody from Whalehurst – anybody from Little Ogburn would probably fancy their chances, too. With varying rates of success. Like I said, everyone knows where the key is, and I know for a fact that the locals visit here regularly and help themselves to the equipment.' He pronounces the word *locals* with a hint of superiority, which makes Gillian cringe. 'Sometimes I think Watson leaves the key out purposefully – you know? To give his *people* a chance to play with the toys round here. His special service to the local community.'

'That narrows things down for us.'

'Sorry to be the bearer of bad news.' He presents a charming smile. This boy must have broken many a girl's heart, and there are plenty left to break yet.

'Would you like to see the rest of the building?'

They traverse through a series of chambers which aren't in the least reminiscent of Gillian's secondary school PE lessons: the archery range is adjacent to a fencing room featuring long and narrow rapier-type weapons and bodysuits complete with mesh-protected headgear; they pass a climbing wall and indoor cricket nets. Finally, they leave the Dark Ages and emerge on a concrete path leading back to the east wing of the main school building.

Back in the auditorium, Gillian notes with dismay, DC Mac-fadyen and DC Whittaker sit bored, looking into each other's eyes and twiddling their thumbs. Gillian thanks Monty Collingsworth for the guided tour of the school and lets him off to his lessons. She approaches her officers.

'Anyone? Anything?'

They shake their heads.

'A conspiracy of silence,' Erin says.

'Or maybe they simply don't know shit? The whole poncy lot of them with their heads up their own arseholes. I bet they don't mingle with the real world out there, where Bradley Watson comes from,' Whittaker summarises in his no-nonsense West Country vernacular. Whittaker is a new arrival at Sexton's Canning CID, but he is a seasoned policeman who in his youth walked the beat in the backstreets of Greyston and – as he puts it – knows his shit. He has come to Sexton's from Greyston. He may be in his fifties, but he is certainly not biding his time till retirement. He moved to Bishops Well to look after his wife, who is suffering from MS, as it had always been her dream to live in the country. (It was never Whittaker's dream, for the record!)

Gillian likes him. He is not a time-waster and he has a sharp eye for detail, plus contacts in all the right places.

Chapter Ten

Back at the station in the incident room, Gillian stands in front of a magnetic whiteboard which displays all the information gathered so far in Bradley Watson's case. The young man's mugshot from when he was arrested for the second time features proudly in the centre of the board. His date of birth as well as the date of his death – this one with a question mark, pending the outcome of the post-mortem examination – sit alongside each other like yin and yang. The Potter brothers, who discovered the body under the suspicious circumstances of being in the wrong place at the wrong time and having no business to be there at all, hold top spot on the board. Whalehurst School is mentioned. Three arrows point towards it: one cross-references it to Watson's place of employment, the second one to the murder weapon, and the third one to Dr Featherstone, mainly because Gillian has a funny feeling about him. Gillian is adding more information to the board as she goes. She writes, *2 drug convictions* and throws Watson's file at Whittaker.

'Read through his file, Constable. Look for his contacts from the old days. There's a chance Bradley regressed into his past. His parents hadn't seen him since Friday. Apparently he was in Sexton's. Who with? What was he doing? Is there any link to Sexton's drug gangs? His father believes he went straight, but I don't buy it. I don't think they'd let him off the hook that easily.'

'Not if they could help it,' Whittaker agrees.

'Use your old contacts, see what you can uncover. I have a feeling there's a connection there. Young men don't get murdered in these parts because of small misunderstandings in the playground. It has to be something big – like drugs.'

Whittaker opens the file and pages through it. A smile of recognition graces his otherwise ungraceful face which nature has vandalised with a bulbous nose and bushy eyebrows. 'Yeah,' he says, 'I'm on a first-name basis with most of them.'

'Good.' Gillian knows she can leave the matter safely in Whittaker's hands. She glances at Erin. 'Macfadyen, go and see whoever's in charge of Ogburn Park. Do they lock the place at night? Do they have any CCTV cameras, though I doubt that squirrels require regular surveillance . . . Still, technically the body was found in the park. Take somebody with you, talk to dog walkers and the staff, see what you can dig out. Somebody might've seen something unless it happened in the dead of night.'

Erin nods. 'We don't have any manpower left to do the digging out, ma'am. They're all looking for the missing girl. I doubt I can recruit anybody for this exercise . . .' She turns to Miller, 'Miller?'

'No, not Miller,' Gillian says. 'I want him to do door-to-door in Little Ogburn. Watson's neighbours, but also any of his friends, people he hangs out with in the village. Damn the missing girl!'

Gillian bites her cheek. It is annoying how cases come by busloads: none at all or all at once, like now. She may have to beg Scarface for more men and resources. Perhaps the drugs connection could yet bring viable co-operation from NCA and that would mean doubling the manpower on this case.

'OK, what are you waiting for? Get down to it, and keep me informed. I'm off to nag Almond for that bloody autopsy he promised me by lunchtime.'

'It's only ten o'clock,' Miller points out.

'That's entirely beside the point!'

'I was just about to call you –'

'What do we know? Time of death? How precise can you be?' Gillian interrupts Dr Almond in her customarily unceremonious way. He doesn't flinch – he's used to her brusqueness. He pulls off his latex gloves and discards them in a bin. His assistant is cleaning the instruments. The autopsy is as good as done and dusted. Gillian has missed most of it. She definitely doesn't have a penchant for the gore of forensic pathology and usually sends Webber to attend. Except that this time Webber is busy finding the missing girl, which hopefully will put another feather in the DI's cap he so desperately covets. He is just a whisker away from promotion. He has asked for Gillian to step back; it's his case.

Almond leans against a stainless steel table and folds his arms on his chest. 'The cause of death has always been beyond dispute: an arrow through the heart. And that's not in a manner of speech. The arrow penetrated directly through the left atrium. Like I said, a damn good shot.'

'That makes every pupil at Whalehurst, ha! Every resident of Little Ogburn a potential suspect. Archery is the favourite pastime over there, they're all at it! I need more than that.'

Almond smiles. You can tell he is smiling because the handles of his huge moustache lift like stringed puppet's arms. 'A healthy, well-nourished male in his late teens. Signs of recreational drug use, going by the marks on his forearms. I'll have more details once I have the pathology report from the lab.'

'Recent?'

'Yes, old and new. The newest, I'd say, a month or so ago.'

'So he was a user . . . Not according to his father, though.'

'Fathers are usually the last ones to find out about their children's sins.'

'Time of death?'

'Early hours of Saturday, maybe as far back as Friday night. He's been dead for more than two days . . . possibly even somewhere in the region of sixty hours.'

'So he was lying there since Friday night and no one's noticed? Two days . . . Could the body have been moved?'

'No evidence of the body being moved post-mortem. I'd say we found him where he fell. It'd be near impossible to move the body and position it in precisely the same position. I say *near* impossible, mind. Also, the amount of blood found at the scene would confirm that –'

Gillian's mobile rings. She checks the caller, intent on ringing them back later. She still has a few questions to ask Michael Almond. But it's Jon Riley from Forensics. 'Yes, Jon, it'd better be important.'

'Hello, gorgeous! Lovely to hear your voice – butter wouldn't melt!' She has an image of grinning Riley with his puffed-up hamster cheeks.. 'I wouldn't be calling you unless it was a matter of life or death. Death, really, in our line of work.'

'OK, so what is it you want to tell me?'

'Lots of things, Gillian love, but they'll have to wait. I need you to come and see me. As in now. Webber is on his way.'

'Webber? Why Webber?'

'I'll explain the way I like it – face to face.'

Riley is slumped in his cosy chair upholstered in soft cream leather, a driver's seat from a Maserati he has had adapted for his office with no expense spared. But then Riley is a nutter and he would do something like that to make a point. Exactly what point is something no one but Riley will ever know. He has developed impressive facial growth over the last year. He looks like a Taliban fighter, only one who has shares in McDonald's. His chubby cheeks shine with an unhealthy glow above his beard. Next to him, Webber looks like an MI6 agent: clean-shaven, slimmed-down, with his hair combed smooth and sleek to the back. He is pacing impatiently, up and down the claustrophobic width of Riley's office corner.

'Gillian!' he exclaims, the exasperation in his voice apparent. 'The bastard wouldn't tell me anything until you arrived!'

'I don't like repeating myself, that's all,' Riley takes his feet off his desk and drives his Maserati seat up to his computer. 'I've got something to show the two of you. Two birds with one stone, as the saying goes.'

Gillian pulls a plastic chair from an empty neighbouring

workspace and says, 'Go on then. I'm in a hurry. Got a dead body on my hands.'

'That's the spirit,' Riley shakes his beard cheerfully. 'This woman needs no foreplay.'

'Oh, for fuck's sake, Riley, get to the point!' It's Webber speaking but it is Gillian's sentiment precisely.

Riley gets the message. He clicks on his keyboard and his computer comes to life, 'So, ladies and gentlemen, these are the contents of a SD card found in Bradley Watson's trouser pocket. Have a close look? Recognise anyone?'

Webber's forehead puckers as he strains to look. He should be wearing glasses, Gillian knows, but is too vain to do so. 'Can you enlarge them? These are thumbnail images.'

'No problem. I just want to show you the context first. They all have one subject – her.' Riley slides his finger over a key on his computer.

Gillian is looking at a pretty young woman, maybe even a girl. She still has quite a bit of puppy fat on her, but also sports fully developed breasts. She is wearing only a flimsy T-shirt top and no bra underneath. The picture isn't very clear. 'Who are we looking at?'

Riley slides to the next picture, and the next, and the next, all showing the same young woman in various poses in what seems like a bedroom. At last, Webber sees the wood for the trees. 'It's Rachel Snyder!'

'Who?'

'Mark's missing girl!' Riley triumphs.

'Are you saying Bradley Watson was stalking the missing girl?' Gillian asks.

'I'm not saying anything, just showing you the pics. But from what I can see she ain't exactly posing for the photos . . . she doesn't even know they are being taken.'

'So he was stalking her.'

'It's your job to draw conclusions. One more thing: the most recent pics were taken on the Friday night –'

'On the night Rachel Snyder disappeared,' Webber says.

'And the night that Bradley Watson was killed,' Gillian adds.

Gillian and Mark are standing in the street behind a large tree facing Rachel Snyder's house and gazing at the top-floor window.

'He would've taken the photos from about here, zooming through Rachel's bedroom window. He must've climbed this tree to achieve the straight angle.'

'A pretty powerful camera then, wouldn't you say?'

'Yeah, definitely not your everyday smartphone.'

'We didn't find a camera with the body.'

'Someone took it. The killer? Maybe they didn't like the photos he was taking?'

'Or maybe they liked the camera? Kids? Opportunistic theft?'

'If only we knew what type of camera we're looking for. It may yet surface somewhere. Riley said it had to be professional equipment. It's probably worth a few bob.'

Riley printed the photographs for them before they left. He obviously would not set foot outside his office even though he would be the best person to talk about the angle and the distance from which the pictures had been taken. There is one of Rachel leaving the house. She isn't looking into the camera so it is still uncertain if she was aware of Watson. The last images are of the girl leaning over a railing on a pedestrian bridge, and finally coming off the bridge, facing the camera. Was she running towards him? Had she discovered he was stalking her? Was she about to confront him? Gillian is asking herself these and many other questions.

The link between the disappearance of Rachel Snyder and the death of Bradley Watson is undeniable, but was one behind the other? And if so, in which order? Had Bradley witnessed Rachel's abduction and been silenced for good, or had Rachel witnessed Bradley's murder, and . . .

Yes, and what?

For the second time, sniffer dogs have been brought to the

area. The first time round, it was to track down Rachel's movements on the night. That was on Saturday. They got as far as the rickety bridge over the river; there they went in circles and lost the scent. There is no vehicular access from this side, only a footpath. It was assumed that the girl had been picked up from the other side of the bridge, from Ascombe Street leading to the main road to Sexton's town centre. This time the dogs will be trying to pick up Bradley's scent. It has been over forty-eight hours now; the scent, if any, will be weak, the dog handlers have warned. Still, this is their only lead at the moment.

Rachel's mother is standing in the doorway of her house. She's been asked to stay inside. The street is crawling with journalists who are just about kept at bay outside the police cordon. Their cameras are flashing and they are shouting out impertinent questions, but she doesn't seem to notice them. She looks dishevelled, her eyes are red and swollen, her hair a mess. She is wearing the same dressing gown DS Webber saw her in when he first came to talk to her after her husband had reported the disappearance.

She is watching and doesn't care about the reporters. She has nothing to hide. The husband has taken the officers' advice and is staying put indoors. So far, no one has explained to them what the hell is going on. They know nothing of the connection between their daughter's disappearance and the body found in Ogburn Park. And maybe there isn't a connection. It is too early to make one, never mind releasing it into the public domain. Webber is itching to go and talk to them, but Gillian forbade him. The information they have is sketchy; most of it – speculation. What matters most is following the leads. Chats with relatives will have to wait. The look Webber gave her when she said that was deeply aggrieved, but he listened – reluctantly. She will have to have a word with him about priorities in their line of work.

The dogs have picked up a scent. They take off across the road and towards the bridge, in the same direction they went following Rachel's scent. Gillian prays they won't come to a dead end in Ascombe Street. She and Mark are walking briskly behind the dog handlers, while Uniform are doing their best to push back the journalists. There was just one reporter to start with, now they have multiplied to at least a dozen.

'DI Marsh! Can we have a word? Do you have new leads?' one of them shouts.

'Stand back and be quiet!' Gillian barks back, 'Don't distract the dogs!' Then she adds under her breath, concisely and accurately, 'Arseholes.'

They approach the bridge, but this time the dogs do not enter it. Instead, they snuffle about busily by the riverside bushes. One of them sits down and releases a volley of excited barks.

'They've found something,' Mark states the obvious and joins the dog handlers in their search through the muddy riverbank. He puts on gloves and pulls out of his pocket a transparent evidence bag. He is holding a mobile phone. Before he places it in the bag, he turns it on. It lights up. 'Interesting,' he mumbles under his breath. 'It's Bradley Watson's.'

Not satisfied with the find, the dogs are pulling, keen to carry on with the job at hand. They are picking up a scent that leads them along a footpath that follows the river west towards Ogburn Park.

Webber is slightly out of breath, though he would never admit it. Gillian however continues with her running commentary as they jog along the path, trying to keep up with the restless hounds, 'So, let's assume he's chasing her . . . But then, why would she have come out of the house in the middle of the night of her own free will to put herself in this situation? That doesn't make any sense!'

Webber grunts.

'No, you're right. So, she doesn't know he's following her. She doesn't know he's there at all. Perhaps she's off to meet someone – a man? They're running away together? Typical teenage behaviour. We've seen it many times before . . . That's why you haven't heard anything from the kidnappers! Because there aren't any kidnappers. They girl's run away with someone, a lover, a sugar daddy . . . That would explain it, wouldn't it?'

Webber gasps for air.

'Yes, I know what you're trying to say: she wasn't dressed for it, didn't take anything with her except for her tablet, which is missing –'

'And her mobile,' Webber wheezes.

'And her mobile,' Gillian echoes absent-mindedly. 'Not even proper shoes . . . I know, I know . . . Let me think.' She jumps over a puddle, agile as a gazelle, whilst Webber lands in it, flat-footed, dirty water splashing in his face. He doesn't have any breath left in him to curse. Gillian continues, unaware of his tribulations, 'This is what I'm thinking: the call came unexpect-edly. She didn't know Friday night would be the night her lover would ask her to run away with him. Perhaps something had gone wrong and they had to do it there and then, or never –'

'Wait!' Webber surrenders. He stops, bends down and rests his hands on his thighs, wheezing hopelessly.

Gillian stops and peers at him, bemused. 'When did you have your last medical?'

'Never mind that! I've got a touch of a cold, all right!' he snaps. 'You may be on to something . . .'

'I always am.'

'Perhaps that other man – the lover, Joe Ex let's call him, per-haps he too had the house under surveillance and realised that Rachel was being watched by Bradley Watson. He called her on her mobile – her mother said Rachel had been on the phone in the middle of the night. So he told her Bradley was outside, snooping. Perhaps the two of them led Watson away from the house and,' out of breath, Webber finishes the sentence with a gesture of slitting his throat.

'That'd explain no ransom demand.'

'And it'd explain why Rachel Snyder hasn't been found, dead or alive.'

'She's still alive, somewhere far away from here.'

'We'll have to widen the search.' Webber takes a deep breath and scans the open plains criss-crossed with gravelled footpaths. 'How much further?' He looks like he has given up.

'Come on, Mark, we're in Ogburn Park. It's only a short distance from here to the murder scene.' Gillian takes off, heading for the familiar spot bordering the grounds of Whalehurst School. Webber decides to arrive there slowly, with his dignity intact.

The dogs are brought to heel at the scene of Watson's murder. One of them is eager to break through the hole in the fence and into the school grounds. 'Watson must've gone that way,' Gillian interprets the dog's behaviour.

The handler looks at her. 'Shall I let her go on?'

'Yes, let's see how far and where exactly he'd been.'

The handler encourages the dog and they scramble through the hole. Gillian follows. The dog leads them across the sports field and seems to lose the scent around the pavilion; it sniffs agitatedly until it picks something up again and heads right back to Watson's final resting place by the wall.

Webber has made it there by that time.

'I'm thinking,' Gillian goes on with her monologue, 'I'm thinking that maybe Joe Ex is someone from the school. If this was their rendezvous point, he may be one of the pupils – or staff – at the school. We'll check if there's anyone not present and accounted for today. But it must be someone who knows the school, who knows where to find the bows and arrows, and how to use them –'

'Rachel knows that. She's a day student at Whalehurst.'

Gillian gazes at him, intrigued. This is the first piece of interesting information Webber has imparted to her in the whole day. 'Do you know something, Mark?'

'I bet I don't, so, go on, tell me!'

'All the roads in this case seem to lead to Whalehurst.'

'OK, I knew *that!*'

'Could it be that Watson and Rachel were running away together? Someone else has discovered their plot, killed Watson and is holding Rachel . . . but not for ransom. They're holding her because she knows the killer's identity.'

'She's as good as dead, then.'

'Not necessarily. Maybe the killer can't bring himself to kill her. Someone close to her? Jilted boyfriend perhaps?'

'But that takes us back to her state of undress when she left the house,' Webber points out. 'If she was running away with Watson, why didn't she at least put her fuckin' trainers on?'

'Maybe she was running *away* from home. Not to somewhere. We need to interview her parents.'

'I have. They'd heard nothing at all. They only found out she was gone in the morning, when they woke up.'

'Let's talk to them again. Together.'

Webber snorts his disapproval. Here she goes again – taking over *his* bloody case. 'Look, Gillian, I talked to them. They're genuinely in the dark. Plus, you're forgetting something: Rachel was unaware of Watson watching her and taking all those photos of her. If you ask me, he was more a stalker than a lover. Lovers do things together, not behind each other's backs.'

'But I'm not asking you, Webber. I'm going to ask people who actually may know something for a fact.'

'Thanks,' Webber grinds his teeth.

'This is our joint investigation, you do know that?'

'You don't do *joint*. That much I do know.'

Gillian gives him a quizzical look and takes off. Webber grimaces with discontent, but follows her. The least he can do when she accosts the poor Snyders is damage control.

The dog handlers are also pulling the dogs out of the school grounds to minimise scene contamination. One of the hounds has found something under the stands by the running track: a buried bone or other doggy treasure. It is digging enthusiastically. The dog handler recalls it back to its proper duties and gives it some telling off when it finally comes to him. Gillian smiles: the canine has brought Corky to mind. Corky, too, doesn't do obedience.

Chapter Eleven

It was purely coincidental that Edwin Featherstone glanced out of his office window at the same time as DI Marsh, accompanied by a John Travolta lookalike, marched across the courtyard, heading for the school reception.

'What the hell does she want now!' Featherstone muttered to himself. He threw his robe over his pullover and bit into a mint. Having spent the morning weeding through his files and his computer browsing history, he was now much more composed. Yet he knew this was not the time to lower his guard. He had to remain on high alert until this nightmare was over. He ground the mint with his back teeth and exhaled into the cup of his hand. Fresh as a daisy! Righteous indignation personified, he descended the stairs to intercept Marsh and her sidekick at the reception desk just as they embarked on grilling Sally for disclosures she was not at liberty to make.

'What can I help you with this time, DI Marsh?' he bellowed, his step steady and his eyes glowing with confidence.

'Mr Featherstone, this is DS Webber. He's in charge of the Rachel Snyder case.'

DS Webber produced an inexplicably placating smile and extended his hand to Featherstone in a gesture of peace offering. At least, this one had some manners. Featherstone shook the man's hand and clarified, 'It's *Dr* Featherstone, actually.'

'You know that Rachel Snyder has been reported missing? She is a pupil at this school.' Marsh would have nothing to do with handshakes and other gratuitous pleasantries. The witch jumped straight to the point – a point she didn't have to make.

Featherstone knew every pupil at his school and it was also his policy to know everything about every pupil's parents and their background. He put on an indulgent tone of voice, 'Yes, we've been informed. Naturally.'

'Then why didn't you tell me that when we spoke earlier?' The accusation in her tone was offensive.

'Why would I? You were looking into the killing of Bradley Watson, not into Rachel Snyder's absence!'

'Didn't it occur to you that the two may be related?'

'No, it did not. Why would it?'

'Is it an everyday occurrence in your school for a staff member to be murdered and a pupil to go missing, all in a matter of twenty-four hours?'

'He was the groundsman's son,' he corrected her. 'And no, it isn't an everyday occurrence –'

'So why didn't you mention it to me? It could've saved us a lot of time spent on putting two and two together.'

'It's not my job to make connections. Isn't that what you are paid for?'

'*Mr* Featherstone, you're being facetious. May I remind you that this is a murder investigation and that a child is missing.'

'No, you don't have to remind me of anything! I am distraught by what happened, for goodness' sake, I am! And no, I didn't make the connection, *mea culpa!*' His indignation was palpable. He could taste it in his throat. He really needed a strong drink to burn through it. 'In any event, Rachel did not disappear from the school – she ran away from home.'

'How do you know she ran away?'

'I . . . I just . . . I assumed she did . . .' His hands began to tremble and he could feel their slippery clamminess as he folded them into fists to control the shaking. He watched, helpless, as the other officer – DS Webber – sauntered off towards Sally and questioned her about something. Sally shot the head an alarmed look. He pointed at her. 'What is that all about? Is DS Webber interviewing Mrs Crowe? She knows nothing. She is a receptionist. She only comes to work at nine in the morning. If you need to know anything, you'll have to ask me!'

DI Marsh raised her eyebrows in mock bemusement. 'You must remain calm, *Mr* Featherstone. We only want to see the school's attendance register.'

'Why on earth?'

'To see if there are any unauthorised absences this morning. Didn't it occur to you that Rachel may have run away – your assumption, as it happens – run away with someone from the school?'

No, it had not occurred to him, not for one second. Perhaps it should have. Perhaps he should be seen as checking these things for himself, carrying out an internal investigation, like any conscientious headmaster should. He pounced on Sally, his hand outstretched, kept still by his sheer willpower. 'Attendance register, Mrs Crowe – has it been processed? May I have it?'

Relieved and grateful for his timely intervention, Sally nodded and passed the register to him. It was an old-fashioned folder. Featherstone didn't believe in electronics when it came to proper record-keeping.

'Here!' He waved the register in DS Webber's face. 'Let's check it in my office. You only need to ask – but you have to ask *me*!'

DI Marsh stood over him as he sat at his desk and let his finger run down the columns of names. The little missy was an insufferable control freak! She did not trust him to tell her – she had to see for herself. 'As you can see,' he said pointedly, 'all present and correct. No illnesses. No unexplained absences this morning. Happy?'

'What about staff members? Has anyone called in sick? Has anyone failed to report for work?'

'Apart from Bradley Watson, you mean, who for obvious reasons . . .' the rest of the sentence died on his lips. His half-baked joke did not go down well. The woman did not possess a shred of good humour. Charming her was not an option. Not that he would contemplate that in the first place. She was a nasty piece of work. Waspish. Persistent. A nuisance! Not in the least –

'Can you spare us your witticisms, Mr Featherstone,' she barked. 'May I remind you that one of your staff is dead and one of your pupils –'

'Is missing. Trust me, DI Marsh, I don't need reminding. Your insinuations . . . your accusations, are insufferable! I am trying very hard to hold things together in the face of your constant impositions!'

'She hasn't even started yet,' DS Webber informed him with stoical calm. Featherstone detected an air of mutual understanding between them. Obviously, the poor sergeant was finding it nigh on impossible to work for that woman. Maybe he would turn out to be an ally.

'Are all your staff members in today?' Marsh continued as if she had heard nothing of what he had to say in his defence.

'I believe they are all in,' he said, his lips pursed with self-restraint.

'DS Webber will talk to them one by one. I want to have a chat with the students.'

'You already have!'

'This time I want to make it more intimate. I want to talk to Rachel's classmates. Her friends. I want names, and I want to put faces to those names. Do you know who her friends are?'

He dug deep into the back alleys of his rather fallible memory. He might have known everything there was to know about his pupils' parents and the depth of their pockets, but any knowledge of his pupils' relationships he found rather elusive. He tried to visualise Rachel Snyder sitting on the lawn with her friends . . . His brow shone with sweat as he worked hard to put names to their faces.

'Starr,' he pronounced at long last, 'Rhiannon Starr is a friend of Rachel Snyder.'

Now he not only needed but also deserved a stiff drink.

Chapter Twelve

They are sitting at a table in the school cafeteria. The girl called Rhiannon is tall but waif-like, she is skin and bone; her voice is also thin; her speech clipped and without a trace of accent. She has long brown hair held together in two French plaits that run from her middle parting and coil together at the back of her head. She resembles a medieval maiden with that hairstyle, especially now that she has taken off her glasses and put them neatly in her lap.

'I wish I knew what Rachel was thinking, but I don't.'

'You two had to talk about something. You were friends – that's what friends do: they talk, they share secrets, their crushes . . .'

'I already explained this to Detective Sergeant Webber. Rachel told me absolutely nothing. I had no idea she was planning to run away. Absolutely none! Do you really think if I knew, I wouldn't have . . . well, done something?' Her bottom lip quivers. She sucks it in, looks around the room, seeking help from the empty walls and the ceiling. 'You can ask DS Webber. I told him everything I knew. He wrote it down.'

'It wasn't much that you told him, Rhiannon.'

'Because . . . I've no idea what you want from me. He wanted to know if I knew where Rachel was. And I don't – I told him. I can't tell you what I don't know.'

'I'd like to know, for example, if you ever saw Rachel talking to Bradley Watson –'

'Mr Watson's son? His dea –' Rhiannon stumbles over the word, '. . . dead son?'

'Yes, him.'

'Rachel and Mr Watson's son?'

Gillian nods encouragement.

'No! Never, I never saw them together . . . Are they?' Rhiannon is blinking away tears. 'I really didn't notice them together, but I couldn't . . . well, I can't imagine . . .'

'That's good. Thank you. You're doing well, Rhiannon.' Gillian makes an effort to look and sound casual. The last thing she wants is to be accused of intimidating a witness – a juvenile witness, at that! 'I only want your help so that I can find your friend and bring her home in one piece. And you're doing very well – assisting me with my inquiries.'

'Am I?' Rhiannon shakes her head in salient disbelief. She gazes imploringly at DI Marsh. 'But what else can I tell you?'

'You can tell me a lot. Because, at this point, I'm in the dark. Anything you can tell me . . . Have you noticed anything odd, unusual, in Rachel's behaviour of late? Any changes in her state of mind? Anything that might bother you as her friend, for example . . .'

Rhiannon plucks at the cuff of her school blazer. Her eyes are nailed to her lap, avoiding contact with DI Marsh. She frowns as if trying to remember something elusive, something that may not be there. She lifts her eyes to look at Gillian. She is on the verge of telling her what has been bothering her about Rachel, but she doesn't. It seems too hard. She either doesn't know how to phrase it or she doesn't want to talk about it with the police. She bites her upper lip and looks like she is in pain. But that quickly passes and she is back to her stony-faced self.

'Well, to be honest with you . . .' This is the point where Gillian realises the girl intends anything but being honest with her. 'Rachel and I have drifted apart in the last few months. She just went her own way, and I mine. So no, I wouldn't have noticed anything. We weren't that close.'

'Mr Featherstone told me you were best friends.'

'We used to be . . . friends. *Best* friends? I don't know . . .

Just – friends. But not so much anymore. We didn't fall out, in case you thought . . . Just busy with . . . things . . . school things, work . . . We tend to mix with different people.'

'So, who does Rachel mix with? Can you give me names?'

Again, Rhiannon puts on an expression of deep concentration. She shakes her head. 'I really can't tell you. She's been in her own world lately, sort of. I wasn't paying attention to what she was getting up to. And who with . . .'

'Surely, you saw her at school every day – you saw who she was hanging out with!' Gillian wants to scream. This is like drawing blood out of a stone. Some witnesses do need to be battered! They need to be hung, drawn, and quartered because otherwise they won't talk. 'You didn't turn blind just because you were busy with school things!'

'No . . . I didn't see her with anyone. Not at school. Maybe she was back with some friends from her old school. She only joined Whalehurst towards the end of year eight, in summer. Maybe you should speak to her old friends. She's a day pupil here. It's not the same as the rest of us . . . well, those of us who board here. Rachel has a life outside Whalehurst, you know, and I'm not part of it. I don't want to be. And I can't account for everything Rachel does. Speak to people who can.'

The medieval maiden shows her claws at last. There is a defiance in her eyes as she glares at Gillian and for the first time holds her gaze.

'That's useful. Her old school, yes . . . I will check that out.' Gillian's tone is conciliatory.

'Can I go now?'

Gillian can tell the girl is being economical with facts: she must know a lot about something that she so vehemently does not wish to be part of. Maybe she isn't lying, but neither is she telling her all there is to tell.

'No, not yet,' Gillian pauses, reflects on something for a long and uncomfortable minute, making the girl wait. She then fixes Rhiannon with a puzzled look, 'You and Rachel are, what? In year eleven now? That gives Rachel three years to settle down at Whalehurst. I take it on your word that you and her are no longer *that close*. So who is? Who else is she friendly with here? Does she have a boyfriend? Bradley Watson? Someone else? Your headmaster tells me you knew her well, but you act as if you two were total strangers. You, Rhiannon dear, you're not telling me everything.'

'Because I don't know *everything*. Like I said, we drifted apart.' Her voice may be thin, but her tone is firm.

'OK,' Gillian takes a deep breath, 'what about before you drifted apart? Go back a few months.'

'There's nothing to tell. She was fine. Happy. She used to be a good laugh . . .'

'That's better . . . So, has anything happened to change that?'

'I don't know. Maybe after Josh dropped her. She never said he broke up with her, but everyone knows.'

'We never broke up because we had never been an item, I'm afraid.' Unlike Rhiannon, Joshua Tyler looks her straight in the eye. He has the open and trustworthy face of a young man brought up to always tell the truth and stand by his word. He has an air of honour and nobility about him. For some reason he brings to mind the image of Lord Byron. It could be the black wavy hair swept away from his brow. It could be his dark brooding eyes with a distant look that elevates him above all mere mortals and their earthly concerns. True to that image, he appears to be outwardly unshaken by the recent developments, but he listens politely to Gillian's questions and demonstrates keenness to be of assistance to the police. 'Rachel and I were on friendly terms, that's true. She was good fun, old Rachel.'

'Why are you talking about Rachel in the past tense?' Gillian won't be seduced by his knight-in-shining-armour airs and graces.

'Nothing sinister about it,' he replies evenly. 'I say it in the past tense because it was in the past. We used to hang out a bit – loosely. You'll probably find out soon enough that Rachel invited me to her home, to meet her parents.'

'That's pretty close, I'd say.'

'You can say that again! I realised she was a bit more serious than me. I couldn't bring myself to say no – I'm not cruel, I don't get off on breaking girls' hearts, so I went along with it. It was so sweet of her and what harm could one visit do . . . But no, I wasn't a hundred per cent comfortable and while I was there I realised, well . . . I shouldn't have strung her along. I mean, don't get me wrong, it wasn't my intention in the first place. I just wanted to be gracious about it, and perhaps it – sort of – backfired,' Even now he looks regretful and slightly out of his comfort zone.

'How do you mean?'

'I don't know . . . it just hit me that perhaps Rachel had somehow misunderstood our . . .' he pauses to search for the right word in his no doubt well-polished vocabulary bank, 'well . . . our superficial relationship.'

'So, tell me exactly how you would describe your relationship with Rachel.'

'At best? We were just mates.' That word doesn't ring true coming from his plum posh-boy mouth. He grimaces apologetically. 'Rachel seemed to think we were more. It would've been unfair of me to milk the situation. She was . . . is – she is only fifteen, and I am well aware of that. I just wouldn't cross any lines with a minor. But it isn't just her age . . . I mean, I'm simply not attracted to Rachel, not that way. I don't know why but I feel like I need to apologise for that.'

Gillian shrugs. 'Not to me.'

Joshua Tyler is still squirming, despite her reassurance. 'I don't take any pleasure from this . . . But to cut the long story short, Rachel and I were – are – not romantically involved. Everything else aside, I really don't have the time for relationships. I'm rather busy with A levels this year. And Rachel is – or should be – with her GCSEs.'

Gillian tilts her head and pauses for thought: he has hit a false note. What eighteen-year-old boy with levels of testosterone rising to the stratosphere wouldn't have time for girls? Unless he preferred boys, of course. Despite her misgivings, she says, 'I can see your reasons.'

'I'm glad you do. It was a matter of priorities for me. I never wanted to hurt Rachel. I humoured her for a while and then, when it got a little too much for me with meeting the parents and all the shenanigans, I slammed on the brakes and let it cool. Gently . . . There was no *break-up*, no dramas – more a cooling-down period. I just let her drift away.'

'You're the second person who has used that term today in relation to Rachel. It looks to me like all her friends *drifted away* from her.'

'Well, I had my reasons, which I've explained, I hope, to your satisfaction. I don't know about her other friends.'

'How long ago was that – when you decided to let her *drift away?*'

He looks up to the ceiling, searching it for dates and times. 'Let me think . . . It was about three months ago. The beginning of December, just before we broke up for Christmas . . . that's when she invited me over. That's when I realised her expectations were . . . well, unrealistic.' He sounds cold; honest perhaps, but cold as a slab of ice. 'Yes, that was before Christmas. I then went home for Christmas – to Herefordshire. That was quite a fortuitous development because I was able to cut off contact with Rachel without her – hopefully – taking it the wrong way. I returned to school on the second of January . . . A bit early, but my father works in the diplomatic service in the Far East. He was going back to his post immediately after the New Year.' He throws that bit of information out almost casually, but Gillian realises it is designed to warn her off. 'So, yes, by the time I returned to Whalehurst, Rachel and I were pretty much on the back burner . . . it was all in the past.'

'You think she took it well?'

85

'I'd certainly hope so. It wasn't my intention to upset poor Rachel, honestly.' His soft, dreamy eyes spark with conviction.

'So why, do you think, did she run away like that?'

'Frankly, I don't think there is a connection,' he says competently. 'December was three months ago. Rachel took off . . . when? On Friday?'

'You think she ran away, then?'

'I guess so, yes,' Joshua shrugs with a slight and involuntary display of boredom.

'Then why now?'

'Embarrassment,' he says and seems to regret it that very instant. He flinches, momentarily losing his self-assured composure, his eyes darting to the left, his eyelids fluttering.

'What would she be embarrassed about?'

'I don't know. I wouldn't want to speculate. Why do you run away, and hide from everyone? I don't know. It's not something I'd do.' He produces his well-practised apologetic smile. 'I think I'd rather like to return to my lessons.'

'One more thing, Joshua. You're doing really well and you're being helpful,' she tries to appease him, then throws a curve ball at him to see his reaction, 'What can you tell me about Bradley Watson?'

He is not appeased. His jaw tightens. 'He's dead,' he says.

'Did you know him?'

'Not really. He worked here with his father, Mr Watson. That's all.'

'Could you think of any connection between him and Rachel?'

'Your guess is as good as mine. In short, I don't know.'

'Would you have noticed if the two of them were . . . close?'

'No. I mean, they could've been close, but I wouldn't have noticed. As I said, Rachel and I drifted apart a while ago.'

'Yes, so you keep telling me . . .'

He gets up – a not so subtle signal that this interview is at an end. 'I hope you find her soon and bring her home to her parents. It's rather thoughtless of her to leave without a word. I'd expect more of Rachel. I still don't understand why she would've done something like that. It's not like her to run away.'

'You think?'

'Yes, I do. Rachel was – is, a . . . a fine young lady. I always liked her. Didn't fancy her – just liked her.'

Gillian releases the boy from her clutches. She watches him slink away back to his lessons. He is slightly stooped, his shoulders rounded and drawn in. Maybe there is a touch of empathy in his posture? Maybe it is guilt for letting his friend *drift away* until she fell off the edge of the earth without anyone out there to grab her hand and pull her back?

Maybe it is neither guilt nor pity. Maybe that's just how he walks.

DI Marsh and DS Webber are traversing Ogburn Country Park, heading back to Lower Horton, the leafy suburb of Sexton's Canning where Rachel Snyder's house is and where they left their car before setting off after the sniffer dogs a couple of hours earlier. The park is sprawled over an area of 150 acres, with Lower Horton to the east and Little Ogburn to the west, and the dual carriageway encasing it from the south and carrying the main weight of traffic to and through Sexton's Canning. The park itself is insulated from the dual carriageway, its noise and its pollution, by a buffer of hedges, a wide parking and picnic area and finally the River Avon that flows through it, wide and lazy. Well-maintained gravel paths wind across a patchwork of meadows, hedges, and coppices. The strip of woodland where the park borders Whalehurst School is particularly dense and impenetrable. That would explain why Bradley Watson's body took two days to be discovered.

Webber is not impressed with the state of the path. Gravelled as it may be, it is also low-lying and boggy, drowning in foaming overspills from the network of streams and ditches which cannot absorb the amount of rain that has fallen in recent days. His elegant black shoes are caked in mud and his socks soaked.

Gillian is unaware of his predicament. She is wearing her usual walking boots. Come rain or shine, she always wears her thick-soled boots and her bomber jacket. She has as much feminine grace as a fence post. Mercifully, she is oblivious to her shortcomings.

'What did you find out?' she inquires.

'That Tara works at Whalehurst School!'

'Tell me something I don't know.'

'I was dumbfounded to see her there. I thought it was some bizarre joke you decided to play on me.'

'Me? A joke?' She glances at him, genuinely baffled. 'You're full of odd ideas, Webber. Why do you think I asked you to interview the staff? Precisely because I couldn't be seen interviewing my own daughter. I have to maintain professional distance.'

'You could've told me. Should you be even on this case?'

'Never mind that.' She shoots him a warning glance. It would be over her dead body for this case to be taken away from her. In any event, there is no one in the whole county more qualified than her to deal with it, keen as Webber may be. 'What did you find out?'

'Precisely nothing. It is like they all live in a bubble. They have zero powers of observation, and that sadly includes Tara.' He shakes his head. 'They sing from the same hymn sheet: Rachel is a hard-working and well-mannered young lady, sensible and promising. Her disappearance is – shock, horror – totally out of character, and no, nobody can explain it. They've noticed nothing unusual about her behaviour, her attendance has been exemplary, she has never missed a day of school. And of course, everyone is extremely concerned for her safe return.'

'Let me guess – they haven't noticed anything going on between her and Bradley Watson.'

'Nothing whatsoever! Everyone was mystified when I suggested that. Even horrified. I had the impression that they couldn't stomach the idea that a girl from a good home, like Rachel, would look twice at, you know, the . . . the . . . the working-class *lowlife*.

88

And if she had, that just wouldn't be the done thing. That'd be a real shame . . . Too embarrassing!'

'Yes, embarrassment . . . Joshua Tyler mentioned that too. But then he wouldn't elaborate on that. Nobody at Whalehurst seems to know Rachel Snyder that well, it turns out. Do you know what I think this is?'

'A bloody toff world I wouldn't know the first thing about, so don't make me guess.'

'It's a conspiracy of silence!' Gillian stops dead in her tracks, lifts her forefinger and delivers her final verdict, 'Do you know what, Mark? I've a feeling that they're all doing their absolute best to distance themselves from that girl. It's almost like they're afraid to be linked to her. Like she's a leper and they may catch what she's got if they come too close . . . I think they're scared.'

'And it's our job to find out why.'

Gillian gazes at him in her typically judicious manner and says without a hint of humour, 'You don't say, Webber. I would've never thought of that myself.'

'Oh, bugger off, Marsh,' Webber mutters under his breath, but he knows she can bloody well hear him. His toes are wet and cold, and it's begun to rain.

Chapter Thirteen

In stark contrast to Whalehurst, Sexton's Comprehensive is a no-nonsense-prefab edifice, purpose-built in the sixties to educate the town's wayward youth. Tragically the letter *t* fell away from the word *Sexton* on the board above the entrance, leading a random passer-by to believe that *sex* is *on* at this educational establishment. The whole school has not had the benefit of a lick of paint since it was built and has never seen what a pair of secateurs can do with rampaging bushes. At least the grass does not pose any challenges, as it has been effectively erased by hundreds of feet crossing the lawns willy-nilly despite the perfectly adequate paved paths aimed at carrying foot-traffic around the school. The rubbish bins are equally redundant, notwithstanding the caretaker's efforts to collect discarded crisp bags and plastic bottles in between the breaks. He waves and shouts a jolly 'Howdy!' to Marsh and Webber as they repeatedly press the intercom button on the gate.

''Ere to see the school?' he enquires upon approaching the gate, a dirty ribbon of toilet paper trailing behind his shoe.

'Police business,' DS Webber informs him and presents his warrant card. 'And that's DI Marsh.' He nods towards Gillian.

'Police? My, my . . . what's the world comin' to?' The caretaker pulls a concerned face and turns on his heel, dragging the ribbon of toilet paper with him as he saunters away. He is clearly not interested in an answer to his question.

'Can you let us in?' Webber shouts after him.

''Old the button firm or they won't 'ear ya in the office. It don't work proper,' the man shouts back.

They don't have to wait long for the head teacher to materialise. She is a breath of fresh air – or rather a whirlwind of pure energy – as she bursts into the reception area. She is a tall blonde, dressed to kill in six-inch heels and a knee-length skirt revealing her shapely muscular calves. Her eyes are quick, but warm, and they carry her enthusiastic smile with authenticity. You can tell she is a tough business woman who knows how to stand her ground but who hasn't lost her tender human touch. Her handshake is firm, but her manner gentle.

'Nora Stanstead, head teacher. What can I do for you?'

'DI Marsh. We're looking into the disappearance of Rachel Snyder. I believe she used to be a pupil here?'

The head teacher's eyes round with alarm. 'Rachel? Little Rachel Snyder? Disappeared? Yes . . . yes, she attended Sexton's school. My God, how did she . . . disappear? Is she all right? I'm sorry . . . this is terrible news . . . I can't imagine what her parents are going through! Please, follow me to my office . . . Of course, I'll help you with whatever I can.'

The journey down the corridors of the school paints a different picture to its exterior. Beautiful and clever pieces of art are on display and the place oozes creativity and warmth. What the school can't buy, it most certainly compensates for in resourceful-ness. The head teacher's office is minimalistic and tidy. DI Marsh and DS Webber are invited to sit down, offered coffee and made to feel more than welcome.

Gillian explains what they know about Rachel Snyder's disap-pearance, though she chooses not to muddy the waters with her connection to Bradley Watson. 'One of Rachel's friends from Whalehurst suggested we talk to her old friends from this school – maybe they can shed some light on this.'

'Yes, certainly . . .'

'Would you know if she kept in touch with anyone in particular at this school?'

Nora Stanstead shakes her head slowly. 'Let me think . . . Gosh, I can't think! It's awful! Right, right . . . Rachel would've left us about three years ago . . .'

'That's about right. She was in year eight.'

'Yes. That'd be my year elevens now . . . She'd . . . she would be in year eleven had she stayed with us. A nice bunch, good kids . . .'

'Do you have any idea why she left?'

'Nothing concrete, as far as I can tell. Neither Rachel nor her parents ever complained about anything or anyone . . . I've always had the feeling that a community school wasn't quite good enough for Rachel's family. I hate to say it, and do not agree with that, but I think they believed she deserved something better. And they could afford it.'

Fiona, the school administrator, takes the police officers to the sixth form common room while the Head embarks on the mission of tracking down Rachel's old classmates.

Mark sports a nostalgic expression, and muses, 'I went to this school – this is my backyard . . . And, believe it or not, it hasn't changed one iota since my days.'

'I believe you. I came here too, and nothing's changed since my time.'

'Since the stone age?'

'Watch it, DS Webber.'

A large Soviet flag hangs on the wall, red like a matador's cape, the hammer and sickle stamped into it in shiny gold. The flag is surrounded by images of what must be the sixth formers' idols: Jesus in the company of Che Guevara, Jeremy Corbyn in his proletarian hat next to Sacha Baron Cohen dressed as a general, and bearded Karl Marx hand-in-hand with Mother Teresa. There are photos of inspired-looking individuals Gillian has never heard of. A few inflammatory slogans, recorded in capitals and poorly spelt, shout from a whiteboard. Other than that, the room is large, airy, and inviting, with its own kitchenette, and comfortable sofas and chairs scattered around half a dozen tables.

'Brings back your rebellious past?' Mark smirks.

'I rebelled in different ways. What about you?'

He has no chance to reminisce because Nora Stanstead flocks in with a group of pimply teenagers: mostly girls and a couple of boys. Unlike their exuberant head teacher, they glare at the two police officers with truculent defiance in their eyes. Give them half a chance, and they'll start a riot here and now, Gillian surmises. One couldn't take them seriously though even if that happened: the girls' skirts are riding up their thighs, rolled up on their waists like sausages; the boys' ties are inexpertly tied and most of their shirts are hanging out of their trousers. They are just hapless and angst-ridden kids.

'So here, sit down and answer the officers' questions.' The Head flaps her arms around her flock. She peers at Gillian. 'I explained to them about Rachel's disappearance – I hope that's OK . . . And I told them you're not here to interrogate them, but you need their help to find Rachel.'

'So, can any of you help?' DI Marsh scrutinises the motley crew of Rachel's old classmates.

There is no response other than grunts of hopelessness. No, they don't know anything. No, they haven't seen Rachel since she left three years ago. And no, nobody has stayed in touch with her.

'Why not? Some of you must have gone to the same primary school as Rachel – known her for years, since you were little . . . Why not?'

One girl, with intelligent eyes and a sombre expression, says, 'She didn't mingle. No one's gonna force her if she don't want to.'

'She kept to herself.'

'Yeah, she did. I hardly remember what she looked like!'

'And why do you think she was like that?'

'Like what?'

'Like keeping to herself and not mingling with the crowd . . . Did anyone do anything to make her feel – uncomfortable?' *As if they're going to admit it if it's true*, Gillian shrugs at her own ill-conceived question.

'No one did nothing to her,' a boy with a thick neck and bulging muscles retorts. He looks like he is on a cocktail of steroids and an intensive body-building programme.

'She just didn't belong – didn't want to belong,' concludes the girl with intelligent eyes.

'And how about Bradley Watson?' Gillian throws in the hand-grenade she has been keeping for later as her secret weapon. She wants to see their raw reactions. 'Do you remember him? He went to this school.'

'Brad? Who was killed in Ogburn?'

The Head rises to her feet, looking none too pleased. She is a tough woman, Gillian has to give it to her. 'You said nothing about interviewing them about Bradley Watson. It isn't really fair on them to ask that. Bradley left the school soon after they came. He didn't even last through to his GCSEs . . . What would they know about Bradley Watson?'

'We know of him.'

'We know he's dead.'

'Fuck, poor Brad,' an anonymous voice from the back commiserates with the deceased young man.

'Do you know if Rachel Snyder would have any dealings with Bradley?'

Webber's innocent enough question meets with a few suppressed chuckles and snorting noises.

'Is that a yes?'

Some are laughing.

'No, we wouldn't know . . . Not likely though,' says the girl with intelligent eyes, who seems to have appointed herself as spokesperson for the group.

'Why not?'

'Not in the same league. Brad and Rach didn't even speak the same lingo,' someone else elaborates.

'Yeah,' adds the girl, 'I can't see them *having dealings*.' They chortle again.

'Would that be all?' Nora Stanstead asks, but it is more of a concluding statement than a question. 'I will show you out.'

DI Marsh and DS Webber rise to their feet. Webber takes out his card. 'Look, guys,' he says, 'we're trying our damn best to find Rachel. You can't imagine what her parents are going through. I won't give up and I will find her with or without your help, but if you know anything, get in touch. She was your friend, once.'

The laughing dies out. They gaze at him, serious and concerned. Finally, the spokesperson says, 'The only thing Rachel and Brad had in common is they both left here and went to Whalehurst. You should speak to them over there.'

That's what you call Catch-22.

Chapter Fourteen

When the security lights came on, Sarah Snyder looked out of the sash window in the lounge facing the driveway. She saw two figures getting out of the car that had pulled up by the front door: a big man accompanied by a small silhouette of a woman, their features obscured by the heavy rain.

It was over! They had found her!

Sarah raced to the door and opened it before they knocked. Detective Sergeant Webber had brought with him a higher-ranking officer: Detective Inspector Marsh. Sarah's knees went soft. She backed into the hallway and pressed her back against the wall. She could feel her blood draining away from her head, leaving her dizzy. Rachel was not with them.

Jonathan came out and told them to come inside, to forget the muddy shoes, and just come in, stop wasting time. Sarah could not say anything – she was still recovering her senses. She followed her husband and the two police officers to the kitchen.

Their kitchen was large and airy; it featured solid oak worktops, with a glass-panelled door leading to a conservatory giving a peek of their beautiful, perfectly manicured garden. Even in the rain it looked idyllic, but right now, it felt incredibly alien. One big fat lie of a garden – a cruel trick of nature.

Sarah gazed at DI Marsh, willing her to unpick all the lies and at last tell her where they were hiding her little girl. Woman to woman.

But DI Marsh wasn't a bearer of good news. She brought with

her more confusion, more pain. Both Sarah and Jonathan stared at her in bewilderment, watching her lips move relentlessly as she went on about the bizarre, inexplicable connection between their daughter and someone called Bradley Watson. The dead young man.

Jonathan's lower lip became slack and revealed his bottom front teeth, yellow and crooked. Sarah covered her mouth with her hand, pushing back in a wild scream. But it was her eyes – they screamed louder than her mouth ever could: the sheer panic, the denial, the plea for mercy. Except that DI Marsh wasn't here to show mercy. She said she was here to establish facts.

Sarah had pressed her body against the sink and was grasping the edge of the worktop with her left hand, her knuckles going white. Her other hand had left her lips and pressed against her stomach. 'Why?' she asked. 'Why was he doing that?'

'We don't know.'

'Those photographs . . . were they . . . inappropriate?' Jonathan's voice seemed to travel from some deep well.

'Not in the way you may think.' That was DS Webber. Sarah trusted the man. He wouldn't lie to them. 'From what we saw, he captured her getting on with ordinary things. Everyday stuff – sitting at her desk, reading, lying down on her bed . . . There are a few pictures of Rachel changing from her school uniform, in a passing state of undress . . .'

'That *is* inappropriate,' Jonathan concluded even more gravely. 'Can we have all those damned photos?'

'Not while the investigation is pending. They're evidence.'

'I'm not sure I ever want to see them,' Sarah heard herself utter her first sentence. 'I don't want to see them, Jon! I don't want to look at Rachel's pictures. I want Rachel . . .' Her throat clogged up. She retched and twisted her body towards the sink.

Jonathan's arm felt heavy on her back. 'Are you OK, Sarah? You sick?'

She swallowed the bile, and nodded slowly. 'Yeah . . . yeah . . . Fine. I'm fine.'

'Are you OK to talk to us? Can we go ahead with a few questions?' DI Marsh was keen to get on with establishing facts.

'Please do.'

'Have you ever come across Bradley Watson? Has Rachel mentioned him, even in passing?'

'No, never. Who is he anyway? Could she have even known him?'

'He worked with his father at Whalehurst School, as a groundsman's apprentice.'

'He used to be a pupil at Sexton's,' Webber added. 'A few years above Rachel, but he was still there – briefly – when she attended the school.'

'They would've – could've – known each other. Perhaps Rachel didn't tell you about him because she was involved with him . . . romantically? Maybe it was her . . . secret crush?'

DI Marsh wasn't making any sense. Rachel didn't have any secrets from her mother. Sarah would have known – she would've sensed it and she would have got it out of her.

'It looks like he was . . . well, to put it bluntly, stalking Rachel,' DS Webber said. 'She may've noticed . . . It would've made her uncomfortable. Did she –'

'She never said anything . . . Nothing about anyone called Bradley Watson!' The name of that dead man tasted vile in Sarah's mouth. She felt sick again.

'But then maybe she didn't want to worry us . . . She's been acting strangely of late, hasn't she?' Jon stepped in. 'She was troubled by something. I thought it was that boy, Joshua –'

'What about him?' DS Webber asked.

'She brought him home . . . when was that? Oh yes, beginning of December – yes, it was definitely the first weekend in December. I remember that because we were celebrating Hanukkah . . . So yeah, I didn't know what to make of him. He acted like he just couldn't wait to get away from us. Answered questions in monosyllables. He looked at us as if we'd killed someone dear to him – his face . . . his eyes! Took the wind out of my sails! Rach had told us what a wonderful young man he was – butter wouldn't melt, but to me the Joshua from her stories and the Joshua stood in front of us were two different people.'

DI Marsh responded with the strangest of comments. 'Oh that! Yes, we know about that.'

Jon didn't seem to hear her. 'He hurt her, if you must know. After that visit, he dumped her. I'm being honest here, Sarah. That's what sent her over the edge. We need to tell the police so that they have something to go on. That boy is bad news!'

'Yes, we're aware of Rachel's failed relationship with Joshua Tyler,' DI Marsh interrupted. 'Was there anything in Rachel's personal life –'

'It was that boy! Let's be straight here, Sarah – let's tell them: we thought Rachel was on drugs, or worse! She was acting like a maniac . . . erratic, aggressive one minute, tearful the next. He broke her heart . . .'

Sarah wished it were that simple: a broken heart. She wished for Jon's sake that they could blame it all on a girly crush, but she remembered clearly how Rachel was that day – the day she disappeared. 'For a while, yes, you're right, Jon, she was out of sorts . . . But that was behind her. Rachel told me they had made up, they were friends again – in an on and off relationship, she said. We had a laugh about it . . . She bought those hot pants – not something a heartbroken girl would care about. She thought he'd like them.'

'Are you sure she was talking about Joshua Tyler?' DI Marsh looked interested. 'Could she have been talking about a different boyfriend – someone new? Did she actually mention his name?'

Sarah scowled, bit her lip – she was trying to remember Rachel's exact words, but everything was a blur and she was confused and didn't trust her own memory. She had missed something; she hadn't listened carefully enough, not paid enough attention that day. She should've known better. As a mother, she should have had inklings that something was terribly wrong, that Rachel's mood swings had more to them than just teenage hormones. 'I . . . I think she was talking about Joshua . . . Who else?'

DI Marsh got up briskly, looking disappointed, perhaps even annoyed. 'OK, thank you.'

DS Webber was more reassuring. 'We'll keep looking for her. We're widening our search. I'll keep in touch with you at all times.'

'Why doesn't she just come back home?' Sarah pleaded with him. 'It's cold, it's been raining – she's not wearing much. She'll catch her death.'

He opened his mouth to say something, but only shook his head and followed DI Marsh to the front door. A pang of panic struck Sarah: she had let them down! She must have forgotten to tell them something important to their investigation, something they couldn't do without, but what was it? She followed them to the hallway, wringing her hands and desperately searching in the depths of her fallible memory for that something. She didn't want them to leave empty-handed. 'There was that phone call, of course – that night. It must've been around ten.'

'A phone call?' DI Marsh stopped dead in her tracks causing DS Webber to bump into her. 'What phone call?'

'What phone call?' Jonathan echoed DI Marsh's question. He was standing in the doorway.

'You never mentioned a phone call in the night, Mrs Snyder.' DS Webber's words sounded like an accusation.

'I'm sorry . . .' Sarah stammered. 'I didn't think . . . I mean, I didn't remember, not until now. I . . . I didn't make much of it. I thought she was talking to Rhiannon . . . That homework project they were doing – all rushed and urgent . . . I thought . . . well . . .' Her eyes shifted frantically from one detective to the other, both staring at her intently, willing her to start making sense. 'She was talking to someone in her room, I heard her . . .' Sarah spat it out.

'I didn't.' Jonathan stepped out of the doorway, frowning at her. 'How come I didn't hear anything?'

'You were in the shower, I think . . . I can't remember where you were but you weren't in the bedroom, anyway. You must've been in the shower.'

Jonathan stared at her, horrified. 'Why didn't you say anything? For God's sake, Sarah, Rachel's gone and you – you . . . Fuck!' He clapped his hands over his head, his fingers pulling at his hair. 'Fuck!'

'That's not helpful, Mr Snyder,' DI Marsh reprimanded him, but that gave Sarah no consolation. She could hardly control the emotion in her gut.

'I'm sorry . . .'

'It's OK. You've told us now,' DS Webber said.

'How do you know she was on the phone?' DI Marsh asked sharply.

'Well . . . I heard her talking out loud in her room . . . I could hear her voice through the wall. I assumed she was on her phone. Wasn't she?'

'There could've been someone else in her room,' DI Marsh suggested.

'But I only heard one voice – Rachel's.'

Chapter Fifteen

Gillian wheels the *Rachel Snyder – missing person* whiteboard into the Incident Room, and heaves it next to the *Bradley Watson* one. 'We're joining forces with DS Webber's team. This is going to be a joint investigation from now on with me as SIO and DS Webber running the missing person inquiry in parallel and in conjunction with us. We'll share resources and manpower on a needs basis, and that means: fairly. We'll share all available intelligence, every shred of information – we'll hold nothing back from each other.' She spares Webber a throwaway glance. He has taken off his shoes and his socks, and hung the socks on the radiator to dry. Sitting with his bare white feet crossed on the floor, he doesn't cut a particularly commanding figure. He doesn't sound it either.

'I'll believe it when I see it,' he mutters.

Macfadyen and Whittaker exchange meaningful glances. PC Baird bites his lips to hide his amusement. PC de Witt is looking away, wisely. They are all puzzled by the announcement. They are deeply intrigued as to why and how this star alignment between DI Marsh and DS Webber has come into being. They are dying to know whether it is done with Webber's prior knowledge and Chief Superintendent Scarfe's blessing. Still, they don't ask any questions, certain that DI Marsh will enlighten them soon enough.

Miller walks in, red-faced and blowing like a puffer fish. He is late and meekly accepts DI Marsh's unspoken reprimand. He sits down like a good boy and tries to stay invisible.

'Let me explain: the two cases are now interlinked. Forensics have produced photographs taken of the missing girl, Rachel Snyder, without her knowledge, by none other than our victim, Bradley Watson. On the night he was killed. We have images of her in the house, in her bedroom, leaving the house, and a few pictures of her crossing the bridge that leads to Ascombe Street.' Gillian draws a straight horizontal line across the two whiteboards, thus connecting the two names. She jots down as she goes. 'The photos are our link number one. We don't know why he was taking those photos – stalking, blackmail, unrequited love? He may have been discovered by Rachel, or by someone else, confronted by them – maybe things got out of hand and he ended up dead. Perhaps Rachel is hiding because she's responsible herself, or because she witnessed the killing. The photos offer a number of new possibilities in this – these – cases.

'We have a missing camera: a good-quality, professional camera with a powerful zoom. We have to find it. Erin, I want you to check all the second-hand shops to see if anyone has tried to shift it recently. Check eBay and other online retailers, too.'

'Ma'am,' Erin nods, business-like.

'Secondly, the autopsy places Bradley's death some time on the night of Friday the second of March, or the early hours of Saturday morning. That coincides with the approximate time of Rachel's disappearance. Another link we cannot disregard.' Gillian rubs out the question mark next to Watson's picture and writes, *2/3 March (Fri/Sat)*.

'Thirdly, Bradley Watson worked at Whalehurst School; Rachel was a day pupil there. The murder weapon is likely to have been sourced from the archery range at the school. Bradley's body was found on the outer perimeter of the school grounds, on the border with Ogburn Park. The school has to be a very strong connection, but we don't know in what way. DS Webber and I interviewed Rachel's classmates, friends, and the staff at the school. We have a few names.' Gillian scribbles down the two names she can put faces to: *Rhiannon Starr* and *Joshua Tyler*. She points to Rhiannon. 'She used to be Rachel's best friend. And he,' she points to Tyler's name, 'used to be her boyfriend – sort of. It is all very ambiguous at the moment. You may have noticed the operative term *used to* in both cases. That's what I find intriguing: Rachel Snyder seems to have drifted away from her friends a few months ago. Something happened. We need to look into it. I'll do that. The possibilities are there to consider: did she get mixed up with the wrong crowd, people like Bradley Watson, for example? He also attended Rachel's old school, Sexton's Comprehensive, and his last year there was when she started in year seven. We suspect Watson had links to county lines because of his previous. He served time, but my guess is he was probably dealing both at Sexton's and Whalehurst. Rachel's parents suspect that she may've started taking drugs. On that note,' DI Marsh pins DC Whittaker with an enquiring gaze, 'did you find out anything about Watson's old drugs connections?'

'Old and new,' Whittaker nods and produces a mysterious smile. His bulbous nose twitches, or rather ripples, with excitement. He gets up and follows his nose to the front of the room. He stands next to Gillian. His huge frame dwarfs everything in its vicinity, especially the minute Detective Inspector Marsh. 'To recap: Bradley Watson had two juvenile drug-related convictions. Like you said, he served time. After being released, he fell off the radar. I don't believe he sorted himself out. What I think is that he got smart. He knew how not to get caught, that's all.'

'His father is convinced Brad's dealing days were over. He had Bradley working with him at Whalehurst since his release,' Gillian interjects, hoping that Whittaker has some hard evidence to contradict that.

'That fits perfectly with what my source has told me – hand in glove,' Whittaker smiles again. He is the smiley type, Gillian observes. Laid-back but damn hard working, he is nothing like Webber. She likes him for being a good copper and not aspiring to anything else. All that blind ambition can get in the way of teamwork. 'My snoop tells me that until about year and a half ago

Greyston dealers had been crawling at the gates of Whalehurst School – rich kids, little sense, easy pickings. Dope, ecstasy, the usual teenagers' stimulants of choice. Then, all of a sudden, the demand dried up. Just like that.' Whittaker clicks his fingers. 'The Greyston lot suspect someone broke onto their turf, using an insider. They think it's Sexton's Mac Brothers. They, in turn, have links to the impenetrable Bristol drug ring that has emerged only in the last two-three years – we don't even know their names . . . they're new kids on the block, possibly Russians or from the Baltic states. So the Greyston lot abdicated without a fight. But the fact remains: a year and a half ago someone started dealing within Whalehurst . . .'

'That is too close for comfort. It can't be a coincidence that Bradley Watson joined his father as a groundsman at about the same time,' Gillian concurs. 'Good work, Whittaker! I want you to follow this lead. Get me names, bring in the runners and small-time dealers to talk to informally. This could be all drug-related. Rachel's parents could be right – she might've got mixed up in drugs.'

Miller musters the courage to add his two pennies' worth, 'The kids I spoke to in Little Ogburn also told me that Bradley was dealing, and that his dad knew fuck all about it . . . Their words, not mine.'

'Follow that up, Miller. Grill them a bit more. They may have some names, or at least be able to describe the faces of whoever was supplying Watson.'

'I'm on to it, ma'am.'

'Any luck at Ogburn Park?' Gillian addresses Macfadyen, who shakes her head.

'Nothing. No CCTV cameras. Well, at least none that work. There's a camera over the entrance to the café and souvenir shop, but purely as a deterrent; it isn't connected to anything but the bloody wall. No one patrols the park at night – no budget for such a luxury, plus there's no need. The gates are locked at seven p.m. Again, they're only tokenistic. Anyone can get through them and there are many *unofficial* pathways feeding into the park from both the Little Ogburn side and from Lower Horton. The place is like Piccadilly Circus: people coming and going, dog walkers, school-kids, joggers, scout groups – you name it.'

'A dead end, then,' Gillian summarises. 'Anything else I might've forgotten?' She glances at Webber and his milky-white bare feet. She's glad to have remembered to give him his moment in the limelight.

'Yes, the phone call.' He doesn't get up but hides his feet under his chair. 'Rachel was heard on the phone, possibly just minutes before she disappeared. We need to find out who she was talking to – it could be the last person she spoke to. They will know what she was thinking. They may've planned it together. Her mobile is missing, but it's a Pay-As-You-Go so may be harder to trace. PC de Witt has been looking into it. Sharon?'

'Yes. It's a Vodafone number. I've sent a request to the service provider. Nothing yet. We just have to wait.'

'They're notoriously uncooperative,' Gillian points out. She is feeling tired. It has been a long day and it is only now that she remembers she hasn't had any lunch. She glances at her watch: it's twenty to six. Never mind lunch, it's time for dinner, a hot bath, and bed. The only problem is that her fridge is almost empty, and whatever may still be lurking there is probably infested with vari-ous bacteria colonies and therefore lethal. She may have to stop at her parents' – to see how Tara and Charlie are settling in, and, with luck, she may be offered something hot to eat. She scans the room and the drained faces of her team. 'We'll resume tomorrow morning if there's nothing else.'

'One last thing.' Mark takes the whiteboard marker from Gil-lian's hand. He writes down *public appeal* and says, 'We've pre-recorded a public appeal with Rachel's parents. It'll be played on local and national news at six o'clock today and again tomor-row. We'll see what that does to raise public awareness and attract potential witnesses ... If we get nothing out of it, we'll do a reconstruction of events from Friday night. I've got Detective

Chief Superintendent Scarfe's authorisation.' He throws in Scarface's full rank for effect, and nods royally to Gillian in reply to her congratulatory gaze. She is impressed. She habitually struggles to have a stationery order approved by Scarface and has to justify (usually unsuccessfully) the need for every paperclip.

Chapter Sixteen

'Immaculate timing, Mum,' Tara raises a congratulatory eyebrow. She is clad in an apron and holding a baking dish. Her hands are hidden in padded oven gloves. She exudes domesticity, something that has eluded Gillian all her life. She has always been a passer-by in her own family. Tara and her grandparents have built a strong bond between them over the years of watching over each other, but Gillian has somehow managed to fall out of that loop. And right now, she is no more than a visitor – one of those stranded travellers that the Bible tells you to feed and water out of charity.

'We're just about to sit down to dinner.' Tara is serving lasagne. This indeed is Gillian's lucky day. Lasagne! She has earned it – she has been through an unrelenting grinder in the last few days. Oh, she's ready for it! And for a second helping; and the third.

'Lovely of you to drop by, dear.' Gillian's mother smiles a slightly lopsided smile due to the partial paralysis of her face following the stroke. 'You are going to join us?'

'You bet she is.' Tara is a cheeky monkey. She knows Gillian inside out. She knows Gillian's main motivation for this impromptu visit is to scavenge for food because, let's face it, she's been at work all day, forgot to eat, has nothing in the fridge and is too tired to even bother to get a takeaway in town. Scavenging is what she has done ever since Tara was a schoolgirl: she would descend on the house like a bat from hell, pack Tara into her car, and drive them both to her parents for a meal. Tara loved it: Gran was a fabulous cook whilst Mum . . . Mum struggled to follow the instructions on a five-minute ready meal packet; she would usually cut corners and shorten the microwaving time by a few vital seconds, rendering her culinary outputs inedible.

Gillian doesn't take offence. She hardly notices the sarcasm in Tara's tone. 'What time is it?' she asks urgently. 'Is the six o'clock news on?' She finds the remote on the arm of her father's armchair and flicks on the TV. The familiar musical score of the news programme blasts out, the volume so high it could raise the dead, due to her parents' combined deafness.

'You should watch this,' she instructs everyone present, 'there's going to be an appeal for witnesses in the missing girl's case. You know, the local girl: Rachel Snyder? You may not realise it yet, but you could be a vital witness – you may've seen something . . . you may know something. Especially you, Tara.'

The camera zooms onto Mrs Snyder's face. She looks tired: black, puffy bags hang under her eyes, her complexion ashen despite the efforts of the makeup team. She has however changed into a suit and combed her hair. The camera shifts focus to her husband; he doesn't look any better, though his face is more inscrutable. He is the one doing the talking. 'Please, Rachel, whatever you think you may have done, it doesn't matter . . . Really, it doesn't. We just want you to come home. We just want to know you're OK. Please –'

He is interrupted by his wife. Firstly, it is her hysterical voice, then her face gives in to her muscles pulling at it in different directions and forming bizarre contortions. 'Please, give us our daughter back! If you're listening! She's done nothing to you! She can't have! She's a good girl, good person . . . Give her up! We don't care! Whatever you've done –' her voice is crushed by the unimaginable possibilities that her words carry, and she finishes in a whisper, 'we'll forgive you . . .'

The cameraman decides to respect her dignity as she dissolves into sobs, and zooms out. There are two other people sitting at the table: Scarfe and Webber. Scarface never misses an opportunity to appear in front of cameras and to display his PR skills to the world. He looks suitably sombre, his Picasso-style fragmented lips pursed with great empathy. Webber looks intent on saying something – probably something important – but it is Scarface who holds the floor.

'We'd like to appeal to members of the public in the area of Sexton's Canning, particularly Lower Horton and Little Ogburn: if you have seen this girl –' At this point, a school photograph of Rachel Snyder fills the TV screen. She has an open, genuine smile, thick dark eyebrows, and keen eyes; her hair is dark brown and bouncy, with a few curls having snaked out of her ponytail. Her cheeks are glowing soft pink. She is wearing the Whalehurst School uniform, 'especially on Friday, the second of March, or in the early hours of Saturday morning, alone or with anyone, contact us on our dedicated free landline. The number is displayed,' and indeed an 0800 number appears on the screen. 'The line is open twenty-four-seven. We're looking for any information relating to Rachel's disappearance.'

'Please!' Mrs Snyder sobs. Her husband pulls her into his arms. DS Webber stares intently into the camera as if he were looking into the kidnapper's eyes.

'That's so awful,' Gillian's mother commiserates, shaking her head. 'I can't imagine what her parents are going through.'

Tara has dished out the lasagne while Charlie is pouring the wine. Gillian nods when he looks at her for permission to fill her glass. He does so; then he pours Tara a glass. He asks her, 'Isn't that girl a pupil at your school?'

'Yes, it's unbelievable!' She gulps the wine down in one go. 'First, Bradley Watson found dead – Mum came to talk to us about it in the morning – and then she was back within a few hours to ask questions about Rachel. We didn't know what hit us!'

Gillian has her mouth full, gorging on the lasagne. It tastes amazing, but then anything would, considering how hungry she is. She washes down a mouthful with some wine. Before another forkful she tells Tara, 'Your school's going to be under a magnifying glass for days to come. You'd better brace yourself.'

'How could these two tragedies have anything to do with our school?'

'You tell me,' Gillian retorts and goes back to demolishing her lasagne, which she does with astounding speed, until her plate is empty. While she is refilling it, she adds, 'What do you expect? The boy's worked at Whalehurst and the girl is a student there. Plus there are other circumstances I'm not at liberty to discuss with you . . .'

Her plate replenished, Gillian settles down to clearing it. She has decided to carry out a spot of investigation while she is here. She grills Tara, 'Tell me about that headmaster of yours. There's something about him . . .'

'Dr Featherstone?' Tara looks at her, incredulous. 'You're not saying . . . ?'

'I'm not saying anything – just asking.'

Tara shrugs her shoulders. 'He's a bit of a pompous prig, but he's all right. I mean, I can't imagine him being into killing people, or kidnapping teenage girls, for crying out loud!'

'People don't usually advertise such tendencies to the world,' Gillian says philosophically. 'In fact, they're usually quite good at hiding them from public view.'

'What reasons do you have to suspect him?' Tara's eyes are burning with curiosity though anxiety permeates her tone. She probably can't make up her mind whether to indulge in a spot of gossip about Featherstone, or defend his – and the school's – good name.

'I'm just exploring possibilities and building his character profile in my head. There's something I don't like about him –'

'Which may not be reason enough to suspect him,' Charlie interjects, for which he receives a critical glare from Gillian. He wonders if his intervention was worth the trouble.

She says, 'There's something called *gut feeling*, young man.

And I've got a gut feeling about him. He's too agitated, too defensive . . .'

'Wouldn't you be, dear, if you were in his position.' Her father tries to inject a dose of common sense into the conversation. 'His employee has been murdered and his pupil has gone missing. How would you react?'

'I'd be offering the police my full co-operation, not blocking their path,' Gillian snorts. Her plate is empty again, but so is the baking dish. She has polished it all off. 'Anyway, he lives at Whalehurst, doesn't he?'

'Yeah, as any headmaster would.'

'And his family?'

'He doesn't have any. He's a widower. No children that I know of. He started at Whalehurst seven years ago, after – I understand – his wife died.'

'She did, did she? What did she die of?'

'He didn't tell me that when I applied for my job, and I didn't ask. I rather think it'd be insensitive to ask him, Mum.' Tara sighs. She knows her mother: she knows that any sense and sensitivity she has as a human being could not have been possibly inherited from Gillian. 'All I know is that after losing his wife, he left his old life behind him – his job, sold his house – and started at Whalehurst.'

'That doesn't surprise me,' Gillian's father comments. 'I wouldn't be able to carry on the same way, look at the same four walls and all the familiar things, if anything happened to Ophelia. It'd be unbearable . . .' He takes his wife's hand and plants a kiss on it. His eyes are glistening, and he blinks rapidly to swallow back tears.

'Nothing will happen to Mum,' Gillian offers her trademark form of vague reassurance, and to avoid dwelling on the matter any longer, moves swiftly to a different topic, 'Any pudding?'

When she gets home, Corky goes berserk with joy; Fritz is nowhere to be seen. In all probability, he has found himself a new home with a set of loving, caring owners who feed him tuna and fresh shrimps for breakfast. By contrast, Gillian feeds Corky dry dog biscuits. He is nevertheless extremely grateful and jumps at her with unbridled delight. Her phone rings. She raises her hand to the dog, 'Settle down, Corky. It's Mark. Let me take it. Then, I promise, we'll go for a long walk.'

She puts the phone down. She has to go back on her promise and let the dog out into the garden for a bit of lone roaming. Gillian turns on her heel and heads for Bishops Well. Rachel Snyder has been found.

PART TWO

A pocket full of posies

Chapter Seventeen

They turned off their respective bedside lamps simultaneously. The night absorbed their fear. They were relieved that they couldn't see each other's eyes. Neither of them had drawn the curtains. It looked as if for the first time in a week the clouds had been lifted, their once heavy bellies empty at last. The rain had stopped. The sky had found its stars. Something screamed in Sarah's head, 'Why can nobody find my baby!'

Sleep was evading them. They had stopped pretending that they were trying to sleep; they were both sitting on top of the bedsheets with their backs propped against the headrest. They were gazing at the stars, which were so far away that no one could reach them. They were safe where they were – in their far, far away galaxies. Sarah kept querying the hopeless silence hanging inside her head, mulling over and over the same question, 'Where is Rachel? Is she safe?'

Sarah refused to take sleeping tablets. What if something happened when she was asleep? What if she missed Rachel's return? Jonathan believed that Rachel had done something stupid and run away. Something ridiculous, like drugs. He was wrong. Rachel would never have done it to them: she would have never put them through hell if she had a choice. She was a caring, sensitive girl. She had her head firmly screwed on.

Someone had taken her. Sarah was convinced of that. She knew. What she didn't know was why – why would anyone want to harm Rachel.

They had stopped arguing over this. It made no difference which one of them was right. As long as Rachel came back home safe and sound, it didn't matter one bit.

When she finally came back, they would have to have a serious talk. They would talk to her about speaking to strangers and trusting people she didn't know. It was a big bad world out there and she was such a naïve, polite girl; she just couldn't say no. She really had to learn to do that. She was fifteen and yet she knew nothing of the real world. Was that their fault? Had they foolishly encased her in a little pink bubble? Had they inadvertently prolonged her childhood that little bit too much? Had they destroyed her sense of self-preservation by shielding her from all the bad things in life? Wrapped her up in cotton wool: public schools, holidays in idyllic, isolated resorts, pandering to her every wish? She had never tasted defeat, never been denied, never been warned. That was why she had let somebody take advantage of her. She had run into the night – an unsuspecting, silly, gullible girl! She had been lured out and now all she wanted – Sarah could feel it in her gut – was to come back home. If only *he* would let her go.

Once Rachel was back, Sarah would make everything better. She would erase the past – all the mistakes she and Jon had made on Rachel's behalf: taking her out of the local school, cutting her off from her friends and neighbours and thrusting her into the alien environment of a boarding school. The poor girl was neither here nor there. It must have been purgatory for her. Because her parents wanted the so-called *best* for her!

Sarah stifled a sob. She gazed at the black shape of her husband who sat next to her, staring at the ceiling, thinking God knows what. Waiting – waiting just like Sarah was, waiting and dissecting the errors of their ways.

Jonathan got up from the bed and walked to the window. A long, heavy sigh lingered in his wake. He opened the window and let air in. Sarah could hear him inhale. His breath juddered like an irregular heartbeat.

'Leave the window open,' she told him and didn't recognise her own voice. It was hoarse and worn out.

They both jumped when they heard the phone ring. It was the landline.

The phone was in the hallway. They raced down the stairs, Jonathan first. He picked up the receiver. 'Yes!' he shouted. His eyes were unsettled. They darted from Sarah's face to the ceiling, back to her face; they shut – tight – and obstinately stayed closed.

'Jonathan!' Sarah reached for the phone. 'Is it Rachel? Give it to me!'

'He's hung up.'

The phone choked in her ear. She slammed it down. 'Who was it?' Her mind was thinking at breakneck speed, faster than she could speak. She wanted him to say it. She wanted Jonathan to spit it out – *the kidnapper has asked for a ransom. How long have they got to put it together? Now! Let's get it all now!* 'Speak to me! What does he want?'

Jonathan's eyes were staring at her, dark and still. 'It was DS Webber. They have found a . . . body. They think it may be –'

'They are wrong!'

'He's sending a car for us.'

119

Chapter Eighteen

Michael Almond hides behind his moustache and refuses to comment. A typical pathologist, he will not commit himself to anything until he has opened the body and inspected every square inch of it. All he says is that she has been dead for a few days. How she died is subject to speculation, though at face value—

'Yes, I can see she drowned,' Gillian snaps. She really doesn't have time for all this tiptoeing, this ludicrous foreplay, this hard-to-get evasiveness. 'But was it an accident or murder?'

'Look at the state of the body. It's been in water for days. We have decay, bloating, discolourations, to name a few factors that may lead to false conclusions if I'm not careful . . . I'll have to examine the body in lab conditions to see if there are any defensive wounds. I can't do it by moonlight. I'm not a wizard!'

Almond can be as bellicose as Gillian when he puts his mind to it. He won't be pushed around. Gillian should understand that – it takes one to know one, and they are made from the same mould when it comes to attitude. Except that she neither has the desire nor the time to psychoanalyse her work colleagues. She now has two dead bodies on her hands and the more time that elapses the colder the scent goes. The murderer has an advantage. He has already had a few days, *give or take a day*, to cover his tracks, prepare his alibi, and calm down and act normally. He is there in the shadows, laughing. Gillian is convinced it is the same person that killed Bradley Watson. Lightning doesn't strike twice on the same night!

'And where the hell is Webber!' She decides to waste not a minute longer bickering with Almond. 'He calls me and then he fucks off somewhere . . .'

'He went to collect the parents.' Macfadyen is looking sheepish. She knows that a storm is brewing. She knows what will come next.

'Parents? Whose parents? Rachel's parents?!'

'He promised to keep them in the loop, day or night He felt –'

'I don't give a shit about how Webber feels! He can't bring the parents here! What if we have the wrong person? Has he gone barking mad! I want him back here   now!' She clutches her mobile, scrolling down her contacts to recall Webber.

It's too late.

Webber's Honda pulls in and stops at an awkward angle to the emergency vehicles which are parked at the top of the access road. Before he switches off the engine, Sarah and Jonathan Snyder spring out of the car. Gillian watches astounded, a sense of imminent disaster swelling inside her head. Sarah screams without forming any words. Jonathan grabs her and pushes her into Webber's arms. He, in his turn, holds on to her despite her efforts to break free. They struggle while Jonathan Snyder tumbles down the bank and directly at the police tape. He cuts through it, shaking off the uniformed officers as if they were nothing but dust. He pushes into the tent and takes just one look. What follows is the agonising shriek of a man who has just discovered his child is dead.

Chapter Nineteen

When a knock on the door brings her back to the land of the living, Gillian remains on the sofa, wide-eyed and still. She is dog tired. She cannot bring herself to open the door, not even to turn her head. Her day has been torture: an endless, repetitive, relentless chain of mind-boggling events. A sideways glance at the yellowed face of the grandfather clock tells her it is ten past two in the morning. It is the middle of the bloody night! She is going to sit this out; she won't answer the door; she will pretend she doesn't exist.

The knocking persists. It isn't loud or particularly urgent – perhaps even slightly timid – but it does persist.

Corky doesn't bark. He has padded to the hallway on low haunches, commando-style, and sat by the door, tilting his head, mystified. The fact that he doesn't look alarmed means that someone he knows is standing on the other side of the door. A friend.

If it were a friend or family, they would have called her first, or texted. Who, in God's name, turns up in the middle of the night on one's doorstep without prior notice? Gillian must find out.

She heaves herself up from the sofa – it takes an enormous surge of willpower to do so, but she does it in the name of burning curiosity. She follows Corky to the door and squats beside him, tuning in to the knocking. Knock, knock.

She wishes she had a spyhole to see who the hell decided to bother her at this hour, but she possesses no such thing and that means opening the door and letting the intruder in. Dropping the pretence that she doesn't exist . . .

Damn it! She turns the old-fashioned key in the keyhole; it squeaks: metal on metal. There is no going back. The uninvited visitor knows she is in. She flings the door open. Corky sneaks out and jumps on –

'Webber?!'

Mark Webber looks guilty. He is gazing at Gillian from behind supplicatory eyebrows. Gillian ignores his imploring eyes, her investigative skills directed at a pair of suitcases positioned neatly on her front step. Two identical suitcases on wheels. Corky is sniffing them. He too is suspicious.

'Sorry, Gillian, I know it's late –'

'You don't say!'

'But . . .' he attempts a strained smile which makes him appear constipated.

'What are you doing here?' Gillian doesn't reciprocate the smile. She wants answers, and then, she bloody well wants to go to bed. 'And what are these suitcases for? You're going away, or . . . what's this all about?'

Webber opens his mouth, shakes his head, his lips contort as he tries – in vain – to control a sob.

'Talk to me!' Gillian grabs him by his elbow and shoves him indoors. 'Come in . . . get those bloody suitcases in . . .' As he is not doing as he is told and merely stands in the hallway, shaking on unsteady feet, she is forced to bring in the suitcases by herself. They are big and heavy as if Webber's whole life were crammed into them.

She shuts the front door and flicks on the lights. She peers into his eyes. They are moist with tears. 'Grown men don't cry, Mark. What's going on?' She can't imagine what the problem is. She only saw him half an hour ago when she gave him a piece of her mind about his stupidity and insubordination in bringing the Snyders to the crime scene. She threatened him with a formal warning and with reporting him to Scarfe, which she fully intended to do first thing in the morning. She is not so sure any more. The man is clearly in an unstable condition. Has her outburst unhinged him so much that he decided to decamp to her doorstep to dissuade her from taking disciplinary action against him?

'Is it about the formal warning?' she asks probingly. She is feeling responsible for his meltdown. His job means everything to him and he has been after that promotion to a DI for months. A written warning would put brakes on that and would bring his career to a screeching halt. She should not have slapped him with the reprimand. It must have got to him. 'Look, it doesn't matter. What's done is done. I have forgotten about it already. Go home, Mark. See you tomorrow!' She opens the door again, tripping over one of the damn suitcases. Webber is under too much stress. His drive towards promotion, his obsession about Rachel Snyder's case – all that must have finally got to him. 'We'll review the case tomorrow. I'm dog tired now.'

'Kate's chucked me out,' he mumbles.

Gillian wonders if he has heard her. He is muttering something. 'What did you say?'

'She told me to go . . . I found the suitcases packed downstairs . . . She said we were done . . . She wants a divorce . . . I don't know what I've done! What have I done, Gillian?' He slumps to the floor, his large frame sprawled across the narrow hallway, and he sobs.

Gillian stands over him with her hands on her hips. She is hopeless when it comes to all those complex degrees of human misery. She scowls. She has no idea what to do or how to relocate this jelly mass of a crying man to the lounge. One thing is obvious: he isn't going home.

She clears her throat. 'You're in luck. Tara and Charlie moved out the other day. I can let you have their bedroom. Just for tonight,' she adds carefully in case he gets any ideas. 'It's the second door on the landing. Mind you, I haven't changed the sheets –'

'It's all right. I don't mind. Thanks, Gillian.'

She nods curtly, not that he is looking at her to see that, and steps over him to take herself upstairs to bed.

Chapter Twenty

Riley is pleased with himself. There is nothing unusual about that; the man has a head the size of a watermelon. The unkempt beard makes it appear even bigger, too big by any ordinary man's standards. But Riley is far from ordinary. For him, the head, the beard and the rest of his huge bulk are perfectly matched. He is smirking under his beard and the selection of crumbs that are trapped in it. He knows he is indispensable and he knows how to milk it.

He produces a list of telephone numbers, stabbing each of them with his square-nailed forefinger, and presents a short *Who's Who* of Bradley's family, friends, and acquaintances. One number is a Pay-As-You-Go, and it is switched off, its owner's identity remaining a mystery. The rest, bar two, are legitimate contacts. The two however are a different kettle of fish. That's where Riley pauses for dramatic effect and, after some impatient encouragement, informs Gillian and Mark that one of the contacts on Bradley Watson's mobile – a frequently accessed contact, as it happens – is Toby Mackenzie. They all know that Toby Mackenzie is the larger half of the infamous Mac Brothers: the drug lords of Sexton's Canning. The smaller half of the formidable duo, Callum Mackenzie, also features prominently on the list of frequently called numbers. And this link to the criminal underworld is bound to pull Gillian's investigation out of the boggy swamp where it has been languishing for the last few, hard-going days. Gillian should be grateful.

'Do I get a thank you?' Jon Riley demands like a small spoilt boy. Well, maybe not *small*.

'Let's bring the brothers in.' Ignoring Jon's cries for attention, she is talking to Webber. 'We'll interview them separately, before they get a chance to compare notes. Just to help us with our inquiries. No need for lawyers.'

'They could choose to help us with our inquiries with their lawyer present,' Webber says.

'Not that we'll be giving them that idea now, will we?'

The two of them are heading for the exit, planning their offensive against the most notorious gangsters in Sexton's, with links to a clandestine Russian mafia operating in Bristol – according to Whittaker. This could be the scoop of the century.

'What about me?' Riley whines from his Maserati seat.

Mark shouts a curt 'thank you' over his shoulder. Gillian can't be bothered. Jon knows he has done a good job; she doesn't have to tell him. But he sulks. 'Then I won't tell you where Rachel Snyder entered the river,' he mutters. 'You can wait for my written report, like everyone else.'

They stop dead in their tracks. Gillian turns to face the bearded maverick. 'Heard of wasting police time? Get on with it, Jon. We've got two bloody bodies on our hands and Scarface is just waiting to pass this buck up to NCA.'

'Maybe they'll be more obliging than you lot . . .' Jon pushes forward his flabby chest.

Gillian skewers him with a sharp glare.

'Come back, then, and I'll take you through it.' He sighs, deflated.

Knowing Riley, both Gillian and Mark realise that this will be a painstakingly thorough and lengthy exposé delivered in technical vernacular. He's got all the minute details in his (big) head and he is keen to share every last shred of them. So they pull up two plastic chairs, prop their elbows on his desk, and scrutinise his panoramic computer screen. Now in his element, Riley takes them through the ins and outs of the River Avon's currents, sediments, and gradient variations; they learn about the weather patterns since Friday last, the strength of the westerly winds and

126

the water level rising due to a few millimetres of recent rainfall. And at long last, Riley puts them out of their misery and pinpoints the exact location where Rachel Snyder's body landed in the river: near the bridge connecting the cul-de-sac where Rachel lived to Ascombe Street.

They are gazing at the satellite map of the area where not long ago they found Bradley Watson's phone. The search conducted at the time did not include the river. Gillian makes an executive decision to send Forensics and divers to re-examine the location. It should have been done straight away, but with the cuts and reels of red tape, no one as much as contemplated taking on the challenge. She pushes her chair back abruptly and asks Jon to email his findings asap to Bobby Hughes, copying Scarfe into it. 'Get him to drop everything else and send his team now. I want a report on my desk by the end of today.'

Mark too is on his feet, raring to go. 'Good work, Jon,' he slaps Riley on the back.

'So she went into the river from that bridge . . . Did she jump or was she pushed?'

Under the false impression that Gillian is talking to him, Webber collaborates. 'That's where the dogs lost her scent the first time we were trying to track her down, before we knew of Watson.'

'And that can mean only one thing: Rachel Snyder never made it to Whalehurst School that night. She couldn't have killed Bradley Watson – she died before him.'

'Could it be that it was the other way around? That Watson killed Rachel?'

'And then what?' Gillian ponders the likelihood of that. 'And then, quite independently of his earlier crime, he went and got himself murdered on the same night? No . . . That'd be too much of a freak coincidence. Whoever killed Rachel Snyder killed Bradley Watson. We have to interview the Mac Brothers.'

Toby is a smooth operator: lean, tall, with the smouldering looks of a blue movie star: clear skin, keen eyes, and the effortless gait of a cat on the prowl. He is wearing an expensive blue shirt that catches the light like the surface of a still lake. He smiles and appears perfectly calm, like said lake. Indubitably, he is not a junkie. He does not take drugs; he deals them. And he makes a good living out of it. The faceless mob of unsuspecting teenagers, young professionals needing a quick boost, and the hopeless addicts that they all become – all feed his expensive tastes in clothes and real estate. DI Marsh and DS Webber have picked up Toby, and his sidekick brother from their converted-chapel estate in an affluent suburb of Sexton's Canning. It goes without saying that Gillian doesn't like the dickhead.

Webber has holed up with Callum in Interview Room 3, which is across the corridor from Interview Room 2 where Gillian is fighting back the urge to punch Toby Mackenzie in his pretty-boy face while interrogating him about his links to Bradley Watson.

'I'd love to help you, DI Marsh,' he feigns citizen's concern, 'but Bradley Watson and I don't mix in the same circles.'

'But you do know him?'

'Of him, yes . . . He went to school with my little brother.'

'Callum?'

'Yes. That's all I know of Bradley Watson. Mmm . . .' he furrows his immaculately smooth forehead in an effort to remember something that he purports is second-hand knowledge to him, 'and I think he served time. If I'm not mistaken, for drugs? You'll know better than me, but I've heard rumours.'

The man has a cheek. He thinks he is playing a game of cat and mouse. He's having a laugh.

'I'm trying to be helpful, but if you don't tell me what this is all about then I can't do much more. I am a busy man, DI Marsh.' He shifts in his chair, gearing up to leave.

'And I'm grateful for your time, Mr Mackenzie. Still, there's something I don't understand: if you don't really know Bradley Watson, how come you're one of the contacts on his mobile? And there has been quite a flurry of phone calls between the two of you . . . For someone who hardly knows the man, you're quite busy staying in touch with him.'

Gillian presents a redacted list of phone calls prepared by Riley, with Mackenzie's number highlighted in fluorescent pink.

He stops smirking, which is an achievement in itself. Without the smile, his face isn't as handsome. He scowls while trying to take in the significance of Gillian's line of inquiry. At last, he speaks, but only to answer her with questions of his own. The cat and mouse game is over.

'How did you get hold of Bradley's phone? And as for his contacts, why don't you ask Bradley? Looks like he got hold of my number from somewhere. So? Lots of people call me, most of them I never heard of.'

'Oh, didn't I say? I can't ask Bradley Watson.' It's Gillian's turn to play games. 'I thought you knew. Bradley Watson is dead, has been dead for four days now. You haven't heard all the rumours then? Yes . . . Murdered. He's been murdered, and all I've got to go on is his mobile phone with your number topping his Favourites.'

The transformation in Toby Mackenzie's face is undeniable. He goes pale and his jaw tightens as he clenches his teeth. He is scared – petrified. 'I want to call my lawyer,' he says through his rigor-mortis teeth. 'I've got nothing else to say until I see my lawyer.'

Slowly, with thoughtful deliberation, Gillian tidies up the papers from the table: Bradley's mugshot and his telephone records. She slides them into her case folder. She gets up. 'In that case, I'd better not waste any more time and call your solicitor. If you don't mind waiting here . . .'

She leaves the room. She is going to let him stew for a while. She is sure though that Mackenzie is not the killer. Neither of the Mackenzies is. And she has an inkling that she has just waded into a drug war. That's why Toby Mackenzie is scared – Big Mac is trembling in his big boots.

★

Having instructed Miller to get hold of Mackenzie's solicitor, Gillian stops by to listen to Webber interviewing Little Mac. For the benefit of the tape, Webber declares that DI Marsh has entered the room and he states her time of entry.

Little Mac, aka Callum Mackenzie, is not in the same league as his big brother. He is nervous; his eyes shift between his well-chewed fingernails and his toes. His dress sense is casual, if not scraggy. He is sweating and it is apparent that he hasn't showered in a while. Unlike his brother, he might well be a regular user and may even be high now. His language lacks sophistication.

'I ain' fuckin' sayin' nothin'! I don' know him! Happy?' He folds his arms defensively on his chest, then promptly drives his thumb to his mouth to have a nibble on his ravaged cuticles.

'But you went to school with him,' Gillian interjects. 'Your brother's just told me.'

'So what if I did?'

'So you know him.'

'No comment.' He digs his heels in and nails his gaze to the floor. He is done.

'Listen, Callum, we only want to know the nature of your business with Bradley. It may be in your interest to tell us given that Bradley is dead and we don't yet know why or who killed him –'

The effect of her announcement is the same as with Toby: Callum stares at her, his eyes rounded with fear. 'Brad's dead?' he mumbles hopelessly.

'Yes. And we want to find out –'

It is not meant to be. The door to Interview Room 3 flings open and in strides DSI Scarfe with DC Whittaker peering timidly over his shoulder.

Scarfe barks, 'A word, DI Marsh!'

It is more than a word. Scarface delivers a cannonade of expletives to express the extent of his frustration with Gillian's performance, and that is done on the hoof as he is marching her to his office. 'You've just undermined months of investigation, Marsh!

Months! Not to mention putting lives in danger – the lives of undercover officers! For grief's sake!'

Whittaker is slinking behind them like a great big tumbleweed of bushy eyebrows and hairy ears. He is riddled with guilt. It was he who brought NCA officers into the equation. His not-so-discreet inquiries with his old snouts in Greyston are to blame. The fact is that DI Marsh had asked him to look into Bradley Watson's connections on the local drugs scene, but of course, she didn't mean him to drag the National bloody Crime Squad into it. And neither did he know about the ongoing undercover investigation of Bristol's organised crime ring from the Baltics – or Russia (the jury still being out on it). He didn't know about it because it was top secret and agencies rarely communicate with each other when it comes to undercover operations. But it's too late. The collaring of the Mac Brothers, even if only to ask them to assist Gillian with her double murder inquiries, has no doubt put the Baltic drug lords on high alert.

Scarfe, followed by Marsh, followed by Whittaker, all burst into Scarfe's office, where they come face to face with an angry-looking man in plain clothes. He tells DI Marsh, in so many words, to get the fuck out of his patch.

Chapter Twenty-one

Dr Michael Almond doesn't like answering questions; he prefers to carry out autopsies in the peace and the dead quiet of his examination room, after which he issues a post-mortem which he believes to be self-explanatory. But DI Marsh won't wait for it. She is a busybody, a domineering little woman running on adrenalin and exuding vapours of bad attitude. She is standing next to him, breathing down his neck and bombarding him with questions: was it an accident? Any evidence of drug use? Was she sexually violated? Did she drown? The exact time of death? Anything of importance?

Almond turns to face her and, due to their considerable height difference, looks down on her with unconcealed irritation. He is pointing a scalpel at her pretty little nose that she so very much likes to poke in anywhere she can. His gigantic moustache hangs ominously over his words. 'You're not helping, DI Marsh. I'm likely to miss vital pieces of evidence due to your distractions. Can you not follow the example of DS Webber and watch patiently from outside?'

'Look here, I appreciate you may like an audience – pathology is an awfully lonely pursuit – but I don't have the time to applaud you from the sidelines. So let's get this straight: I don't do *watching*. Webber attends autopsies. And he's only behind the glass because he can't bear the sight of blood.'

Outside, Webber smiles sheepishly and adds, 'Nor the smell . . . There's something about the smell that turns my stomach.'

'Anyway, it's not about Webber.' There! She's doing it again: an abrupt change of subject. 'So, was she murdered?'

Almond would love to argue and stick to his rules, but he has come to know DI Marsh and he is in no doubt that she won't go away until she gets what she has come here for. In telegraphic shorthand he delivers his verdict, 'There are no defensive injuries anywhere on the body. I can't tell you with certainty that she wasn't pushed or coerced, but I'd be more comfortable with the hypothesis that she went into the water voluntarily.'

'Went? As in waddled in?'

'Or dived . . . But the river isn't deep enough in that section by Ascombe Street. There is no bruising to indicate that she hit the surface of the water falling from a considerable height, like the bridge . . . I'd say she just – went in.'

'Suicide?'

'That's not my conclusion to draw. I can't account for the victim's intentions.'

'But you can account for the time of death?'

'Late Friday night or the early hours of Saturday morning. I can't be any more specific. And before you repeat yourself,' he raises a forbidding finger in response to Gillian's mouth forming the opening of her next question, 'yes, she drowned; no, she wasn't violated – in fact, she is still a virgin; and no, there's no external evidence of drugs, no needle marks or any suspicious bruising, but you'll have to wait for the lab results to have a definitive picture as to what she may, or may not, have ingested.'

'How long?'

'Expect everything by close of business tomorrow, alongside my post-mortem report.'

DI Marsh expels an exaggerated sigh and asks her sergeant poised outside the glass window, 'Close of business – what's that?' DS Webber retains a straight face and thanks Almond.

'What is it with people wanting to be thanked for everything these days,' Gillian despairs as they are walking back to her car.

133

'They're just doing their bloody job. Correct me if I'm wrong, but they are being paid for it, aren't they? Isn't that enough?'

'It's just common courtesy, that's all,' Mark explains patiently, safe in the knowledge that such a concept will be lost on her. 'Anyway, thanks for putting me up last night.'

'Don't mention it,' she shrugs. 'When are you leaving? Going back home, I mean . . .'

'That's the thing: Kate won't have me back.'

'What exactly have you done?'

'Nothing.'

'That's what they all say.'

'Nothing, really nothing. It's just my job – late nights, I'm never there. And, more to the point, she's still battling with her depression. She's all over the place and she can't rely on me to be there to help out with the kids.'

'I can see where she's coming from.' Gillian nods and reaches over him to get a wine gum from the glove compartment. She pops one in and offers one to Webber. He shakes his head. 'Please yourself.' She chews loudly, relishing the rubbery texture.

'I've been wondering if I could stay another couple of nights,' Webber mumbles like a boy with a guilty conscience. 'Until I get something sorted.'

'Yeah, no worries.' Gillian nods her head slowly. 'But you should really sit her down and explain to her how things work when you're a copper.'

'She knows; she's lived with it for more than ten years!'

'Ha!' Gillian exclaims and, before elaborating on that exclamation, picks a stubborn piece of wine gum lodged in her molar. 'But what she doesn't know is your priorities. The job comes first.'

'Sometimes I wonder about that.'

'Then you're in the wrong job . . .' She gives him a prolonged sideways glance, which gets him worried that she isn't looking at the road. 'But I don't think you are, for what it's worth. You're a damn good copper.'

'Yeah, thanks.'

'I'm not telling you this so you can bloody well thank me! I'm stating facts. And I'll give you another fact for nothing: good coppers and families are a contradiction in terms. You want to stay a good copper, you're guaranteed to wake up one day a lonely, miserable old git with no life of your own. Your choice.'

'You've made it too,' he points out.

She fixes him with a sharp glare. 'Pass me another one of those wine gums,' she says, 'the dark red one that says *Port*.'

The riverbank by Ascombe Street is buzzing with activity when they arrive. They park in the cul-de-sac by Rachel's house as the immediate vicinity of the bridge is cordoned off and the access road is chock-a-block with double-parked vans. Somehow the press had got the scent and decamped nearby for a picnic and a touch of news-mongering. A reporter with a vaguely familiar face sticks the fluffy end of his mike in Gillian's face. 'BBC Points West. DI Marsh, may we have your comments on the new developments?'

'Can I first find out what they are?' She pushes the mike out of her way.

Bobby Hughes spots her and Webber, and hurries to talk to them. The journalist hurries too to eavesdrop, but he is stopped by Uniform and redirected back behind the tape.

Bobby is wearing waterproof gear and it is evident that he has been in the water alongside the divers. There are no limits to his dedication, and that's what Gillian has always valued him for.

'We've found a few telling clues,' he says as he extricates himself from his bodysuit. 'Based on what we found we could probably – tentatively – hazard a provisional reconstruction of events from Friday night.' He presents an evidence bag containing a muddy slipper sock. 'We found this embedded in sediment, about a metre from the riverbank, directly under the bridge. It compares with the slipper socks she was wearing on the night, based on the photographs we retrieved from the memory card found on Bradley

135

Watson's body. So, I'd say, she went in from the bank; her foot got stuck in the muddy bog, she pulled it out – and the sock came off. She didn't jump from the bridge, she just went in –'

'Dr Almond would back you up on this,' Webber nods.

'Oh yeah?'

'He says there are no injuries or bruising consistent with her hitting the surface of the water from a height.'

'OK, it makes sense.' Bobby puts the evidence bag away and picks up another one. 'And this is what, I think, she was trying to get to. We found it stuck in the lowest-lying branches of that tree tucked under the bridge. The cables from her headphones became entangled in branches and held it up hanging just over the water surface. It was well obscured by the reeds. We couldn't see it from the bank, but once the divers got in, it was right there in their faces. Rachel Snyder's missing iPad.'

Gillian turns the bag containing the tablet in her hands. It isn't even wet. It has hung there for four days, waiting to be found to tell the tale. 'So, she drops the iPad from the bridge – or throws it in the river for some reason or other – realises it didn't go in, or perhaps changes her mind and decides to retrieve it, wades into the river, gets stuck, gets sucked in, and that's it?'

'It certainly looks like that's what happened.'

'But why? Why was she on that bridge? In the middle of the night? In her bloody pyjamas!'

'We may never find out, but it looks like it was an accident.'

'And that bastard, Bradley Watson, saw it happen and did nothing to save her,' Webber concludes, his jaw locking as he swallows his anger.

'Possibly. But it's also possible that he couldn't help her. Don't forget he ended up dead just a couple of hours later. Maybe he was already on the run, trying to save himself ... We found his mobile only a couple of yards further down the footpath. Maybe he was being chased and he dropped it ... Maybe he had to choose between himself and Rachel Snyder?'

'Or maybe he didn't see her go in at all? It was a dark night and the last photo he took of her was on the bridge,' Bobby adds another layer to this mystery.

'Oh yes, he did see her!' Webber sticks to his version obstinately, 'and he let her drown.'

Gillian gives her sergeant a sharp look. 'That's pure speculation, Webber. You're becoming too emotional about this case.'

'Someone should, for crying out loud!' he retorts. 'She was a young girl with her whole life ahead of her, and that scumbag –'

'Let us pass judgments when we're in possession of all the facts.' DI Marsh cuts him short and turns her attention to Hughes. 'Did you find her mobile? Did she have it with her?'

He shakes his head. 'Nope. Only that iPad tangled in the branches.'

'Get your men to look for it – for a mobile phone. It's missing.'

'It could be anywhere between here and where the body was found!'

'Yes, I know, but it is somewhere and there's a chance you'll find it if you look for it. Right?'

Chapter Twenty-two

Back in the briefing room at the station, DI Marsh finishes updating her team on the latest developments in the Watson/Snyder double murder inquiry, which may just turn into a singular murder and accidental death crossover. 'So, it is possible that Bradley Watson witnessed Rachel's death and walked away from it, or that he didn't see anything at all. Certainly, the photographs from his SD card do not support the supposition that he saw her die. Yes, he was following her – stalking her – but that's as far as the evidence at hand takes us. In the end, we have nothing to verify the hypothesis that these two cases are related other than by the time of death and Bradley's clear obsession with Rachel Snyder.'

DC Macfadyen wades in. 'Not one of Bradley's family or friends has even heard of Rachel Snyder. I spoke to all of his phone contacts.' She shoots a look gingerly towards Detective Chief Superintendent Scarfe, who is in the room with the sole purpose of ensuring that the briefing doesn't stray into the drugs connection. 'I spoke to all of them except the Mac Brothers,' Erin clarifies for his benefit, 'and those I spoke to haven't heard him mention Rachel Snyder – not ever. If he was so obsessed with her that he followed her every step, day and night, why didn't he as much as mention her name to his closest friends?'

'The true nature of obsession,' Webber is all of a sudden an expert on the matter, 'is that you don't talk about it.'

'Yes, we can't rule that out, not yet,' Gillian agrees. 'Anything worth a mention about Bradley's contacts, DC Macfadyen?'

'Spoke to all of them, as I said. All pretty ordinary. There's that one Pay-as-You-Go number that is switched off and we don't know the identity of the owner. It was the last number Bradley dialled before he died. I put a trace on it. We'll know as soon as it is switched on.'

'That wouldn't be Rachel's missing Pay-as-You-Go?'

'No, boss. That was the first thing I cross-referenced.'

'Good job, DC Macfadyen.' Scarface nods his approval. Then he addresses Gillian in less favourable tone, 'Treat these two cases in isolation, Marsh. Rachel Snyder was a good girl from a decent family. We shouldn't be tainting her memory with drugs and the like. Her parents want to take her body home and put her to rest. Let's arrange for an inquest. It looks like we're going to get an accidental death verdict. And then we'll release the body to her family. Let's concentrate on Bradley Watson, but whatever you do in his case I want to be informed first. Do we understand each other?'

Gillian nods though she isn't in full agreement. She may have understood the Detective Chief Superintendent well enough, but he is far from even beginning to comprehend her.

Chapter Twenty-three

'It feels like unfinished business to me.' Webber doesn't look happy. 'And to her parents. You could tell from their faces. They've got no real answers, no closure. The mother looked . . . I don't know . . .'

'Bewildered,' Gillian helped him.

'You've noticed?'

'Yeah, I watched them.'

'Poor people . . . The father – Jonathan – he's blaming himself for everything. It's hard to watch . . .' Webber is already drunk. He tips his glass to his mouth and drinks with a loud gulp.

'At least they can have her body and bury her.'

'Yeah, there is that. It's important to them to do it quickly. It's called *k'vod hamet*, honouring the dead.'

'How do you know that?'

'Jonathan told me. Still, for me, the best way of honouring Rachel is to find out who the hell is responsible for her death. Someone is.'

'Yeah, and the Coroner seems to agree.'

After hearing the open verdict at the inquest, Gillian and Webber decided to go for a pint before heading home. Gillian's home is still Mark's home. The contents of her fridge just as the contents of her mini bar are severely depleted. A pit stop at The Bull's Eye for a steak and ale pie, plus the supplementary couple of pints, was inevitable. They have finished their pies and are on their fourth pints.

'Another one?' Gillian asks.

Mark nods.

'This one is on you.'

'You're sure? I could swear I bought the last one.'

'You may have, but this one is on you, take it or leave it.'

He shakes his head but gets up and staggers for the bar, muttering under his breath his dissatisfaction with this arrangement. He returns with the two pints. His eyes are brighter now.

Gillian dips her lips into the white froth. It's a funny thing, beer: the more you drink it, the more you like it. She was never a beer drinker but, stuck between Mark and Erin on their now customary Friday nights out, she has become fully converted.

This is a Friday night like any other except that Erin is absent. She is on a blind date. Gillian is unnerved. She wishes she had the guts to do something like that, but she suspects she would end up whipping out handcuffs and arresting the guy if his face didn't match his dating site profile. That's a common occurrence, Erin told her: everyone lies a little. Unlike Gillian, Erin can live with that; she has more common sense and a higher level of tolerance. She has more experience, too. This is the twenty-first century's preferred method of social – and romantic – interaction. What's next, Gillian marvels, tantric sex and video-conference orgies?

Apparently, the guy is a doctor. Hopefully, he didn't lie about that *a little*.

They bundle in over the threshold a few minutes past eleven. Gillian has lost count of how many pints later that is. Fritz is out and about – he too likes late nights out on Fridays. Corky is pleased to see them, though he stays out of their way knowing that neither of them could take his weight without losing their balance and tumbling to the ground. Gillian's head is swimming. She puts the kettle on and throws generous teaspoons of instant coffee into two mugs. She perks up the moment she pours the boiling water into the mugs. The aroma alone does the magic. Mark needs a similar pick-me-up. She carries the mugs to the lounge and hands one to him. 'Don't you drop it,' she warns him, seeing that he is already half asleep with his eyelids drooping and his body splayed on the sofa.

'Thanks,' he takes the mug and holds it unsteadily over his stomach.

'If you spill it – you'll burn yourself.' Gillian sits next to him, leaning forward and sipping the hot liquid reverently like it was the elixir of eternal youth. 'Ahhh,' she exhales her words with a satisfied smile. 'That's exactly what I needed. I love coffee after a few pints.'

Mark makes a whimpering noise. She gazes back at him and sees that he is crying.

'I've lost them, Gillian. I know I have . . .' he mumbles. 'It hurts here.' He punches himself in the chest. 'It hurts like hell, but I . . . I've no fight left in me. I've accepted it. Would you believe it – I have accepted defeat . . .'

She hopes he hasn't accepted anything like that because that would mean he wasn't going home any time soon. 'Come on, Mark, don't give up. Call Kate, talk to her . . .'

'Don't you think I've tried!' He jumps forward.

And screams.

The steaming hot coffee from the mug precariously perched on his stomach has spilled all over him. He is up in the air; his mug is down on the floor; what's left of the coffee is soaking into the rug. Corky has arrived and is barking at Mark to – presumably – tell him to calm down.

'Shit! Shit!' Gillian and Mark curse their displeasure, she with the state of her Persian rug, he with the state of his expensive shirt. Mark attempts to tear the shirt from his body, not very efficiently. 'It's burning!' he yelps. 'Take it off! Help me take it off!'

A reluctant Good Samaritan, Gillian abandons the idea of cleaning the carpet and starts unbuttoning Mark's shirt. Together, they succeed at pulling it off his back. And this is where their bodies and their lips meet. Mark pulls Gillian into him. She can

142

feel his body heat (probably enhanced by the coffee spill). He holds her with an unexpected ferocity and starts kissing her.

'No, Mark! I don't think it's a good idea.' She tries to push him away. But he can't hear her. He is feverish with lust. His lips press into hers. His hands begin to fumble with her zip.

'Stop it, Webber! I said STOP it!'

It is pure instinct when her hand curls into a fist and the fist lands squarely in Webber's face, making direct contact with his left cheek. He squeals and recoils, clutching his face. He trips over the dog, and travels on a sharp trajectory towards the coffee table holding Gillian's mug. Mark's head crashes against the mug, which tumbles to the floor and joins Mark's mug. The bulk of Mark's body follows his head and smashes the coffee table to smithereens as he finally becomes still and harmless, lying on the floor.

Intrigued by the commotion, Fritz walks in and stares at the carnage, assessing the extent of the damage. Then he gazes at Gillian. His feline face is stern, but his eyes say clearly and unequivocally, 'Respect!' If he was wearing a hat he would be tipping it to her.

'What the hell's happened to your face?' Erin is impressed with the size of the blood-laced bruise on Mark's left cheek.

'I walked into a door,' he mutters.

Gillian bites her lower lip and shakes her head when Erin directs an enquiring glance at her. Erin knows that 'walking into a door' stands for something totally different, but she doesn't know what that something is. Gillian won't be telling her and neither will Mark. The cause of his black eye sits between them uncomfortably and they are both trying their best to ignore it. Mark starts the engine. They are driving to Rachel Snyder's funeral.

'How was the blind date?' Gillian changes the subject.

It is Erin's turn to look hangdog. In the rear-view mirror, Gillian watches her face undergo an intriguing transformation from carefree to despondent. 'I don't want to talk about it,' she says flatly.

'Oh, come on, you're amongst friends. Should we be worried?' Mark insists, glad that the focus has shifted away from his black eye.

'Well, if you must know – it was embarrassing for both of us.'

Their appetites whetted, Gillian and Mark round on her like a pair of obnoxious mosquitoes. 'You'll feel better if you talk about it. Go on, Erin, we won't tell . . .'

'It was Michael Almond.'

There is a short, but loaded, pause.

'Our Michael Almond?'

'Dr Almond, the pathologist?'

'Yes! Yes! Precisely. The most embarrassing moment of my life . . . We were meeting in the market square by the Cross. I think the plan was to go for dinner. It didn't occur to either of us at first. I saw Almond, said hello – he asked me what brought me there – I said I was meeting a friend. Wasn't gonna confess about my date, was I?' From the back seat, Erin glares into the rear-view mirror where she meets Gillian's gaze.

'Course not!' Gillian nods keenly.

'So how did you find out he was your date?'

'My *friend*,' Erin puts the word *friend* in the inverted commas of her fingers, 'wasn't coming and neither was his . . . And then we, sort of, had this eureka moment – we looked at each other like a pair of utter arseholes, and finally he goes, "Does your friend go by the name of *Sleepless-in-Sextons*?"'

'Sleepless in Sextons? Is that his dating alias?' Mark is howling with laughter. 'What's yours?'

'Never mind that.' Erin purses her lips and clips Mark round the ear.

Gillian is gobsmacked. 'How come you didn't recognise his mug from his photo? I mean the man has the greatest ruddy moustache the world has ever seen!'

'That's the problem: he has no facial hair in his avatar picture – a picture taken before he grew the damned thing . . . He's totally unrecognisable without it!'

'But then, he should've known you the moment he saw you,'

Gillian continues to apply logic to the utterly illogical business of online dating.

Erin's face twists with contrition. 'I had my photo touched-up. There's this brilliant app . . .'

Gillian tut-tuts, 'Serves you right!'

Mark's body is shaking as he tries to suppress an outburst of giggles. He receives another clip on the ear.

'I told you: it's not funny!' Erin acts like she is livid but it is obvious from the twitching in her eyes that she, too, is struggling to keep her face straight.

'So how did you get out of this macabre comedy of errors?'

'Well, we both apologised for the misunderstanding and went our separate ways.'

'As you do . . .'

'At least he didn't lie about being a doctor.'

'Yeah, that much was true.' Erin hangs her head to hide a wide grin.

'Don't know about that! I've never known him to make any of his patients better.' Mark is in fits of laughter. Only Gillian sits there sombre and sympathetic, contemplating the trials and tribulations of modern-day mating rituals. Why does it all have to be so complicated?

Chapter Twenty-four

The synagogue is bursting at the seams. Tara is there along with other teaching staff from Whalehurst School and a large number of pupils, all immaculately dressed in their demure school uniforms. They came in two coaches and filled the place with their uncanny silence – the last thing one would expect from a crowd of full-blooded teenagers. They all huddled up together, bewildered and tearful. Some are holding hands. Many have brought cuddly toys and flowers: white lilies. Gillian, Erin, and Mark are tucked out of the way up in the gallery from where they can observe the mourners, their faces and their reactions. Gillian recognises Josh Tyler, the five-minute boyfriend. His head is hung low, his eyes drilling the floor – she can't tell what he's thinking or feeling. He is flanked by Monty Collingsworth on his left and another tall young man on the other side. Both are staring straight ahead with no shadow of expression on their faces. Their backs straight and their chests pushed forward, they look athletic and invincible, the vigour of youth shielding them from mortality. Only, what good did it do for Rachel Snyder?

Gillian's attention drifts to Featherstone, the tiresome headmaster. He has come wearing his school robes, unlike other staff members who chose not to make any loud statements and leave the floor to the dead girl. Gillian finds the man so irrepressibly irritating that she wants to growl. Even now, his eyes shift quickly and stealthily from side to side as if he is checking whether anyone's watching him. He is like a naughty schoolboy caught on camera. There is something about him that provokes suspicion.

There are a few young people from Sexton's Comprehensive. Their uniforms are navy blue and their dress code more relaxed than that of Whalehurst School. The girls are wearing nail varnish and their hair isn't tied up; their skirts are shorter than convention would dictate. Gillian recognises some of them: the girl-spokesperson, the thick-set boy; she also recognises the headmistress, who shares a pew with her flock of misfits, and like them, looks like she can only hold back her tears for a second or two longer.

A silver-bearded rabbi chants a blessing over a simple pine coffin, 'Baruch dayan emet . . . Baruch dayan emet . . .'

Rhiannon steps forward and faces the congregation of mourners. She is holding a crumpled piece of paper in her hand, which she fails – or forgets – to unfold. She squeezes it as if it were a stress ball. The poor girl looks frightened – overwhelmed by the proximity of the coffin, by the unfamiliarity of this place and by what is expected of her. She must have been asked to deliver a eulogy for her once best friend; it clearly hasn't been her own idea. She is palpably nervous. She clears her throat and utters the first few words. They are so feeble and so tentative that they drown in the echoing silence that pervades the place. Someone shushes the crowd though there is hardly the need for it.

'I don't know what more to say,' Rhiannon carries on unaware of the fact that no one has heard her opening words. 'Rachel was my friend . . . she was there for me when I needed her, and . . . and I wasn't.' She swallows hard. 'I've let her down. She had nobody to go to . . . I'm sorry . . . I'm so sorry!' She gives in to crying. She sobs and runs back to her seat, into her father's comforting arms.

Another father, the dead girl's father, stands up and takes over. He only says a few words, 'Rachel didn't kill herself. She wouldn't have done that to us – to her mother.' The sympathetic eyes of the congregation are set on Sarah Snyder. She is staring vacantly into the space above her daughter's coffin and remains unresponsive. Her husband clenches his jaw. You can hear the grinding of his teeth in his voice. 'Someone out there is responsible for her death. I won't rest until they're brought to justice. Rachel won't rest . . . She won't be at peace.' He sits down. A low, ill-omened murmur replaces the silence and follows Rachel's casket all the way to the cemetery.

The students and teachers of Whalehurst School are packed onto the coaches to be transported back to the bubble of their privileged existence. Though that bubble has recently been pierced and they have lost one of their own. The silence that has enveloped them inside the synagogue still hangs on and smothers them. It is uncanny how lost for words they are. Jonathan and Sarah Snyder step into that silence and watch the coaches depart. They have received condolences from Dr Featherstone on behalf of *all pupils and staff*. Meaningless, really. There is a longing in their eyes to hear more, to know more, to understand what has happened to their child. There is a sense of unfinished business.

Just before Gillian, Erin and Mark get back into their unmarked car, they are approached by a bald man with a rotund midriff whom Gillian recognises as Rhiannon's father. Rhiannon is with him – cowering behind him; she did not get on the coach with the others.

'Detective Inspector Marsh?' the man enquires.

'Yes?'

'Can we have a word?' He eyes Erin and Webber with distrust. 'In private.'

'This is DS Webber and DC Macfadyen,' Gillian points to them, 'my investigating team. You can talk freely in front of them.'

'It's not me who wants to talk to you. It's Rhiannon.'

The girl peers from behind her father, her eyes red and swollen. She looks like she is finding it hard to find words. It looks like she is in two minds whether to talk or to flee.

'It was heart-wrenching,' Erin says, 'what you had to say back there. You must never blame yourself. This guilt you're feeling – it's irrational.'

'No . . . It's not . . . I should've . . .'

'I told her the exact same thing,' the girl's father sighs, 'but she insists she wants to tell you something. It'll explain her state of mind. I've taken Rhiannon out of Whalehurst – before anything happens to her. We're going home, to the Midlands. Next term, she'll start in a new school, hopefully one with a lower death toll. Things are not right at Whalehurst. It's not the place for my daughter.'

'What is it that you want to tell us, Rhiannon?' Gillian gets to the point. 'Whatever you have to say could make a huge difference – it could help us find out what happened. You've heard Rachel's dad. He wants to know. He deserves to know.'

'Yes . . . I want to help you. I should've helped Rachel . . .'

'You can now help her parents to understand. Talk to us.'

'Should we go somewhere more private?' Erin offers. 'There is a small café on the corner. We can sit down and talk.'

'We *were* friends, Rachel and I . . . We were real friends – best friends. She's been there for me when I was crying my eyes out – homesick and . . . The girl I'd been sharing with had left, her parents had moved her, and I was sure it was something to do with me, like I wasn't good enough. I was in pieces and . . . and Rachel came and made it all bearable. And I paid her by dropping her when she most needed me!'

Rhiannon's voice rises to a hysterical level. Her father rubs her back and tells her she can stop if she wants to; she doesn't have to put herself through this if it hurts so much.

'No, Dad, I have to tell them.'

Gillian is relieved. For a split second she was tempted to punch the guy in the gut for trying to sabotage her interview.

'Rachel was my . . . like, she was my mainstay, like she understood everything and could explain everything away . . . She was cool – I mean, like cool under pressure. But lately . . . it was like she's gone crazy . . . She made me so angry! The things she's been posting . . . they was sick! Filth! Like she was on something . . .'

'Do you mean, drugs?'

'Yeah, I guess. She wasn't herself. She was insane!'

'What exactly was she doing to make you think that?'

'The stuff she posted on Facebook and Snapchat! I mean, I mean . . . It was disgusting! And I was there too, in the pictures . . . And it wasn't fair!' Rhiannon's face is flushed livid red. It is anger and shame combined. 'I didn't want anything to do with her. I told her to stop! But, by then, everyone had seen it. It was insane and I was beside myself. I wasn't thinking clearly, you must understand!' Her eyes dart from face to face, seeking some form of absolution. Gillian nods hers. Mark and Erin do the same. The father's lips are twisted with pity.

'It was true, Dad! None of it was real!'

'I know,' his voice is hollow. 'You were just dragged into something . . . nothing to do with you . . .'

'I was . . . I didn't want to be . . . I told her. I was incensed with her! We were done! She tried to tell me it wasn't her. I didn't believe her. It was her Facebook, her Snapchat! How come it wasn't her? I . . . I really wasn't thinking straight. I should've believed her . . . And I should've been there for her . . . It's my fault she killed herself –'

'Did she tell you who was doing it? Did she mention any names? Think, you were her best friend, Rhiannon!' Gillian hopes that Rachel had an inkling about the identity of the perpetrator and what better person to confide in than her best friend?

'No. I don't think she knew. But she was telling me it wasn't her! And I didn't care. I didn't want to have anything to do with her. I pushed her away and . . . and she killed herself!'

'We don't know that – we're not sure Rachel killed herself,' Erin tells her, interjecting before Gillian ploughs on with her line of insensitive questions.

'She did! I know! I would've killed myself if it was me!' Rhiannon dissolves into tears.

Her father gives Gillian a hard look. 'That's why I'm taking her out of the school. I'm not taking any risks. She told you everything she knew, so now we just want to go home.'

Gillian ignores him. Her focus is on Rhiannon. 'What was in those pictures? What was so bad?'

'I don't want to talk about it,' Rhiannon clams up.

'We're leaving.' Her father pulls her up by her elbows, which she is pressing defensively against her torso, her wrists crossing on her chest. He leads her away, his arms wrapped over her like a blanket.

'If I need to contact you to ask more questions, how do I –' Gillian shouts after them. She hates it when witnesses start to slip through the holes in her net.

Rhiannon's father turns. 'That's all we have to say. My daughter has endured enough pain and self-blame to last her a lifetime. You don't need to contact her anymore. She's got nothing else to say.'

Gillian frowns, about to make a comment, but Webber stops her. 'We have to handle this sensitively.'

'I know, I bloody well know that, Mark. But we also need to get to the truth.'

'I don't think that girl knows the truth,' Erin ponders aloud.

'No, she doesn't. You're right. But she mentioned drugs,' Gillian hangs on to snippets of information which she may be able to somehow match with the other pieces of this incongruous puzzle. 'That takes us back to Bradley Watson and the Mac Brothers. That is something.'

'She didn't quite explicitly –'

'Oh, Mark, let's not split hairs . . . We're not going anywhere with this – we have to be more imaginative, try out theories, see what fits . . . I mean, I can see now why those kids from Whalehurst were acting the way they were when we interviewed them. They were scared that those images Rachel was posting included

151

them . . . Rhiannon's admitted it. Joshua Tyler probably will if we confront him with this . . . Let's think about it: was Rachel into drugs – dealing, maybe, alongside Watson – and was she being blackmailed because she wanted out, for example? Were those Facebook and Snapchat posts a way of warning her off against leaving the ring? That would explain why Bradley was secretly taking photos of her . . . Were his photos used in those posts? We must get Riley to retrieve those posts, see what was so terrible about them. How bad they really were . . .'

'Snapchat streaming doesn't last beyond a few minutes, Boss.'

'Riley will have a way of finding them, he's a bloody wizard.' Mark is in agreement with Gillian.

'Yes, he will. What we have to find is her damned mobile.'

Chapter Twenty-five

When everyone was gone, Sarah and Jonathan sat in their lounge, frozen in their grief. No words would take them out of it, so they said nothing to each other. Their silence witnessed the darkness descend on the room like a thief in the night, and still it said nothing.

There had been no closure in the funeral. Not for Sarah. Despite all the people attending, some of them so young and bursting with life-force, the synagogue had felt cold and empty. It had made Sarah shiver for the best part of the service. Her lips had gone blue with that all-pervading chill. Rachel was not there. Sarah couldn't feel her presence – she could not feel anything. She stood up and, putting an apologetic hand on her husband's shoulder, left him alone in the room and climbed the stairs to Rachel's room. She hoped to find that last ray of her daughter lingering there and to warm herself up on it.

The room was as it had been left by Rachel *that night*. DS Webber and the other female officer had been through it, looking for clues as to Rachel's disappearance, but they made no mess – well, no more mess that Rachel herself had made in her teenage-girl customary fashion. That thought put a feeble smile on Sarah's blue lips. Rachel had been a paragon of mess creativity! Her wardrobe was gaping open, showing a gutful of its untidy intestines: clothes bundled up rather than folded, dirty underwear crammed on the floor, dresses half-suspended on hangers, held by a lone strap. Schoolbooks scattered on the desk alongside unsharpened pencils and discarded fountain pen cartridges. Bedsheets convoluted and crumpled into a shapeless heap, littered with cuddly toys, hairpins, and a few empty sweet wrappers.

Sarah slid onto the bed and spread her arms wide, gliding with the palms of her hands across the bed as if she were making snow-angels. The sheets felt warm – here was the warmth that she so craved. It was trapped in the sheets and in all the objects abandoned between them. She inhaled that warmth and it made her feel better.

She kicked off the uncomfortable black shoes that she had been wearing since this morning, throughout this whole day of good-byes and tears, and lay down on the bed. She curled up, pressing her head against the pillow that was still out of place and still indented with the shape of Rachel. She pushed her hand under the pillow and caressed the space beneath it.

Her hand came across an angular and cold shape. She pulled it out, sat up, and held it up to look at it closely. Despite the paucity of light in the room, she recognised the object as Rachel's missing phone.

A sudden wave of anxiety clogged her throat.

Repeatedly, Sarah pressed the Power button but the phone remained unresponsive. She searched the room for a charger. It was plugged into the wall under the desk. With shaking fingers, Sarah tried to connect the phone to it. She couldn't. She switched on the desk lamp. This time it was easy. Two long seconds later the phone lit up with an animation of a charging battery. As soon as it hit one per cent, Sarah pressed the Power button again, and this time the phone came to life.

'Jonathan! Come here! Come now! I found her mobile!'

They were gaping at the small screen, holding their breaths. And holding back the bile that was building up in their mouths. In Rachel's inbox a long string of names indicated recently received Facebook notifications:

JoshTosh commented on your post . . .

Machiavelli commented on . . .
LazyBoy commented on your . . .
Rhiannon commented on your . . .
Floral_Arrangement commented . . .
LadyNoTramp commented on your . . .

Sarah's fingers were too numb to operate the phone. Jonathan took it out of her hand. He opened Rhiannon's message. Without saying much, it said it all: *WTF! U@itagain*

'JoshTosh – that's that boy, Joshua.' Jonathan opened that text. Again, it wasn't long: *Am enjoying ur Snappy output.* Plus a string of shock-grin-steam-out-of-ears emoticons.

Jonathan could not help but torture himself and Sarah with more of the same:

Its always the quiet ones LOL
Didnae no u had it in u babe!
Cut it out u made me puke
Sick shit bring it on!

All of that was followed by Rachel's response to multiple recipients: *It's not me! I swear I'm not doing this!*

Sarah retched and brought up the meagre content of her stomach onto the floor.

Chapter Twenty-six

Gillian puts the phone down and leans back in her chair to digest the facts of this convoluted, twisted case. Is it one case or two? Was Bradley Watson Rachel's dealer or were they in it together up to their eyes? Why was he stalking her? Did he die because of Rachel? Are their deaths related in any conceivable way? The information she has before her contradicts that. No traces of drugs were found in Rachel's bloodstream. There is no evidence of those two being in direct contact with each other except for the memory card in Bradley's pocket – full of photographs of Rachel (though not posed by her). And now the girl's mobile phone has been found. What connections will it reveal? Riley is working on it. Gillian cannot wait, but she knows that leaning over him will only distract him and slow him down. She is best advised to take this time to think and let the wizard do his magic.

An onslaught of pressing questions pounds at Gillian: was Rachel's death accidental? Or did she kill herself? Rhiannon, her closest friend, Forensics and Dr Almond seem to think that she did. Again, there is no evidence of a struggle, no defensive wounds – a straightforward death by drowning. She waded into the river seemingly of her own accord. Did she have a reason to commit suicide? If it wasn't drugs or blackmail, or both, then what was it that made her do it? Gillian has just got off the phone with Jon Riley. He will look into Rachel's online activities before her death: the *crazy filth* she was allegedly posting on social media. *Allegedly* because she denied it. And if it wasn't Rachel Snyder parading the filth online, then who was it? What was it? Why? Was it really so bad as to cause her to take her own life? Then again, it doesn't take much for a moody teenager to descend into the depths of despair. Gillian should know; she went through a few ups and downs when Tara was going through the minefield of puberty.

Of course, it could've been an accident: Rachel drops the iPad, tries to retrieve it, wades into the river, fights against the unpredictable current, gets trapped in the treacherous muddy bog, and loses the fight. Only what was she doing on that bridge in the night, with Bradley Watson in attendance?

Whittaker waddles in and disrupts Gillian's musings. He is heaving with excitement, his arms flaying, his huge frame threatening to come apart. 'I knew it was only a matter of time!' he bellows in his deep voice. 'It's a war!'

He towers over Gillian's minuscule person, not waiting for any encouragement. 'Just got the latest on the Mac Brothers and co.' Webber and Macfadyen crowd behind him, all ears. 'NCA have just got themselves two corpses: two small-time runners from Greyston. It looks like retaliation for Watson's death. It has all the hallmarks of an execution.'

'Now, now . . .' Webber nods as if he has seen it coming all along.

'And that's not the funny bit,' Whittaker chuckles.

'Is there a funny bit?' Gillian is genuinely puzzled.

'Oh yeah! Our new friends, the Mac Brothers, are on the run, fearing for their precious little backsides. They're deep in shit with the Russians, or whoever the bastards running the show in Bristol are. But whoever they are, they went to Greyston with guns blazing to show them who's in charge. Two corpses on Greyston turf is a declaration of war. More's to come – just watch this space.'

'So, they must be thinking Watson was taken out by the competition,' Gillian is thinking aloud.

'And that proves that he was working for them.'

'Dealing at Whalehurst.'

'Is that enough for a search warrant?'

'No!' Scarfe has nothing else to add. He is not letting Gillian wade in on the raging drug wars. It is a matter for NCA. They are dealing with it. Their investigation is in full swing. New matters are coming to light and they've got experts to tackle them. She will not tread on their patch. Full stop.

'But, with all due respect, sir –'

'Respect, Marsh? Don't make me laugh.'

'I don't intend to.' Gillian is seething. She is fed up with Scarface and his never-ending, higher-ground manoeuvres. 'But I can't close my murder investigation if it is – and it IS – drug-related. This is an open investigation and it will sit on our books with the dead weight of other unsolved cases –'

'Don't try it with me, Marsh.' He raises a silencing hand and gestures to her to plant her backside down in a chair and stop buzzing over his head. His face says it in so many words. She takes her seat reluctantly, perching on the edge, ready to shoot off as soon as it is feasible.

'Right,' Scarface is temporarily appeased, 'you can listen now. Firstly, Rachel Snyder's case is as good as solved: it was either suicide or an accident. Either way, there'll be no charges. Done and dusted!'

Gillian disagrees – it was actually an open verdict – but realises any resistance to Scarface's ideas will be futile.

'Secondly, Bradley Watson's case will be solved, though not thanks to you, DI Marsh,' he rounds on her with a critical stare. 'You see, if you just sat down and listened from the start, you'd know by now that the Mac Brothers want to talk. They approached NCA for a deal: they'll grass on their Russian masters in return for false identities and a new life in the Bahamas. So, sooner rather than later, we will have the names of those involved in Watson's murder.'

'If it had anything to do with his drug running, that is . . .'

'Didn't you just say that it had?' Scarfe is incredulous. He waves Gillian away, 'Just leave, DI Marsh, leave this to the experts.'

Gillian is not one for complying with direct orders, especially when they double as insults to her professionalism. 'Sir, I want to sit on those interviews with the Macs. I must satisfy myself that Watson's death is drug-related. NCA want the names of the Russians. I want the name of Watson's killer. We aren't after the same thing. I must insist –'

'All right, all right . . . I'll see what I can do. And, Marsh?'

'Yes, sir?'

'This is confidential. No one is to know about the Macs' deal, not even Webber. Are we clear?'

'Sir!' Gillian walks out, smiling under her breath. Everyone always knows. Everyone must know. One stupid 'top secret' and the trust is gone from the team.

Chapter Twenty-seven

Without stopping, Mo watched the coach arrive and the others trickle out of it to go straight to their dormitories. None of them looked in Mo's direction, and frankly, Mo didn't waste much time looking at them. They could be strangers in the street, popping out of a city bus. From day one in this school, Mo had been regarding his peers as *the others*. Nothing would change. He would always be an outsider at Whalehurst.

At least they weren't his enemies. They didn't pick on him. They simply ignored him.

It used to bother him. In fact, it tormented him and he had spent many a sleepless night thinking of how to fit in. How to change his skin colour. How to burn all the bridges to his past on the cheap Bristol estate. How to kill off his own parents . . .

But he had stopped that madness. He didn't care to be liked – not any more. From now on Mo would be admired. His future was mapped out and he no longer needed Whalehurst and its stuck-up protégés to achieve his goals. He was not one of them, he never would be. They were rich kids from privileged backgrounds, sitting on bags of money and thrusting their coats of arms in his face. He was the son of a Somali refugee and a Nigerian nurse. All he had was his talent.

Yes, Mo had a talent – something most of them could only dream about. He was a prodigy. He was an athlete, a winner. He had been head-hunted and in two days' time, after two more nights of restless sleep, Mo's fate was going to be sealed and delivered. His official selection to the national squad for the Commonwealth Games was only a formality. He knew he had it in the bag. The two English squad officials were coming to the county tournament here at Whalehurst just for him, for Mo.

He had not gone to Rachel Snyder's funeral with the others. It had been voluntary anyway, and Mo had chosen not to volunteer to go. This wasn't the best time to miss his training and tag on with the others to spend hours in a pew and then on the coach. Nobody would have noticed whether he was there or not, and nobody would have given a toss. Rachel was beyond caring. She had killed herself, so it was pretty clear she did not care for all that ceremony.

There had been times when Mo had lost the will to live too: when as an eight-year-old he had to sneak into the school gates after the bell went off so that his tormentors had gone to lessons instead of punching him in the stomach and telling him to 'go back home' . . . Those times when, cornered in the toilets or in the changing rooms, he would have to clench his fists and bare his teeth like a wild animal. Those times when he would bite them and draw blood, because that was his last resort, and his parents would be called in to see the head teacher and bargain and plea in their broken English for their son not to be expelled. Those days were in the past. Now, Mo was on form. Top of the world. Winning.

His high-knee kicks punched the air as Mo, buoyant and invincible, began to warm up for what was coming his way. For his due.

Chapter Twenty-eight

The commotion upstairs is baffling: hurried pacing, a squeak from the springs in the bed mattress, something being wheeled across the floorboards. What is Mark getting up to? Gillian and Corky are standing at the bottom of the stairs, listening. As soon as Mark and Gillian arrived home, ten minutes ago, he shot upstairs and shut the door behind him. Nothing has been said between them about the previous night. His black eye speaks volumes and that is enough said. Gillian considers that subject closed. There are however subjects that can't wait. For example, she really needs to know when − or if − he is coming down for dinner. She's hungry. Should she throw something in the oven for two, or just for herself? Is he planning to sulk upstairs for the rest of the night? It makes no difference to her, but she doesn't want to come across as inhospitable. Or worse yet, as holding grudges. It's all water under the bridge, as far as Gillian is concerned.

Not so for Mark.

He has abandoned the sanctity of his room and is huffing and puffing down the stairs, dragging his two suitcases with him, bashing them against the wall.

'What on earth are you doing! Where are you going?'

'I don't know yet − just getting out of your hair,' he mutters, avoiding eye contact.

'It may not be the best of times to look for a room. It's night-time in case you haven't noticed . . . well after nine − not your normal check-in time.' She points to the grandfather clock because she knows he won't take her word for it.

'I can't stay here, can I!'

It's an outburst of self-pity worthy of a snotty toddler. Gillian doesn't like it. 'And neither can you go home! From what you're telling me Kate isn't going to welcome you with open arms. Is there anywhere you *can* go? Your parents'? I don't even know where they live.'

'Taunton.' He purses his lips, a martyr to the cause of selective homelessness.

'That's no good. It'll take you well over two hours to get to work in the morning. It's not a good idea. It's a crap idea, actually. We're way too busy for you to spend the best part of the day commuting.' Gillian is not planning on allowing him any excuses, his personal dramas notwithstanding. He is supposed to be in charge of the Rachel Snyder case; he has to have his head screwed on properly.

'Gillian, after last night . . . I can't stay here.'

'Don't be an idiot, Mark!' she snaps. 'Last night was last night. I was perfectly capable of looking after myself, as you well know. You – as it stands – have nowhere to go. So, you're staying in your room – grounded. No!' She wags her forefinger at him. 'Shut up and do as you're told. If you must go, find a room first, or preferably swallow your pride and talk to Kate so she takes you back. You'll perish on your own.'

She ignores his indignant expression and pushes by him in the direction of the kitchen, 'We're having fish and chips, that's all there is in the fridge.'

'I'm not hungry.'

'I am. You can't watch me eat while we're discussing the case. You may as well join me. And, for God's sake, put those bloody suitcases out of the way. I don't want to trip over them.'

As she switches on the oven she can hear some more commotion on the stairs, accompanied by some more huffing, puffing and

163

cursing. Webber is again regrouping to higher ground with his luggage. At least he has listened.

Fritz has strolled into the kitchen and sits on the floor, fixing Gillian with a questioning glare.

'Men!' Gillian explains to her cat.

Chapter Twenty-nine

Up with the lark, DI Marsh and DS Webber are camping on the doorstep to Jon Riley's kingdom, waiting for His Highness to arrive. He does – at twenty past nine – carrying two laptop bags strapped across his chest and what looks like egg yolk attached to his Taliban-fighter beard. The man needs a mother to wipe his breakfast from his face, and while she's at it she might just see to wiping his arse, a prospect Gillian refuses to entertain any further.

'What time do you call this?' she vents her frustration instead.

'This? This'd be twenty-one past nine,' Riley is happy to inform her upon consulting his high-tech wristwatch. 'Lovely to see you both – my very own fan club! Come in, I've got things to tell you.'

'I bloody well hope you do! We've been waiting for two damned hours!'

'I'm on flexi-time – working from home . . . Anyway, I'll make it worth your every minute, love.' His eyes sparkle with mischief and his beard lifts in a wide grin. The egg yolk cracks and peels off, landing on the equator of his rotund stomach.

He ushers them to his cubicle and takes his driving seat in front of the computer. He takes his time setting up his laptops, plugging them in and signing into the intranet network. Gillian is biting her lips, scraping off the chapped skin with her teeth. Any more of this posturing of his and she will be biting Riley's head off.

'Where should we start?' he teases some more.

'The mobile.'

'Oh yes! Interesting – very interesting . . . So nothing you wouldn't expect from a teenage girl's phone: games, long history of trawling YouTube, crap taste in music —'

'Spare us your opinions, Jon.'

'Obviously all those Facebook notifications of the night she died — we know about those . . . Texts — boring: mum, dad, a few friends, all identified, all but one! And that's where the plot thickens, ladies and gentlemen . . .'

'Yeah, OK — tell us.'

'That one contact — that is a Pay-As-You-Go number. It's off and hasn't been in use since that night. And . . . wait for this . . .'

'Riley, for fuck's sake, you aren't on stage and we've got other things to do today!' Webber finally snaps and opens his mouth to bark at the maverick forensic expert.

Riley throws up his arms in mock surrender, 'All right, all right . . . Take it easy. Here goes: it is the same Pay-As-You-Go number as the unidentified number on Bradley Watson's phone.'

'We've got the connection!' Gillian slaps Riley on the back. 'Good job!'

'At your service, ma'am! Told you it'd be worth your while. I'm a man you want by your side.'

Gillian chooses not to lecture Jon on the merits of work ethics and not mixing business with pleasure. She could — she could tell him to get a fucking life, but she won't. She likes him too much to be the one opening his eyes to his sad reality. Instead of lectures, she asks about the images supposedly posted by Rachel Snyder.

'Not a decent job. Amateurish. Some pics have been taken with a huge zoom, especially the ones in her bedroom. The zoom, the angles and the quality of those images would point to Bradley Watson — I mean to the photos on the memory card found on him.'

'So, that's what he was doing . . .'

'Well, he can't have been doing the doctoring at the same time as he was taking the photos. The live stream on SnapChat for example was going on while Watson was taking the photos that we found on the SD card. So someone else was involved, someone working in the comfort zone of his, or her, armchair at home.'

'Couldn't he have pre-programmed it somehow?' Gillian doesn't want to let Watson off the hook that easily.

'No,' Riley sounds definitive. 'You see, Rachel tried to deactivate her accounts several times, and several times someone, who had access to her passwords and email, re-activated them within seconds. It was a game of cat and mouse. She stood no chance.'

Webber exhales slowly through his teeth.

'Like I said, they've made a crap job of it. They used snapshots of Rachel in her home and school environment, cut out her body and superimposed bodies of naked models, probably resourced from some cheap porn site. The pig head could've come from any pigsty.' Riley smirks but no one likes the joke. They are not in the mood for jokes. 'From what I can ascertain, the other girl's pictures came from her online gallery. She went by the name of *RhiannonB12*. Her account is now deactivated too. But yeah, some images came from her profile. Not very good. Going by the quality, the pixilation –'

'Yes, we've got the picture,' Gillian tells him. 'The other girl is Rhiannon Starr. We've met her. They were best friends. She went to the same school as Rachel: Whalehurst in Little Ogburn.'

'Is that so?' Riley nods knowingly. 'Why am I not surprised?'

'Why? What do you mean?'

'You see, naturally, I was able to track down the IP address of our graphic-designer psycho. Oh, he tried to go through a host in Luxembourg to get me off his scent, but you know me, old fox –'

'Yeah, all right, Jon.' Gillian is burning to know without having to pay tribute to Riley's grand investigative talents. 'Where did that IP address take you?'

'Well, that's the thing! Whalehurst School, in Little Ogburn. That's where the bastard operates from.'

Chapter Thirty

No! Mo called upon Allah to do something drastic to get rid of the cops.

They had descended on the school at the crack of dawn. A dawn raid, something he had heard about often enough from other families on the estate in Whitchurch Park where he had lived since he was born. Those dawn raids used to hang low in the air and cling to the rooftops like soot – everyone knew the coppers were coming; you could smell them a mile off. The word would get around, travelling with the speed of light along the graffitied streets of Bristol's poorest estate.

But the Sexton's coppers weren't looking for failed asylum seekers or visa-overstayers; they came to search the office building and dormitories for some kind of evidence, and to confiscate all computers. They asked that everyone brought all their electronic devices to the auditorium. Mo wasn't worried about that. He didn't have a computer, or a laptop, or an iPad, or anything other than his mobile phone. In any event, boarders weren't allowed private computers in their rooms, but not everyone abided by that rule. If they wanted to break the rules, then it served them right that their equipment would be taken away. That was water off Mo's back. But he was anxious about the races; about the distraction to his training regime.

Only one sleep left.

He closed his eyes and his fists, and muttered prayers. He prayed that the tournament wouldn't get cancelled. It would kill him if it did.

Dr Featherstone was running around like a headless chicken. His face was bloated and flushed red – he'd had a few already or maybe he was just hung over from last night. Alcohol always lingered on his breath and in his bloodshot eyes. As a rule, Mo didn't approve of drinking, not only because it was forbidden to indulge in alcohol at the school, but also because it was stupid. Alcohol made you weak. His views had nothing to do with religion because, deep down, Mo did not subscribe to his parents' faith, or any other faith. Mo believed in himself – his own ability and hard practice.

The spooked headmaster was shouting at the policewoman, threatening to take her to court.

As if! She was the law, wasn't she?

Dr Featherstone was shouting in her face that she was jeopardising the safety of his pupils; she was telling him calmly to step aside. When he refused, she simply went around him, followed by four uniformed officers, as well as the other policewoman who had been here interviewing the pupils in the auditorium a couple of weeks ago, and a fat man with an unkempt beard, pretending to be Muslim or something. Unsuccessfully because his hair was long and greasy. A hippie? His body wobbled as he walked. That made Mo feel sick. Mo couldn't bear people who didn't look after themselves. Dr Featherstone was another such example. With all those degrees of his, he knew nothing. He did not respect his own body and he abused his mind. Mo knew. He could see through the man.

The hapless fool.

Even the Knights Templar were looking agitated. It was a rare sight to see Monty Collingsworth unsettled. Eddie, Archie and George were flustered as well, but that was to be expected; they would always be his second-rate sidekicks – do as he did, do as he said; have no imagination of their own. Mo could just envisage them losing their heads in this hullabaloo, but not Monty. He was a cold fish – normally. A man in charge. Stiff upper lip. An Englishman through and through. Like Josh Tyler. They were made of steel. But today, they buckled under the pressure. At least, Monty did. Josh was nowhere to be seen. He had been acting strangely ever since Rachel had killed herself.

She had killed herself, hadn't she? Mo knew those two used to be an item; he had seen them behind the pavilion, kissing and fondling each other like love-struck puppies. Maybe Josh was grieving, though Mo found it hard to believe that Josh was capable of that.

Like Monty, Josh was a cold fish. They were Knights Templar after all – the Medieval Martial Arts Society of bloody Whalehurst. Ha! They called themselves *knights!* Pretentious twats. What century did they think this was? *Altar boys*, that was what Mo called them, but not to their faces, naturally. The clever nickname had come to him just like that: like a snap of his fingers! It was a perfect name tag for the lot of them: altar boys tending to their 'Mass', their fancy Medieval Martial Arts Society gang. All bollocks, airs and graces, really. Mo had seen it all before. He instantly recognised them for what they really were: a gang.

It was perfectly normal for similar guys to gang up together. He had seen it on the estate. They would be stronger together, in a group. Alone, life sucked. Unless you were a fast runner.

Mo was a damn fast runner. He could outrun all of them. He could run circles around them. But he knew to keep his head down and not to cross them. Especially not Monty. It was important to be on Monty's good side because he could be useful. If Monty put his mind, and his heart, to it he would look after you better than your own father could. But it had to matter to Monty – *you* had to matter to Monty. You had to have something that Monty valued. Otherwise, like all Head Boys, he was just full of shit and couldn't hide it if he tried. Luckily, Mo was a great athlete and represented Whalehurst, and that mattered a great deal to Monty.

The policewoman – was her name Marsh? DI Marsh? – she had just got on Monty's bad side. She stood there, right in his face, demanding access to the Knights Templars' den. Monty handed her the key. His lower jaw spasmed as he did that. Archie started explaining to DI Marsh that the room was where the Martial Arts Society had its private headquarters – big emphasis on *private*. DI Marsh looked him up and down like he had said something funny. Even she could tell what a bunch of pretentious losers they all were.

The battle on the doorstep to the Mass was fought briefly and lost, before the cops went on to commit the sacrilege and entered the den.

Mo peeped in. Out of curiosity. He had never been inside the den, had never been invited. It was reserved for the top sixth-formers, only the crème de la crème of the whole lot. The select few, and Mo was not one of them. Even Dr Featherstone had limited access to the goings-on in there, though he was the one who had started this hocus-pocus shortly after he had come to run Whalehurst.

Inside the den, Mo noted, the walls were wood-panelled from top to bottom, as was the ceiling. Two banners were displayed, clashing with each other on the wall: one was the St George's cross, the other a starkly black and white background with a fanciful red cross stamped in the middle. Jousting lances hung on iron braces beneath the banners. Boys and their toys! They had not seen the real world out there, that was for sure.

'You won't find any electronic equipment in this room,' Archie informed the police, his freckles darkening in his face. 'It's against the rules.'

'We'll have a quick sweep nevertheless.' DI Marsh stormed in, leaving Archie to eat her dust. Mo was beginning to warm to her. He remained at his post by the door, tuning in.

'Be our guest,' Monty told her through his teeth, but he concealed his anger with a courteous bow of his head. You had to give it to him, he hadn't quite lost his charm in the face of adversity. He was still a pretty well-chilled fish.

George was breathing down the coppers' necks, following them wherever they went. Eddie was doing the same.

'Can you step back, please?' DI Marsh ordered them.

'There are a few very valuable objects in this room,' Archie said, and that was a big mistake.

DI Marsh fixed him with a hard glare. 'Are you implying my officers are likely to steal? Whatever items we remove, will be removed under the seal of the search warrant. In any event, this is none of your business, young man. You are just a pupil at this school and I can't imagine that any of the school property belongs to you.'

Archie shrunk under that glare and mumbled something semi-apologetic. Mo smiled. This whole situation amused him no end. He only hoped that it would be over and done with before tomorrow's races. In the hope that this was the case, Mo decided to take himself outside, onto the fields, to get on with his training.

At that very same time, DI Marsh lost interest in the den and left her officers to carry out the search. She caught up with Mo on the stairs. This was as good an opportunity as he would ever have to put his mind at ease.

'Do you think you're going to be done with this . . . the search by tomorrow?' he asked her.

'We should be finished within a matter of hours. You don't like us poking our heads everywhere, do you?'

'I don't mind,' he shrugged, trying to sound indifferent, 'but we're scheduled to have an athletics tournament all day tomorrow. Lots of other schools and some important people are coming. It'd be a catastrophe if it was cancelled.'

'I can't see why it should be. By tomorrow, you won't even remember we were here.'

Mo grinned with relief. He had a big, toothy grin – he couldn't restrain it if he tried. It would usually spring up of its own accord. Like it did now. He negotiated two steps at a time as he hurried outside, nearly bumping into the fat hippie man.

'Gillian,' the man was out of breath, but then anyone would be if they had to carry so much extra weight on them, 'we found that phone! We've got it!' He had lifted a transparent evidence bag with an old-fashioned mobile in it, the sort that still had push-buttons and a tiny screen. Mo's mother had one of those. She was a self-confessed technophobe and couldn't handle anything more technologically advanced than an electric iron. Who would think that one of the brats at Whalehurst would be using a similar relic? Maybe it was to do with being *medieval,* Mo chuckled at his own pun.

'Which one is that?' DI Marsh wanted to know. And so did Mo! He paused by the door to tune in to the forthcoming clarification.

'You know, that Pay-as-You-Go from Watson's contacts that we couldn't locate. Guess where it was!'

'I'd rather you told me.' DI Marsh was clearly not one for mind games.

'Of all the places – you wouldn't guess!'

'That's because I wouldn't be trying. Just tell me, Jon.'

'Behind thick volumes of yearbooks in the headmaster's office. Fancy that!'

DI Marsh didn't look particularly surprised. Neither was Mo – if anyone at this school was into prehistoric mobile phones it would have to be Dr Featherstone. Mo sprinted out. Behind him, he heard DI Marsh say, 'OK, it's time we brought the man in.'

Chapter Thirty-one

Edwin Featherstone was like a rabbit in headlights: dazzled, spooked, and poised to run. He had never been to a police station, in whatever capacity, never mind that of a suspect. They had advised him that he was being interviewed under caution. It felt as if a bucket of cold water had been poured over his head. It gave him a thorough shudder and then he began to shiver. His hands in particular. God knows if it was the shock of his predicament or his desperate need for a steadying shot of gin.

They were treating him like a criminal: fingerprints had been taken from him and a sample of his saliva had been sent for analysis. They had confiscated his laptop, his vehement protests being treated with disdain.

How much would that cursed laptop tell them?

He feared that despite his feverish efforts, they would uncover everything, every last unsavoury bit. He was experiencing waves of cold sweat; his blood pressure must have gone bungee-jumping.

He hated the interview room: it was stuffy and impersonal; it had no windows; it was suffocating him. He had rejected off-hand the idea of a solicitor being present – far too embarrassing. He wouldn't be able to take the shame. He would prefer to go down without any witnesses watching his disgrace. A fish out of water, he was swallowing air; his mouth was dry and felt wooden. He tried to look dignified when DI Marsh and DS Webber entered the room.

They sat in front of him, facing him in a challenging,

confrontational way. Especially DI Marsh. She took her time just to stare at him, her eyes steady and focussed on him like a laser beam. He pulled his elbows off the table and straightened up his back. It was an impulse. He had regressed to his schoolboy self; in those days he had always been reminded not to slouch.

After the introductions and stating his name and personal details for the benefit of the tape, he was presented with a black mobile phone. DS Webber fired the first question, 'Do you recognise this phone?'

'No. Never seen it in my life.'

'Take a close look, Mr Featherstone,' Marsh insisted. He had to resist the urge to correct her that he was *Dr* Featherstone.

'It isn't mine.'

'That's odd because we found it in your office.'

'Well, I don't know how it got there. It's not mine.' He was blinking rapidly: the dazzled rabbit syndrome. This line of questioning had taken him aback. It was not what he had expected.

'Would you be surprised if I told you that this phone was used for contacting Bradley Watson and Rachel Snyder, and no one else at all? This directly links the two dead people to your school – and to you.'

'Well, um . . . I don't . . .'

'I take that as *no comment*.'

'I have no idea what you're talking about . . .' he stuttered.

'How about the fact that this number was the last number Bradley Watson called? The last person he contacted before he was killed? The owner of this phone may be the last person to have seen Bradley alive. And what if I told you that it was also the last number Rachel Snyder contacted? A lot of coincidences here . . .'

'I told you, it's not mine. I've never seen it! You're trying to frame me – someone is! I want a lawyer!'

'You told us you didn't want a lawyer.'

He buried his face in his hands, trying to focus his jittery, alcohol-starved mind. Of course, he had rejected the idea of a lawyer, but at that time he didn't know they would be interrogating him about some wretched mobile device. This was totally new, so he might change his mind and ask for a lawyer . . . Then again, he didn't trust them – he most certainly did not trust this snake of a woman. As soon as a lawyer, no doubt a respectable member of the local community, were to enter this room, the line of questions might meander into something much more uncomfortable. DI Marsh would see to that. 'No! I mean, yes, that's right – I don't need a lawyer.'

'Can you please reiterate for the tape – do you want a solicitor present at this interview, or not?'

'No. No, thank you. I'm innocent.'

'OK.' DI Marsh thumbed through a file she had brought with her and kept, until now, unopened. The rustling of the papers sent a shiver down his spine. She noticed that straight away. 'Are you cold, Mr Featherstone?' Her tone was incisive; she clearly took some sort of sick, sadistic pleasure from his discomfort.

'A little, yes.'

Ignoring his affirmative answer, she said, 'We have reason to believe that the owner of this phone is implicated in a drug-dealing operation at Whalehurst School. Do you know anything about drugs being peddled within the perimeter of your school? Would you care to comment?'

'This is preposterous! An utter fabrication!'

'And yet . . .' Marsh's eyes were locked on his like a vice. He seemed unable to look away. 'Bradley Watson, your employee, had links to a notorious drug gang.'

'He was only a groundsman's assistant. His father brought him here to teach the boy the ropes. I . . . I, I . . .' he puffed, losing his breath. 'I don't know anything about him and his contacts. What he did outside his school hours was his business –'

'I think it may have been in school hours as well. Would it not matter that much to you if he only sold ecstasy or cannabis to your pupils after hours? Don't you owe them a duty of care at any time of day or night?'

'I didn't know! I would've stopped it had I known anything! Who do you take me for?'

'Have you heard of the Mac Brothers?'

'No!' He tore his eyes away from the snake-woman. It felt tortuous, as if his optic nerves had been torn in the process. His head was hurting. He pinched the bridge of his nose to release the pressure on his temples.

'Of course not. You wouldn't! Not a man of your standing. What was I thinking . . .' DI Marsh raised her eyebrows and let him brew in pointed silence, which contained more unspoken accusations.

Featherstone resolved to act decisively. He was no psychologist but even he could tell she was playing sick mind games with him. Anyway, if this was all they had on him – mind games . . . 'I have no further comments. I've no idea what you're talking about. The phone has been planted . . . so I can't help you. I'd like to go now, please.'

The other policewoman, DC Macfadyen, entered the room. She put a form in front of DS Webber, and left after shooting Featherstone a filthy look. He wished he could crane his neck without losing his dignity to read what was on that form. DS Webber scanned the form and passed it to DI Marsh; she took a couple of minutes to go over it. The couple of minutes felt like eternity. Featherstone listened to the clock on the wall marking every second with a loud click and watched the second-hand twang along. DI Marsh and DS Webber looked at each other in such a way that he couldn't shake the impression that they had just read his death warrant.

'So,' DS Webber took over the interrogation, 'you were previously employed as headteacher at St Vincent's Comprehensive in Yate?'

'Yes. What of it?'

'They have a serious drug problem there.'

'Not while I was there. I left St Vincent's eight years ago.'

'To join Whalehurst?' DI Marsh inquired.

Featherstone suspected the question was a trap. She knew. She was a cunning snake. He swallowed back the bile rising to his throat. He braced himself. He would have to come clean.

'Not exactly. I took a one-year career break.'

'You did? Why was that?'

'I was unwell. Suffering from depression, if you must know. Though I can't see how this has anything to do –' Something tickled the side of his face. It itched. He scratched it. It was wet and his fingernail slid down with it. It was a trickle of sweat from his temple. It was coming back to him: the night terrors, the sweating, the palpitations. He needed help. He needed a drink.

'You lied to us.' DI Marsh had no sympathy, but he wouldn't expect any from her. She looked at him and his sweaty face without any emotion. He swiped his tongue over his upper lip, which tasted salty. All that sweat . . . his palms too. 'You told us you were a widower. That's what it says in the school's official records. But your wife isn't dead, is she?'

Featherstone was unable to answer this question. Any question. His throat was tight and dry; his vocal cords convulsing as he again tried to swallow thick mucus. His lips buttoned up.

'We will check that.' Marsh paused and waited for some kind of comment, exclamation or denial from him, but he still couldn't bring himself to speak. He blinked the sweat out of his eyes. She went on, 'However, as it stands, your wife left you eight years ago following an incident. You attacked her –'

Featherstone's muscles surrendered to a wave of emotion. He broke into violent sobs where tears mixed with his sweat and snot. He used to worship the ground Emily walked on. She had been young and beautiful, full of life, full of laughs. She had been the lady of his heart. There was so much they would do together. He had waited for her to leave school, never once showing how utterly and hopelessly he was in love with her. He had been her teacher. Not once had he compromised his position. But three years after she left school . . .

She had been everything he wanted in a woman. He would do

178

anything for her: steal, kill . . . but he couldn't let her go! He had tried everything to stop her, to keep her where she belonged: by his side.

He told her he had already forgiven her, it had been nothing – just a fling! That guy she had fallen for was nothing – a nobody! He was a damn car salesman, for pity's sake! But she wouldn't listen. It was her turn to be utterly and hopelessly in love. Only her love wasn't meant for him. So, he hit her. And he hit her again. To make her listen. To hold her back until she came to her senses. To fight for her. To keep her safe at home . . .

'I see your wife dropped the charges against you, but good Lord, her face doesn't look a pretty picture!' DI Marsh pushed a photograph of Emily in front of him. He did not have to be reminded. Her face, tarnished with a stitched-up cut along her eyebrow and a black eye, was etched in his memory for life. With his trembling fingers he caressed the photo as if to wipe away her bruises and her pain. He still could not speak. The words he couldn't let out in the open were clogging his windpipe.

DI Marsh continued with her cruel narrative, 'So, that was eight years ago. She left you. You were divorced nine months later. You lost your home, your job . . . Your mind, I'm guessing.'

Featherstone refused to look at her – the viper. Instead, his eyes sought solace in DS Webber. He discovered a tiny glimmer of understanding in DS Webber's expression. There was something there that DI Marsh – a woman – could never comprehend. Man to man. He recovered his power of speech. He addressed DS Webber, and only DS Webber, 'It was as if she had died. I didn't lie. It isn't a lie. She is dead to me and I will always mourn her. I lost her and everything else – now – everything, everyone else is just a poor imitation of the real thing we had.'

DS Webber nodded slowly; he seemed to agree. That gave Featherstone strength.

'So now you can charge me or let me go. I don't care anymore.'

Chapter Thirty-two

The search of the dormitories looked amateurish, to say the least. Josh waited outside, calm and bemused, as a uniformed officer opened and closed a couple of drawers and half-heartedly peeped under his mattress. Josh had told him there was nothing there to find, and the cop believed him.

Josh had this effect on people: he came across as a reliable young man – a model citizen in the making. It couldn't be further from the truth. People should know better than to trust him. Sometimes Josh wasn't sure that he could trust himself. The thing was, he was not comfortable in his own skin, nor in this school. This wasn't what he had in mind when he twisted Father's arm to send him to a public school, far away from home and away from Mother's suffocating, clingy love.

She had lost Father's attention a long time ago, at about the same time as she had abandoned her legal career to be a stay-at-home mum to Josh, to provide her boy with a stable, loving environment while his father travelled the world, moved from one placement to another, from one world capital to the next. It was precisely the thing Joshua was dying to do with his dad because that was so much more exciting than rotting in an isolated, gated house, wrapped in the cotton wool of Mother's unsolicited devotion. Joshua had resented it from an early age. Starting from Reception, school had not agreed with him, and so he had stopped agreeing with Mother. Well, she had lost not only Father but Josh too. Shortly after that, she had lost her figure and her confidence. Josh never needed a stay-at-home mum; he needed to be left alone. Especially by her.

She had to stop asking him stupid questions and telling him how to live his life. He didn't want to make friends and keep them for life; he didn't want to try hard so that he could make something of himself when he grew up; he didn't feel sorry when he patently ought to be, and he didn't feel happy when everyone else did. He felt fed up and isolated, so he had come up with the idea of a boarding school. Far away from all of that cotton wool. His plan beyond school had always been to join the armed forces. He got the idea of a foreign legion from some book he had read, but with time he lowered his sights on to something less exotic, like the navy.

The membership of Mass had seemed like a good idea to start with: he would learn discipline and how to handle weapons. He would have to tolerate the comradeship that came with it, though never quite adopting it as his own way of thinking. All that cheap, passionate indoctrination was tiresome. All that laughable posturing made him cringe, like *having each other's back*, like *loyalty above all else*, like the idiotic *sacrifice in the face of adversity,* or the pompous *will of steel,* but most of all the infantile, *all for one and one for all*. To Josh they were just empty words and empty gestures. He went with it on the surface, because deep down it was and always would be just him and him alone. Joshua Tyler was a lone wolf. That wasn't a crime.

Back in his room after the uniformed officer had taken himself out of it with a curt nod in reply to Joshua's polite smile, Josh put up his feet. He retrieved his iPad from under the floorboards and stuck his headphones on. The objective was not to listen to the music, which was sputtering into his brain with irritating flatness, but to cut out the rest of the world. He was sprawled on his bed, his legs wide apart, with his arms flung out. His face was aimed at the ceiling and his eyes glazed over. This mess was not what he had in mind.

181

The idea had been to distance himself from Mother and her high expectations, to become his own man, but instead he had ended up embroiled in things he didn't give a fuck about. He frowned, annoyed at how life seemed to have manipulated him into a corner. He ought to get himself out of it. This was not his war. He had never asked to take on any commitments, any blood-oath bullshit. He was allergic to relationships and to society at large. People who insisted on getting close to him had a cringe-worthy effect on him. He had to fight the urge to kick their faces in, and sometimes he would give in to it.

He didn't hear the knock on his door and so he became even more irritated when Monty and co. casually sauntered into the room. They should've knocked and waited for his *Go away! Not now! I'm busy!* Josh was resisting the urge, but only just . . .

Monty pulled the headphones away from Josh's ears and pressed one of them to his ear. 'REM?' He laughed like he had an opinion about music. 'Don't tell me you're losing your religion!'

He threw himself next to Josh, forcing him to shuffle to one side. Archie sat in the chair by the desk while George and Eddie took George's bed and started pushing each other, fighting for the pillow. They acted relaxed and unruly – full of unspent adrenalin – like soldiers after a battle which they counted themselves lucky to have survived unscathed. Josh had read somewhere in his notes that it was called de-escalation.

'The cops have arrested Featherlight,' Monty informed him, using the nickname they had coined for the head. 'They took him away in a police car. You should've been there to see his face! Priceless!'

'They took the bait.'

'You've got to feel sorry for the man.'

Monty stretched and gave out a huge yawn of indifference. 'They just need a scapegoat, and who better than Featherlight?'

'Yeah, he's a brilliant arsehole!' Archie chuckled and swivelled in the chair.

'I saw the policewoman with the mobile sealed in a bag,

holding the bloody thing like a trophy. She must be pleased with herself.'

'That's the last we see of her, I bloody well hope!'

Monty flicked a screwed-up piece of paper at George and Eddie. 'Cut it out for fuck's sake!' He turned to Josh and eyed him with cool interest. 'Why weren't you there? You don't know what you missed.'

'More of the same old, same old?' He raised his eyebrows and shook his head like he wanted to shake off the question. 'To be honest with you, Mont, I don't give a monkey's arse. I s'pose it's become a bit repetitive: Rachel, Brad, now Featherstone. A hamster wheel – round and round it goes. I need a fucking break.'

'A break?' Monty laughed, and Archie joined him, looking like he wasn't sure what the joke was. George and Eddie were laughing too but for their own reasons. The pillowcase had burst at the seam.

'Yeah, a break, all right? If that's OK by you?' Like Archie, Joshua didn't think there was anything funny in what he had said. He tore the headphones out of Monty's hand and shoved them back on, giving Monty an evil eye. Monty should take a break too. He was too bloody excitable. He was talking bollocks most of the time, like an old woman. Joshua was sick and tired of all that patriotic drivel. It had gone well past its sell-by date.

Monty was staring at him as if he could read his mind.

'Anyway,' Josh added in a conciliatory tone, 'they'll let Featherlight go. They're bound to. Much ado about nothing.'

'That mobile was the final nail in his coffin. He's a goner.' Monty disagreed.

'OK, fine, it's done. Let him rest in peace then.'

They all hollered with laughter. Josh turned up his music.

Chapter Thirty-three

The team bonding exercise over a pint and a steak and kidney pie in The Bull's Eye has been long overdue. Riley has tagged along too, despite the evidence of recently consumed egg-fried rice smeared on his desk and the smell of stale cooking oil. A thought crosses Gillian's mind: that Riley is stocking up on fat and carbs to prepare for hibernation over the summer season, indulging in nude takeaways. She decides not to picture that scenario. She much prefers the image of him contained in his overstretched jumper and a pair of baggy jeans.

They take their regular table by the fire and order food and drink. Webber is resolute about his orange juice – he is planning to visit the Snyders to update them about the latest developments. He wants to have a clear head. Gillian wonders how finding out about their dead daughter's vicious bullying is going to help them heal their wounds and find internal peace, but upon reflection she chooses not to point out the obvious to Webber's face. It is his case; the Snyders are his *customers* in a manner of speaking, and the importance of customer satisfaction is something Detective Chief Super Scarfe impresses on the team at every opportunity.

'I wouldn't have let him off the hook that quickly,' Erin is referring to Featherstone's release from custody.

'No evidence to hold him on, I'm afraid,' Gillian replies, her mouth full of mash and gravy. 'There were no fingerprints on the phone – no proof that he had ever held it in his hands. Anybody with access to his office could've put it there. His defence would tear us to shreds on this.'

'I agree,' Riley concurs, expertly rolling half a pie into his mouth. The pie seems to come to life between his teeth, pushing against his cheeks and exploding in small splinters from under his tongue.

'He could've wiped it clean,' Erin persists.

'Why would he? If he was sure he'd found a good hiding place where no one would find it, why bother wiping his fingerprints? He didn't expect it to be found! And if it was him who hid it, why hide it in his own office? Why not take it somewhere else, as far away from his office as possible?'

'Another thing is that the phone was always topped up using cash. No credit card has ever been attached to it, only top-up vouchers you can get at any supermarket. We can't link that phone to that man,' Riley elaborates whilst sucking bits of meat from between his teeth.

'Plus, he seemed genuinely surprised when we showed him the phone. I had the impression he was expecting something entirely different. Is there anything of interest on his laptop?'

Riley is chewing rapidly, waving his arms to Gillian to let him swallow his food before answering her. 'If you consider a recently deleted history of visiting mildly pornographic chat-rooms interesting, then yes. But in my opinion, the bloke is a virtual virgin.'

'By your standards everyone would be,' Gillian points out.

'You'd be surprised how restrained I am, DI Marsh. Online porn doesn't hold any appeal for me. I prefer blue movies – a true romantic, me!'

Webber chokes on his orange juice, coughing and spluttering bits all over the table.

Riley shrugs. 'Believe it or not, I don't care.'

Gillian slaps Mark on the back to help him get over his chok-ing. 'So,' she says casually amidst her Heimlich manoeuvres, talking over Mark's persistent coughing and retching, 'I gather it wasn't Featherstone who doctored and posted all those vile images of Rachel Snyder?'

'He wouldn't know where to start! Honestly, a virtual reality virgin. If you analyse his IT profile, his online activities, and everything he gets up to on his device, the man is clueless. A Neanderthal! He just doesn't have the know-how.'

'So who does? Have we found the source?'

'Yeah, a computer from the school's IT suite was used. He – or she – disabled the filters, so obviously they had access to the administrator's password. I'm talking to ArmIT – they are the IT support people at Whalehurst – to find out who had access. But I won't hold my breath – they could have easily stolen the password. The damned thing is hanging on the noticeboard in the reception office, I could read it from three yards away! It was typed in bold, font size sixteen, believe it or not. It could be anyone at that school, even a visitor, who used the administrator's password – anyone but Featherstone. I will stake my professional reputation on this.' Riley raises his beer and drinks it in one long glug. Then he burps and asks, 'Another round, everyone?'

'Not for me. I'm off.' Mark stands up, recovered from his bout of coughing. 'I promised I'd see the Snyders tonight.'

'I'll see you later,' Gillian shouts after him.

Riley squints knowingly and taps his nose. 'You're living together, you two, aren't you?'

Gillian rolls her eyes. 'Mind your own business, Jon.'

'Everyone knows. I was only verifying at the source,' he mutters in reply and totters towards the bar.

Chapter Thirty-four

DS Webber's discomfort was palpable. Sarah detected it the moment she opened the door and saw the detective's face. It was ashen; its muscles were tied into a knot. Instinctively, she held off his revelations by playing the good host. She offered him a cup of tea and insisted he took it despite his protestations that his visit was only a flying one – just to let them know the latest. She took a long while in the kitchen making the wretched tea and composing herself. Jonathan and DS Webber waited for her in silence.

She had to overcome her dread and joined them in drinking the tea. She and Jonathan hid their emotions behind the steam from their cups as DS Webber relayed to them the horror their daughter had been living through behind the closed door of her bedroom, right there under their noses, without them knowing.

DS Webber was clumsy with his words, failing miserably to understate Rachel's abuse, but the brutal truth began to hit home all by itself: the vile images shooting out in rapid succession like bullets from a gun pointed at their little girl's head.

Whoever was holding that imaginary gun had killed her.

Sarah and Jonathan were painfully aware of that fact. DS Webber couldn't hide it from them, hard as he tried to spare their feelings. He was a good man. Good but hapless. He said the police weren't treating this as a murder investigation anymore. The culprits were guilty of cyberbullying, but not murder. All the officers at Sexton's CID, the forensics team, everyone was doing their best to identify them, but DS Webber could make no promises that they would find them – cyberspace seemed greater than the whole universe.

Culprits? Sarah contemplated that term and found it lacking in gravity. Surely, they were talking about a killer. Plain and simple: a killer.

'Whoever is behind this . . . this . . . cyberbullying campaign, is responsible for Rachel's death,' Jonathan said, expressing out loud his wife's thoughts. 'They as good as pushed her off that bridge. It's one and the same thing, what they did. It's murder.'

The word *murder* hit Sarah like a ton of bricks. It winded her and took her breath away. She gasped and cradled her stomach. She could not settle the commotion in her heart. The pounding didn't show signs of relenting. It seemed to her that everyone in the room could hear it. She could hear it loud and clear. The cup she was holding began to rattle too. DS Webber gawped at it. She put it down on the table to stop herself from spilling her tea. The cup was still full. She hadn't had a single sip – she had only been pretending to be drinking it.

'You must find that murderous bastard.' Oblivious to her trepidations, Jonathan laid into DS Webber. 'Bring him to justice. It's your job – do it right!'

'We're doing everything we can,' DS Webber said, looking guilty, looking as if he wasn't actually doing everything he could. His eyes were averted, lowered, submissive. 'It's a wide circle of possible suspects. Anyone at the school . . . But we'll get to the bottom of it. We'll do everything . . .'

'You do that.'

DS Webber got up, thanked Sarah for the tea, which he had not touched either. He again assured them he would stay in touch – at all times. He again reminded them that if they could think of anything, no matter how insignificant it may seem, he was at the other end of the phone – day or night. He was a good man, DS Webber, but Sarah was beginning to tire of his goodness. She wanted blood. She wanted someone to pay. She wanted

Webber to bring that someone to her so that she could tear out their heart.

Her own heart was beginning to slow down. 'Thank you, DS Webber, for everything you're doing.' She took his hand and held it between hers, passing onto him her will, her burning desire for blood.

They saw Webber to the front door. He got into his car and drove away. She watched his rear lights disappear at the end of the lane.

Back in the lounge, Jonathan dropped to his knees and gave in to sobs. His face was hidden in his hands. He was rocking his body as if he were praying. Sarah touched his shoulder, and that made him jump. He looked at her with tearful eyes and said, 'It's all my fault. I had a go at her, remember? I didn't have a clue what she was going through . . . A father should've known . . . She had no one to talk to. I stopped her from talking to us.'

'No!' Sarah knelt in front of him and commanded him to stop, her hand pressed against his lips. 'Don't you dare blame yourself! He made sure she couldn't talk to us – to anyone. He made her feel ashamed. There's a killer out there – our child's killer. He is to blame and when they find him, we'll make him pay.' Her hands were surprisingly steady as she wiped the tears from his face, gently and thoroughly.

A sizeable crowd had gathered in the stands. Everyone was there: all the pupils, the teachers, even Mo's mother on annual leave from her nurse's duties and his father in his best and only suit – every conceivable person with a vested interest had come to watch the event. But Mo only had eyes for Joe Wigan, the head scout for the national squad.

He was a small man, wiry and wrinkly, his skin weather-beaten like he had sailed the seven seas in his heyday. He used to be a triathlete. He knew talent when he saw it. Mo had talent. And he had been training tirelessly, six hours a day, looking after his diet, taking vitamin supplements, keeping his wits about him.

Today was his day to peak. His competitors would eat his dust – choke on it.

Mo flashed a wide grin towards the spectators – his so-called *peers* who today were a hundred per cent behind him, all as one. Because his success would be Whalehurst School's success, and they would all bask in his glory. They were rooting for him. Monty Collingsworth smiled back at him and gave him the thumbs up. Oh yes, they all wanted Mo to win! They had been with him on this journey for months. Off the running track they wouldn't notice that he existed, but when it came to this, he was their one and only hero. They were cheering for him. He was not imagining it. He reciprocated Monty's gesture.

'Go, Mo! Go, Mo! Go, Mo!' George started the chant and *the others* joined in. Soon the whole school was throbbing with it.

Mo's body was throbbing too, with adrenalin. His fingertips were tingling. He couldn't stay still. The air raced, sharp and voluminous, into his lungs. He could feel it flood his limbs. The energy surge was galvanising every cell in his body. His heart was pounding in his ribcage, his temples and his feet. He was jogging on the spot. He couldn't steady his buzzing body. He was bursting for action. If the race didn't start soon, he would explode.

The pistol went off.

Mo shot out, straightaway to the front of the pack. He would stay there to the end. He didn't need to ration his energy or pace himself. He had enough determination to circumvent the globe. What was a mere ten-thousand metres to a superhuman like Mo?

Go, Mo! Go, Mo! Go, Mo! was ringing in his ears. *The others* were all behind him, and indeed he left them there. He was focussed on the run. His head was thumping to the rhythm of his pace.

It was a bizarre feeling when his left leg seemed to give in as if it had detached itself from his body. He stumbled but picked himself up by sheer willpower. Still, he was unaccustomed to his body not listening to his mind, not doing as it was told. His body was steering away from him, going off on a tangent until it was gone altogether, pulled from under him, and his head hit the ground and rolled to one side. His eyes saw the spectators pour from the stalls and run towards him. His mother and his father, in his best and only suit, *the others*, the teachers, even Joe Wigan.

Mo would not live with the shame of his fall. He shut his eyes the moment the first person reached him.

'I am a nurse! Stand back!' Mo's mother screamed. She pushed through the hapless crowd of onlookers and dropped to her knees. 'Mo! Mo! It's Mum! Can you hear me, Mo!' She slapped him on the face and his head rolled from one side to the other.

'Call an ambulance!' she shouted. She lowered her cheek to his lips to feel his breath. She felt nothing.

She pressed her lips to his and gave him the kiss of life. Then she started the chest compressions. 'Come back, Mo! Come back, Mo! Come back, Mo!' She sounded like the beat of a heart, only it couldn't possibly be Mo's heart. His heart had come to a standstill.

PART THREE

Atishoo, Atishoo
We all fall down

Chapter Thirty-five

The mortuary is Dr Michael Almond's office. He keeps all sorts of ungodly hours here. He has no time or room for cultivating indoor plants or for swivelling armchairs and desks that would bear coffee stains and mug rings, like in any other self-respecting workplace. He has had a computer installed in his examination room, complete with a screen mounted on the wall and a stool. Gillian fears that she may find a kettle near the fridge where bodies are kept. It bears no guessing what may be lurking in that fridge aside the bodies.

Almond greets her with a handshake which feels most bizarre as he is wearing nitrile gloves. His head is adorned with a plastic hat resembling Bobby Hughes' shower cap. The gigantic moustache curled over his mouth resurrects the image of the very hungry caterpillar from the picture books she used to read to Tara when she was a toddler. All in all, Michael Almond is not male model material.

'Sorry I can't offer you a seat,' he gazes at Gillian apologetically from his stool by his computer keyboard, 'but I want to show you something.'

'Don't worry. I'm not here for the cosiness factor.' She attempts a smile. She came on her own, Webber is out and about checking on flats for rent and as for Erin a consensus was reached in the team that she should steer away from Michael Almond until the dust of their aborted date settled. 'How did the boy die?'

'A massive heart attack caused by an overdose of Epoetin.'

'Drugs?' Gillian asks herself, allowing her mind to wander to Bradley Watson and the Mac Brothers.

'Not that kind of drugs. I mean, not the casual sort you can score in the street. Epoetin is a prescription drug given to people suffering from anaemia or recovering after chemotherapy – that sort of drug.'

'Was the victim suffering from any of these conditions?'

'Nope. I'd venture a guess that he used it as a performance-enhancing stimulant. It's not uncommon amongst cyclists or endurance athletes. Epoetin is a synthetic derived from erythropoietin, a type of hormone. It boosts the production of red blood cells and haemoglobin, which in turn increases the intake of oxygen to the muscles. It looks like Mohammed Abdikarim was a cheat.' Almond gets up from his stool and proceeds to the fridge, opens it and pulls out a trolley with a body on it. 'I want to show you a needle mark,' he says and twists the corpse's arm to point to a very faint dot. 'This, you see? I almost missed it. He must've injected to start with, then he took tablets. I'm judging by the concentration of the hormone in his blood stream that he took a considerable overdose. His body couldn't process it. After all, he was only sixteen, and quite small for his age.'

Gillian peers at the body. It is lean and well-toned, without an ounce of fat on it. Death has rendered it waxy and deprived it of tone and depth. 'He kept asking me if the race could go on. He was so anxious that it did,' she speaks, seemingly to the boy's corpse. 'Winning obviously meant everything to him, but to this extent?'

'I don't know if he was aware by how much he overdosed, or what the acceptable dose should be for that matter.'

'How did he get hold of this Epoetin? I'm thinking Bradley Watson, am I right?'

'Like I said, it's not a substance supplied on the street. You get it on prescription, especially the ampoules for intravenous use. Tablets you can buy online.'

'Or you can get it delivered to the school gate by the likes of

196

the Mac Brothers and their minions. Thanks, Dr Almond. We may finally have a connection here to the Bradley Watson case.' Gillian has a whole new angle to explore: prescription drugs. She will have to get Whittaker on the case.

Almond wheels the body back into the fridge and nods. His eyes linger on Gillian and he appears to be smiling under the caterpillar of his moustache. 'Gillian,' he starts, addressing her in a most unorthodox manner by her first name, 'I've been wondering if you may want to have dinner with me some time . . .' He gets an attack of coughs.

Gillian strives to look beyond the caterpillar, the rubber gloves, and the shower cap, not to mention the whole sorry episode with Erin. In the end, she thinks, a forensic pathologist is not the worst possible candidate to fish out of the pool of potential dates a policewoman is likely to come across in her line of work. At least, he isn't a criminal! She smiles back at him. 'Why not?'

The caterpillar comes to life and performs a little wriggly dance of joy. 'I'll call you once I've made a booking.'

'Great,' Gillian retreats. She hopes the date isn't going to be too soon – she's got so much on her plate at the moment, her heart isn't quite in it.

Chapter Thirty-six

The Epoetin phials, three of them, were bought with cash on prescription at Boots pharmacy on the High Street, Sexton's Canning. In February. It was a legitimate purchase on the face of it and it was duly recorded in the dispensary log. Erin has found two operational CCTV cameras in the vicinity of Boots; the recordings from one of them are kept for only a week and then deleted, but she has struck gold with the other one. Bradley Watson appears on film entering Boots on the date on which the prescription was collected. The evidence is irrefutable – it had to be Watson who bought the drug. Erin has done an excellent job.

Gillian is leaning over her desk, the case file contents strewn across it in a manner which makes sense only to her. She has added Mohammed Abdikarim's school photo to the board and linked it with an arrow to Bradley Watson's mug shot. She has labelled the arrow with two words: *dealer/victim*. Somehow, these words grate with her. The evidence that she has compiled in this case points clearly and unequivocally to a link between those two. Bradley was Mohammed's dealer; their partnership went sour – maybe Mohammed couldn't pay (he wasn't stuffed with money like the rest of Whalehurst's live-in residents), or maybe Mohammed didn't need Bradley any longer and wanted to get rid of an inconvenient associate who represented a blemish on his rise to glory? Perhaps Bradley threatened to expose Mo as a cheat or blackmailed him for more money – money Mo did not have. He had no choice: it was either kill Bradley or wave goodbye to his bright and promising future. A keen sportsman on all levels and in all disciplines, Mo must have been proficient with a bow and arrow.

Yet, the whole scenario doesn't sit well with Gillian.

'You wanted to see me?' Whittaker appears from nowhere, giving her a fright. She had been so deep in thought she didn't see him coming.

'Yeah. Sit down, talk to me about the Mac Brothers' line of business. I need to make sense of this case. As it stands it just doesn't gel.'

'Well, the turf war is temporarily on hold since we got the Mac Brothers into hiding. I think the Russians are biding their time, or they've already wound up their business and moved on. At this moment, it's all quiet on the western front. Either that, or NCA aren't telling me everything since officially I'm no longer part of the team.'

'That's not what I want to know. It's the prescription drugs business – is that something you'd describe as one of their regular lines of merchandise?'

Whittaker heaves the bulk of his huge frame into a chair, which creaks in weak protest. He doesn't have to think for long. 'No, I wouldn't say so. Too much trouble for too little profit: a paper trail left behind, buying on individual prescriptions, small scale petty crime, nah . . . Stolen prescription pads are reported fairly promptly and then they are useless – there's little mileage with such a micro-scheme. Negligible takings. No, that's not how they operate. They bring in mainstream merchandise from overseas en masse: amphetamines, cocaine, speed, you name it. It's wholesale uncut stuff. We know they use boats, old smugglers' routes – anything goes: small Cornish bays or large ports like Bristol. They vary the routes constantly so we won't catch up. It's a big operation. Prescription drugs don't fit into it. Not to my way of thinking, and trust me, I know how to think just like them; I've been in this long enough.'

'So Watson must have gone solo on this one. Why would he

take that risk? Mohammed would've had to make it worthwhile for him, but that's the problem, you see – the boy was skint, from a poor family from one of the poorest estates in Bristol. He only got into Whalehurst because of his athletics. He won a full bursary. So, why would Watson do it for him, stick his neck out for no conceivable incentive?'

'Dunno, guv.' Whittaker isn't one for speculation. He either knows or he doesn't know. Everything in between isn't worth considering. In a last-ditch attempt to be helpful, he scratches his chin and says, 'His mother – Mohammed's, I mean – she's a nurse. It'd be easy for her to organise a prescription.'

Gillian peers at Whittaker, her lips twist into a tight scowl. 'You may have something there . . . If she was as keen as the boy for him to win, she'd have tried to help him. Let's bring her in.'

Gillian would have charged full steam ahead into the Abdikarims' grief had it not been for Erin. She managed to convince Gillian to abandon the idea of bringing Mrs Abdikarim in and instead to travel to see her at her own house, purportedly to appraise her and her husband of the latest developments. That would give her a valid excuse to ask her a few innocent questions. Gillian agreed only because she believed catching the woman unawares with her guard low would make it easier to work her out. She was more likely to slip up in the comfort of her own living room. She now realises how misguided she had been and thanks her lucky stars (and grudgingly, DC Macfadyen) for stopping her from coming down on the poor grieving mother like a ton of bricks.

They have found her and her husband at home with their curtains drawn in the middle of the day, sitting in the dark. The two of them are holding hands like two frightened children as Gillian tells them about the drug Epoetin that killed their son.

'Is that what gave him the heart attack?'

She nods.

They frown and seem to think long and hard when she asks

them if they have any idea as to how Mo would have got hold of it. It's not easy to obtain: you have to have a prescription or resource it on the black market. Mo happened to have a prescription. Do they know how it might have come into his possession?

'Are you saying Mo was taking drugs?' Mr Abdikarim speaks with the heavy accent of a first-generation immigrant. His voice is thick with indignation. 'So, it's all his fault, you saying, that he's dead!' He stares at his wife, round-eyed. 'She saying that, is she not?'

'I don't think she is, Abdul. Never in a million years would anyone say that of Mo! He is so health-conscious, everyone knows that.' Unintentionally, Mrs Abdikarim comes to Gillian's rescue. She sounds like she genuinely can't believe Gillian could even imply such a preposterous possibility. Her motherly trust in her boy is unshakable. There isn't a shadow of guilt in her voice, and there would be bound to be plenty of it if she knew she was instrumental in Mo's death. No, she didn't source the prescription, Gillian is sure. The poor woman hasn't even absorbed the information; the idea of drugs hasn't as much as penetrated her conscious mind.

'So what she is saying?' Mr Abdikarim persists with his indignation, which is so strong that he can't bring himself to address DI Marsh directly.

'She must be talking about the supplements, I reckon,' Mrs Abdikarim has an answer ready. 'He was taking supplements like all sportsmen do, that much I know.'

'Supplements?' Gillian and Erin repeat in unison, amazed at this novel use of the word *supplement* for the performance-enhancing substance that killed their child.

'Well, yes! Mo would've never taken drugs – not deliberately. He did say he was taking vitamin supplements that a boy at school had recommended to him. He said everyone at Whalehurst wanted him to do well, didn't he, Abdul? They were helping him to peak at the right time, for the championships.'

'Hm.' Mr Abdikarim is uncertain whether to join his wife in

201

her praise for the school. He shrugs his shoulders and folds his arms on his chest. He is no longer holding her hand.

'Don't tell me you don't remember! Mo was forever telling us how he was looking after his diet and how the school cook was giving him extra meat on his plate at dinner time – for protein to grow his muscles. And about the vitamins to keep himself fit and healthy. He thought they were vitamins and minerals . . . They came in standard capsule sizes . . . What were they if they weren't vitamins?' Her tone ominous, she seems to have caught up at last with the absurd circumstances of Mo's death. She stares at Gillian and Erin, her head wobbling slightly as though she is finding it difficult to hold it up.

'So who gave him those *vitamins?* Did you give him money to buy them?'

Mrs Abdikarim lowers her eyes and gazes at the floor apologetically. 'We don't have much, not enough to make ends meet. Mo did as well as he did all by himself. He got into that school on scholarship. Do you think we could afford to give him money for vitamins? We struggled to pay for the uniform and a new pair of shoes each year. Do we look like we can afford luxuries like health supplements?' Her eyes lift and sweep the room, which is dingy, dark, and minimalistic in its furnishings. It is a room in a flat on the sixth floor of a dilapidated building with no lift and with graffiti smeared on all accessible (and inaccessible) wall surfaces by someone with little or no artistic ability but possessing lots of raging anger.

'Do you remember the boy's name?'

'Who?' Mrs Abdikarim's eyes are glazed over with something that she subconsciously uses to block from her mind the things she is hearing about her son.

'The boy who recommended the supplements to Mo,' Gillian elaborates, impatient to hear the name Bradley Watson.

'No . . . I'm sorry. He was an older boy, a young man. I think Mo looked up to him, or maybe he was a bit wary of him . . . He spoke of him with . . . you know? How do you say it? Reverence?'

202

'Was it Brad? Bradley?'

'I don't know. Bradley doesn't ring a bell. I'm not sure Mo mentioned the name more than once.'

'Is that who killed Mo? Is that who gave them drugs to him? Bradley, his name?' Mr Abdikarim rises to his feet, the bulks of his fists ramming against each other like two boxer's gloves hungry for a fight. 'He killed my boy and I kill him now, as God is my witness!'

'He is already dead,' Gillian levels with the man. She knows she shouldn't have mentioned any names. That would be leading the witnesses. She is regretting it now, but there is no point in withholding the truth. 'Bradley Watson was murdered. Someone beat you to it.'

Chapter Thirty-seven

Webber is making a second attempt at leaving Gillian's impromptu B&B whilst noting in passing that neither of the Bs represents her strength. He has packed his suitcases (or perhaps he never unpacked them in the first place) and lined them up by the front door. Corky has sniffed them and found them of little interest. Fritz on the other hand is sitting guard on top of one of them and is licking his backside. Gillian hasn't noticed. She is bent over her coffee table, ploughing through the files and shouting occasional throwaway comments to Mark. 'I think Watson was building his own little empire on the side. He had those rich kids eating from his hand. He was their only link with the outside world. They had to go through him if they wanted something they were not allowed to have in Whalehurst. That's what it looks like to me. What you do think?'

The flushing sound from the toilet upstairs muffles his response, if there is one. Mark checks *his* bedroom to see if he has left anything behind and everything is tidy and in good order.

'And I can't imagine Mo would've killed Watson, can you? He didn't even realise Bradley was pumping him with lethal hormones – he thought it was vitamins. Watson was executed in cold blood. It's the gangs. It all goes back to the gangs: his own people or the rivals from Greyston. My bet would be on Bradley's own masters – once they found out he was double-crossing them and dealing behind their backs, they took him out. I need to interview the Mac Brothers, wherever the hell they are. They know more than they're letting on.'

Mark is standing in the doorway, leaning against the wall. He waits for Gillian to look up at him from her pile of papers. She does. 'Why are you standing there like a lemon? Get down on your knees and help me with this . . . A few details still bother me. No,' she waves her arm, 'not details, but something's bothering me and I can't figure out what it is. Cast your eye over –'

'I'm leaving, Gillian. I told you I've found a place.'

'I know, I remember. Is it tonight?'

'Yep.'

'All right then, good luck. Do you need help with anything?'

'No, but I want to say thank you for your hospitality, putting up with me, and –' he blushes like a schoolgirl.

'Don't mention it.'

'I've booked a table for dinner tonight. Just a token of my gratitude, nothing more.'

Gillian wrinkles her nose and looks disappointed. 'Oh, bugger! Not tonight!'

'Yeah, tonight. What's wrong with tonight? It's only a dinner.'

'I'm having one already. Michael Almond's asked me out, and it's tonight at eight.' She shakes her head. 'Damn it! It's always like that: nothing happens for months on end and then two free dinners come at once. It's not fair that I should be forced to choose. I don't particularly like making choices.' It is one of the very few deeply philosophical observations Gillian has made in her whole life. It raises Mark's eyebrow. 'Sorry, I don't think I can squeeze two meals in, as much as I'd love to.'

He puts on a brave face. 'Never mind, I can cancel. We'll make it another day. The invitation stands.'

'Great, thanks. You don't have to, you know, but I am free tomorrow,' and she turns away to bury her head in her case files. She still has a good half an hour before she is due to meet with Almond in the town square.

Chapter Thirty-eight

Firstly the caterpillar-moustache appears in Gillian's peripheral vision and when she turns in its direction she finds the rest of Michael Almond. She waves to him and reminds herself not to refer to him as *Dr* Almond. His name is Michael. Michael waves too, and it's all smiles from there.

The table is booked in a quaint Italian restaurant called The Scent of Tuscany, and frankly there is little more than a whiff as the restaurant consists of a mere six tables huddled in a cosy basement; above, on the ground floor, the scents and flavours of pizza mingle with the scents and flavours of pasta, and takeaway orders are shouted out in a dramatic baritone by the Italian chef. The exotic smells and even more exotic sounds drift down to the basement lazily until a hyperactive Italian waiter with a moustache rivalling that of Dr – Michael – Almond approaches their table to take their order. In his unquenched enthusiasm, he has twice as much to say as they do. In the end they give up trying to talk over him and it is he who gives orders to them as he tells them that they *should prefer* the chef's special seafood risotto, of course if they like seafood, all of which he articulates part in English, part in Italian, and part in vivid gesticulation. They gratefully accept his choices. He fills their glasses with a flourish and springs away to conduct a loud exchange with the chef on the ground floor, all in Italian. Listening to that, Gillian and Michael gaze at each other in terrified silence: going by the volume and rapidity of that exchange, it seems like a third world war has erupted in the kitchen. Gillian wonders whether she should have mentioned earlier that she isn't a great fan of Italian cuisine, but it is too late now. Walking away could cause a vendetta to be taken out on their heads. Anyway, she shouldn't stir trouble – she isn't paying for this and beggars can't be choosers.

'Were you surprised when I asked you out?' Almond's moustache asks her.

'Well . . .'

In all frankness she hadn't had a chance to consider the implications of this dinner. Is this a date? The man is on the prowl, that's common knowledge ever since Erin kissed and told.

'Well . . .' Gillian repeats.

'I surprised myself,' he informs her. 'It just came out.'

'Well . . .'

He lifts his hand, palm out. 'I mean, don't get me wrong. I find myself attracted to you as a . . . a . . .'

'A woman?' Gillian only tries to be helpful, but it comes out as if she is mocking him.

'Yes, as a woman.' So he took it in good faith, thank God! 'I know you live alone . . . I mean you're not seeing anyone at the moment, unless I am wrong of course.' An unspoken question mark is quivering over his last sentence, prompting Gillian to explain.

'As of tonight I do live alone, as it happens. Webber's found a flat to rent.'

'You've been living with Webber?' The surprise in his face is sobering. His moustache handles drop.

'Well, not exactly living with him. He's been staying with me – at my place, you know: couch-surfing . . .' No, it doesn't sound right. It sounds as if they've been making waves and riding them on her couch, and that can be interpreted in many suggestive ways. 'What I mean to say is Webber needed a roof over his head while looking for a flat to rent. But we – we haven't been living together as in having regular sex.' This should do. She looks at Almond deadpan, trying to read his face to see if she has expressed herself clearly.

'So, no *regular* sex . . .' His face looks clouded – it's more like storm clouds are gathering on the horizon, behind the hedge of his moustache. Perhaps she has given him too much information, perhaps not enough. Luckily for both of them, the animated waiter enters the equation with garlic bread and marinated olives.

'Enjoy your *food-der*!' he enthuses and refills their glasses. 'More wine, I enquire?'

'Yes, please.' Gillian steps in before Michael has a chance to act like a man and take charge of the liquor.

'No problem!' The waiter departs with a mysterious smile, which may be sympathetic or derisive towards Michael, or both in equal measure.

Gillian indulges in a glassful of Dutch courage, as does Michael. She says perhaps too quickly and too intrusively, 'And you, I take it, you live alone too?'

'Yes, I do.'

'Good.'

'Well . . . Yes, I guess it's not bad. Living alone.'

'I quite enjoy the peace and quiet. My daughter and her boyfriend recently moved out to live with my parents. I was enjoying it till Webber moved in.'

He smiles, appreciative of her efforts to put Webber's cohabitation with her in proper perspective.

The omnipresent waiter re-enters the scene with a second bottle of wine. He refills their glasses and collects the empty plates. Gillian intercepts the last olive from the bowl before the dish is cleared away. She chews on it, desperately trying to think of something to say.

Michael is quicker, 'So, do you enjoy solving murder cases, chasing criminals?'

'I was just about to ask you the same question.' She won't be outdone. 'Do *you* enjoy cutting corpses up and peering into their stomach contents?'

It is at that moment that the waiter reappears, carrying two plates of seafood risotto, which upon reflection does resemble the contents of one's stomach. The waiter squints slightly, not quite certain whether the snippet of their conversation he has just caught means what he thinks it means. Just in case it does, he tells them to enjoy their *food-der* in a rather aloof manner, a far cry from his former enthusiastic self, and promptly withdraws to his other duties. He stops at another table and has a loud and cheery conversation with its occupants.

'It's a job,' Michael answers Gillian's question.

'So is mine,' she agrees.

They distract themselves for a while with the risotto. Instantly, Gillian's mind wanders to the case at hand. She can't help it. 'How, do you think,' she drills Almond, 'did that boy get hold of a prescription? A genuine prescription. You are a doctor, after a fashion, you should have an idea of how these things can be procured . . .'

'Well . . .' It's his turn to be vague. 'There are plenty of prescription pads lying around in doctors' surgeries and hospitals. Doctors sometimes use each other's pads. It's hard to tell, but I'd say –'

She stops him halfway through his sentence, 'My God! I've been so stupid! How did I not see this? It was staring me right in the face!'

'What was?'

'The name, the name on that prescription. Something was bothering me. I went through the papers over and over again, and something was bothering me. And I couldn't figure out what. It was the name of the doctor. Dr Collingsworth! Blimey, I never! Thank you. Thanks a million!'

She jumps to her feet, leans over the table and kisses Almond on his moustache. 'Doctor bloody Collingsworth . . .'

'And that name is significant because?'

'Because it takes us back to the school, to a sixth former, Head Boy going by the name of Monty Collingsworth. I've got him. He has a few questions to answer. Let's go!'

Almond stares at her. 'Surely, not this very minute? It's nine o'clock at night. Surely, it can wait until the morning?'

Gillian glances at her risotto, which is surprisingly tasty considering it does resemble the contents of one's stomach; then there is the promise of pudding and she has already eyed up the tiramisu. She sits back to finish her main course. She'll have that nasty little Head Boy for breakfast tomorrow morning. 'Yes, it can wait. And we may as well finish this bottle.' She gestures towards the wine. Almond adopts his manly duty with delight.

They are both irrevocably plastered when Gillian sweeps her plate for that last smudge of alcohol-soaked biscuit. 'So, your place or mine?' she asks in all her direct innocence, 'considering that both of us live alone.'

It is hers, mainly because it is within walking distance from the town square and neither of them is in a position to drive. Michael Almond (she really has to stop reciting his surname each time she thinks of him, or this relationship goes nowhere fast) lives in the village of Bishops Well, a fifteen-minute drive.

The drizzly cool night helps with clearing their heads, but their respective bloodstreams would catch fire if a burning match was anywhere near them. They stumble through the deserted streets, talking in monosyllables. Almond confesses to having never been married, which sets off alarm bells in Gillian's head – the man is in his mid-forties, heading for a midlife crisis before he has had the chance to grow out of his little boy's short trousers. Surely corpses wouldn't have adequately filled the gap in his sex and family lives?

Gillian finds herself re-assured. At least she was married once upon a time, and though now she is wedded to her job, she has been known to have casual sex every now and again with a living person.

A young couple emerges from a small alley at the corner of the town square, and heads towards Gillian and Michael. You can tell they are young and in love because they are holding hands and have suddenly stopped in the middle of the pavement for a random kiss. The girl's arms are draped over the boy's neck and the boy's hands have strayed towards the girl's bum. Michael and Gillian are keeping their hands to themselves as they pass by the kissing couple awkwardly and guiltily. The girl throws her head back and Gillian recognises Tara's friend Sasha. Gillian has hardly seen her since the bomb blast that killed her boyfriend Ross and could have done the same to Charlie.

A hint of embarrassment crosses Sasha's face, which she attempts to cover up with an over-the-top big smile. Gillian grins at her. She is happy Sasha is beginning to put Ross behind her. What other choice does she really have? Staying faithful to his memory doesn't mean staying celibate. The girl has a whole life ahead of her. She must live it.

'Good on you, Sasha,' Gillian says, gesturing towards her new boyfriend. Sasha bites her lip. She looks like she has been chastised. 'Good on you, I mean it,' Gillian repeats.

'Yes. Good to see you, Gillian. Say hi to Tara.'

'She has moved out and lives with her grandparents now.'

'With Charlie?'

'Yes, with Charlie. You should go and visit.'

Sasha shakes her head. 'No, I don't think I'm ready to see them, still together, as if nothing happened.' She takes her new boyfriend's hand and walks away. She has clearly burned all her bridges with the past and all the people in it, not just Ross.

Michael Almond doesn't ask any questions. Gillian likes that about him. She wouldn't know where to begin to explain this to him.

In her lounge, she asks him if he wants coffee, but she doesn't intend to go and make it. She sits next to him on the sofa. As the convention requires, he says that yes, he would love a cup, and he kisses her, giving her a valid excuse to forget about the coffee. As they begin to relieve themselves of their clothes, Corky enters the periphery of Gillian's vision. He sits down and gazes at them. His soulful, brown eyes are sad. He is hurting, poor boy, remembering his former master, Gillian's old flame Sean. Gillian can't bring herself to carry on in front of the dog, and she doesn't want to think about Sean now.

'Let's go upstairs, to my bedroom,' she whispers into Michael's ear, 'and do it like two civilised adults.'

He looks at her, puzzled.

'The dog isn't allowed in the bedrooms,' she explains, then remembers the upstairs resident, Fritz, so she adds, 'We'll only have the cat to worry about . . . but the cat is very discreet. He won't say a word.'

'Right . . .' Michael sounds even more confused than he looks, but gets up and follows her up the stairs, hopping on one leg as the other one is still caught up in his trousers.

'It's a weird night,' Gillian mumbles as she pulls him towards her, 'full of ghosts from the past.'

He doesn't comment. His lips are sealed with hers.

Chapter Thirty-nine

Monty Collingsworth acts as if being interviewed under caution by the police was an everyday occurrence for him. He knows exactly what to do. When he was being escorted from the school, he told Dr Featherstone to 'relax, this was just a misunderstanding, he'd be back in no time' when Dr Featherstone went on the offensive, shouting *'police persecution!'* and almost lying prostrate across the school threshold to stop the arrest. When later, at the police station, Monty was offered a duty solicitor, he declined, but asked to be afforded one phone call. That was all he needed to have this mess resolved in no time.

In the interview room, sitting across the table from DI Marsh and DS Webber, with the tape running, Monty remains unfazed. His posture is upright, his shoulders square and confident; his pale eyes are resting unflinchingly on whichever officer is asking the question. There is an air of fractured and bruised nobility about him – the police have got it all wrong.

Gillian pushes the Epoetin prescription across the table. 'Take a look at that, Monty. Do you recognise it?'

Monty examines the paper without lifting it from the table. 'Insofar as it has my father's header on it . . . Is it from my father's prescription pad?'

'Let us ask the questions.'

'Do you recognise the signature?'

'It looks like my father's, but then my father's signature is just a squiggle. Anyone could have forged it, even me.' He smiles, amused.

'Did you?'

'Why would I do such a thing?'

'Like I said,' Webber repeats, 'we'll ask the questions. You just answer them.'

'No, I didn't sign it.'

'Can you explain how your father's prescription found its way to one of Sexton's pharmacies?'

'I wish I could. Maybe one of his patients happened to come to Sexton's for whatever reason? It's a small world we live in.'

Gillian ignores his smart-arse witticism. 'Would you be surprised if I told you it was for Epoetin, the drug that killed Mohammed Abdikarim, and it was collected by Bradley Watson, who was not your father's patient. Do you know anything about this?'

'Yes, I'd be surprised, and no, I've no idea what you're talking about.' For the first time since the interview started, Monty's eyes shift nervously as he peers at the door, willing it to open. His Adam's apple buoys in his throat as he swallows.

'How did Bradley get hold of this prescription?'

'I don't know.'

'Did you give it to him? Did you take it from your father's surgery? Did you forge your father's signature? Did you write the prescription out?'

'No, no, no, and no!' A slightly elevated pitch in his voice betrays his discomfort.

'Were you just trying to help Mo?' Gillian has softened her tone. She is gazing at the boy, feigning sympathy. 'I can understand what you were trying to do, Monty. You just wanted to help Mo win, right?'

Monty shakes his head.

'For the benefit of the recording, Monty – speak up.'

'No. I don't know what this is about. I don't know anything about any prescriptions.'

'But surely you can see why I find it hard to believe you? It's your father's prescription, and you father is far away from Sexton's . . . where is his practice?'

'Taunton.'

'Taunton! That's quite a distance for his patient to travel to collect a prescription. You know, Epoetin is prescribed for people suffering from anaemia and people recovering from cancer. Would such a person travel this far to collect a prescription?'

'I can't comment on that.'

'You see, Monty, we've come up with this scenario, which makes much more sense than a patient of your father's travelling across two counties to get a prescription. We think that you stole the prescription, you gave it to Bradley Watson to collect, and then you gave Epoetin to Mohammed Abdikarim. You convinced him that it was a vitamin supplement. So you see, Monty, it looks like you are directly responsible for Mo's death.'

'No!' Monty has lost his cool. He has taken his hands off the table and is rubbing them against his thighs; his eyes dart between the table, DI Marsh and the door. He is thoroughly unsettled.

'Look, I can see that you acted with the best of intentions. Mo's parents told us that another boy at school – a boy Mo really looked up to – was helping him with vitamin supplements. Was it you, Monty?'

'No.'

'I have a strong suspicion that it was you. Did you think that Epoetin was an innocuous vitamin supplement? You may've heard about it somewhere. You thought you were doing Mo a favour. The school's reputation is important to you, isn't it? You are the Head Boy. I remember you telling me how important sports and martial arts were for everybody at Whalehurst. It's understandable that you wanted Mo to win, to put Whalehurst on the map. Am I right?'

'No, you're wrong.' Monty is back to himself. His eyes are steadily focussed on Gillian. What did she say to restore his composure? He even leans forward and speaks directly to the tape recorder, 'I don't think, not for one minute, that Whalehurst's reputation could be enhanced by someone like Mo. We don't support drug cheats at Whalehurst. Mo was a drug cheat.'

'But Mo didn't know he was taking drugs –'

'And you've got what to support that? His word for it?'

The door swings open and in quick succession, Scarfe and two unknown men dressed in suits march into the interview room. One of the suits plonks himself at the table, in the spare chair next to Monty, facing Webber. He puts his hands on the table, palms down, and says, glaring Webber straight in the eye, 'William Jones. I'm Mr Collingsworth's lawyer. I need time with my client before this interview continues.'

DS Webber winces as if the man has just spat in his face.

'Monty, you don't have to say anything. Just listen to William. He'll get you out of here,' the other suit speaks in great agitation.

'And who are you?' DI Marsh regains her power of speech.

'I'm his father, Dr Collingsworth. You had no right to interview him without his lawyer being present!' White spittle settles in the corner of his mouth.

'He refused a solicitor,' DI Marsh informs the man.

'He's only a boy, for God's sake!'

'He's over eighteen years of age, not a boy. And neither is he a vulnerable adult,' DI Marsh points out. 'He can make his own decisions, and you can't be here while he's being interviewed under caution. He is not entitled to be supported by his parents.'

'But he is entitled to a solicitor, so can I please have some time with my client,' William Jones insists, his voice low and cold.

Scarfe, who has been watching the goings-on with admirable self-restraint, takes charge of the situation. 'DI Marsh, DS Webber, Dr Collingsworth, can you all please step outside with me. We'll go to my office. This way.'

Scarface's polite manner does not fool Gillian. It has been put on for the benefit of Dr Collingsworth. Without him in attendance, Scarface would right now be biting Gillian's head off. She can see it in his burning face: it is flushed red and rigid with displeasure. Gillian can read him like a book: her actions were thoughtless and with utter disregard for due process; she has jeopardised the relationships between the police and the local community; Whalehurst School – a symbol of status, not to mention the sole employment provider in Little Ogburn – is on the verge of being closed down; the parents are withdrawing their children from the school in droves. It is Gillian's fault.

'Would you like to sit down, please,' Scarfe points Dr Collingsworth to his black fake-leather sofa. 'I'm sure this misunderstanding will be cleared up in no time.'

DI Marsh and DS Webber are left standing in the corner.

Collingsworth doesn't take the seat. He is in his late sixties, older than one would expect the father of an eighteen-year-old to be. He is tall and stooped, his shoulders hunched and rounded, indicative of him having spent most of his life sitting at a desk in a nice country practice. He glares at Gillian from behind thick glasses that make his eyes bulge. 'What I'd like to know is why my son's been dragged here. What are the charges against him?'

'There've been no charges laid against Monty,' Gillian says.

'So why the hell is he here, being interrogated like a common criminal!'

'Could you explain that, DI Marsh? I'd be curious to know.' Scarface will never comprehend the meaning of the term 'team spirit'.

'Mohammed Abdikarim, a student at Whalehurst, died as a result of an overdose. Epoetin. He obtained the drug on prescription, apparently on the recommendation of another boy from the school.'

Dr Collingsworth is blinking behind his thick glasses without comprehension.

'And you assumed that other boy was Monty Collingsworth because . . .' Scarface is seething. No explanation will be good enough. Nevertheless, Gillian tries.

'The prescription was purportedly issued by Monty's father – by you, Dr Collingsworth.'

'Me?' Collingsworth is blinking with such rapidity that it is beginning to look like an attack of convulsions.

'Of course, we realise your signature must have been forged, but there is no denying that the prescription is authentic. Mohammed Abdikarim, or rather Bradley Watson who collected it, had no way of obtaining it from you personally. The only way they could get it is through your son. We were just talking to him to find out how it happened. You'll appreciate –'

Dr Collingsworth's face has undergone several stages of utter shock, disbelief, consternation and white fury, but at last he looks like he is back in possession of all his faculties. He interrupts Gillian, his tone didactic, 'No, I do not appreciate anything you have insinuated because everything you said was just insinuation, speculation, and pure fabrication. If you'd only cared to ask me I would have told you that one of my prescription pads has been stolen recently from my . . . my car. I left it open, inadvertently, and a . . . So, as *you* will appreciate, anyone but my son could have . . . would have used it.'

There is nothing like a loving father who will take the fall for his child, Gillian marvels. She feigns interest in his obvious lie. 'Oh, stolen? Have you reported it? As a practising GP you will know, naturally, that such thefts must be reported without delay. We checked and there's no record . . .'

'It only happened a few days ago. Give me a chance, I'm a busy man.'

'Just a couple of days ago?'

'Well, yes, late last week. Coincidentally, Monty hasn't been home since Christmas so it couldn't have been him, could it?' Dr Collingsworth triumphs.

Gillian smiles at him, all innocence. 'But you see, the prescription was collected in February and that'd be soon after Monty returned to school after his Christmas break at home.'

'You are wrong!' Having no other arguments to advance, Dr

Collingsworth raises his voice. 'Prescription pads go missing all the time. Besides, they are easy to forge.'

'Let's just ask Monty, shall we?'

Webber and Gillian exchange a knowing look. She has played it well, but they both know that by now the lawyer has had an opportunity to coach Monty and their chance to take the boy by surprise has passed. They are proven right within seconds of re-entering the interview room.

Gillian resumes the recording and states for the tape that Monty's lawyer, William Jones is now sitting in on the interview. He then immediately takes charge and speaks for and on behalf of his client, 'My client is keen to do everything in his power to help you with your investigation. He therefore feels compelled to admit that he indeed had a prescription form in his possession. He had obtained it from his father's pad, without his father's knowledge.'

'I'm sorry.' Monty makes an effort to sound contrite. 'I shouldn't have done that. It was in case –'

Jones touches his client's arm ever so gently and takes over. 'Let me speak, Monty. We agreed.'

Monty nods, even more confounded and meek.

'My client regrets his actions, but it was meant well. He took the form in case he or any of his friends got ill and needed a course of antibiotics or anything that can be obtained only on prescription. Unfortunately, medical care at the school is not easily accessible.'

Bollocks to that! Gillian and Mark share an unspoken sentiment with just their body language. Gillian leans back in her chair; Mark rolls his eyes.

William Jones ignores their fidgeting. 'My client is now aware that it was a mistake to take the form without his father's permission and he is remorseful about that. To compound his distress, the form was stolen from him as soon as he returned to school from the Christmas break. He was obviously unable to report the theft as it was about something he should not have had amongst his possessions. Although someone had gone through his belongings the

219

only thing missing was the prescription form. Reporting it would mean confessing to removing it from his father's surgery in the first place —'

'Who knew about it? Who knew you had it?' DI Marsh interjects.

'Everyone . . .' Monty makes sure the radius of suspects is wide enough for the scent to go cold. He smiles apologetically. 'Students, and some staff members, like Bradley.'

'I would like to make this statement on your behalf, as agreed. Is that all right, Monty?' Jones reiterates, this time a note of irritation stealing into his smooth delivery of the statement. 'So,' he sighed, 'as my client has already told you, he had no idea that the prescription form would be used to buy Epoetin. He had no knowledge of that until the prescription was presented to him by yourselves. He has never seen it completed and there is nothing else he can add with regard to this matter. As he has already indicated, he regrets taking the form foolishly and then not reporting the theft. He is prepared to take full consequences for his actions . . .'

'Right . . .'

'. . . but not for the actions of whoever stole the form and the subsequent overdose suffered by Mohammed Abdikarim.'

'Thank you for your frankness, Monty.' Gillian drills the young man with a knowing glare. He holds it, his face crumpled with fake remorse – a foolish puppy that chewed his master's slipper, no more than that . . .

'Can he now be released to go back to school? Unless you wish to charge him?' The lawyer's eyebrows quiver on top of his forehead. If they were to go any higher, they would fly away.

DI Marsh terminates the interview, though she is not done with Monty Collingsworth – not by far.

Chapter Forty

The wood-panelled chamber housing the Medieval Martial Arts Society of Whalehurst was their bastion. All their secrets were kept locked within its four walls, away from prying eyes. But the secrets had multiplied lately and were now refusing to stay out of sight. People, the wrong sort of people, had been asking questions, hovering closer and closer to the truth, beginning to scratch the surface. Not long ago the headquarters' sanctity had been violated by the police breaking and entering to search for the phone that had been tucked away safely in Featherlight's office. That had been a close brush with the long arm of the law and their arses had been saved only thanks to Josh's quick thinking. But the danger of slipping in the shit left behind by three untimely deaths still hung thick and heavy over their necks – the sword of Damocles wielded by that bitch detective, Marsh. It would take more than a good lawyer to get her off their scent. She had her nose close to the ground and was bound to sooner or later dig out the long-focus lens Nikon CoolPix camera alongside the memory card and all the other incriminating paraphernalia buried under the stands in the sports field.

The fucking equipment had cost them an arm and a leg. They all had to chip in together to buy the damned stuff but trying to sell it would have brought the cops right to their doorstep. So, it had been condemned to rot in its own shoebox-sized grave.

Monty couldn't bring himself to bury the iPad. It was his tool of trade – he lived on the damned thing. He had insisted that they would be able to use it once the dust settled, so they had switched it off, locked it in a metal box, and stashed it behind one of the hundreds of indistinguishable wall panels. They were sure that they had disposed of all the incriminating evidence – except that nobody had thought of the flaming prescription.

It had been Monty's baby – his responsibility to sort it out. He had fucked up. He was beginning to seriously piss Josh off.

Monty was sprawled in the bishop's chair, an antique throne-like seat upholstered in tough, well-worn leather, and he looked pleased with himself. His father had plucked him by the ears out of the shithole he had got himself into, but he was acting as if he had achieved it all by himself. And what achievement exactly was that?

He was going to drag them all down with him. Arsehole!

Josh had no illusions about that bitch detective. Now that she had latched on to their scent, she would keep going. She would sniff around the school until someone threw her a bone to get her teeth into. She wouldn't go for cheap tricks – it had to be something real, something close to the nerve. Something or someone.

Apart from Monty, no one was in the mood for celebrations. Even Monty was running on pure adrenalin and not much more. George and Eddie were scrambling for some kind of inspiration from their fucking *führer*, but none was coming. Monty was an ideological bankrupt. Gone were his one-liners about honour and purity. He was sitting in his own shit, finally looking like himself: an arsehole.

Josh had always known Monty for what he really was: a psycho. Perhaps Archie did too. The two of them were in it for the ride. But George and Eddie, the faithful bloody disciples, had been following the gospel of Monty as if he was God Almighty. The poor, pathetic bastards!

'They had to let me go, and they won't dare to pull me back in,' Monty sneered, distorting his perfect, sensual lips into an ugly convulsion. 'It's called double jeopardy.'

'No such thing. You're talking crap,' Archie snapped. Josh was behind him on this, but he couldn't be bothered to say it. There was no talking sense into Monty.

'This entire holy shit's behind us, all right? They've got nothing on us.' Monty tensed up. 'Cool it.'

'Dream on. You're such a sorry cunt!'

'Take that back!' Monty jumped from his throne and grabbed Archie by the collar. Monty's spittle hit Archie's face when he repeated, 'Take it back.'

'Fuck off!' Archie wouldn't be dictated to. Not by someone who had messed up big time. He tore Monty's hands off his neck and punched him. His fist made direct contact with Monty's lips. Blood appeared on his gums and began to colour his teeth. Monty licked it off his lips and spat it on the floor. He rammed into Archie head first and knocked him to the ground. Archie hadn't expected that. He went down with a thud, but quickly shook off the surprise and started to pick himself up. Monty wouldn't give him the chance. He seized one of the lances from the wall and charged blindly forward with a wild scream.

Josh had to step in.

He intercepted the lance mid-flight and wrestled it out of Monty's hands.

George and Eddie had finally decided to take the right side. Jointly they grabbed Monty from behind and were holding his head in a lock, his arms twisted behind his back.

For a split, adrenalin-charged moment, Josh was tempted to plunge the lance into Monty's chest. It would've felt good and it would have been right, but it would take too much explaining later on. He lowered the metal head to the floor and safely replaced the lance on the hook. It sat neatly and precisely in its place as if it had never left.

Josh peered at Monty from under his long, girlish eyelashes, 'Have you again lost your fucking mind?'

'I told him to cool it! He started —'

'Both of you, sit the fuck down.'

'I'm good.' Archie was already sitting down on the floor, holding his stomach.

Monty wriggled to free himself from the headlock; they let him go. At least he had stopped smirking and, satisfyingly, his gums were still bleeding.

Chapter Forty-one

What is missing is an overarching motive. Why? Watson had to be killed because he became an inconvenient witness, maybe a blackmailer – his death makes its own twisted sense. Whether it was Mo or Monty who shot Bradley Watson to cover their tracks is yet to be established. Gillian's money is on Monty, but then again: would he have done it before Mo's accidental overdose? Unless it wasn't an accident and Monty knew Mo would die; then he would have had good reason to dispose of Bradley early on, before Bradley put two and two together. But Mo would've had his own reasons, too. If he qualified for the Commonwealth Games squad, he could not afford to leave behind any loose ends, like his supplier. So that's Bradley Watson: dead and buried. But why Rachel Snyder? How is she implicated in this mess? That is the one conundrum which breaks this case into pieces that don't fit back into the puzzle box no matter which way you try to squeeze them. Unless Rachel Snyder's death is totally unrelated. Except that there are too many circumstantial links: her photos on the memory card found in Bradley's pocket, the online bullying campaign against her that was run from the school. She is connected. But how? And why?

Gillian carries on with her inventory of facts with her feet up on Michael Almond's lap. She has a captive audience in Michael, she believes, for he gazes at her attentively, hanging on her every word. Little does she know. Michael is hungry. He is hungry for her and he is hungry for something to eat. He can't tell which hunger is stronger, but whichever is satisfied first, he will be a happy man. So he is very attentive and doesn't interrupt, but he silently eggs her on to get to the end of the evidence trail so that they can get on with the evening.

'What do you make of it, Almond?' Sometimes she forgets herself and calls him by his surname. It would be cute in a way if it wasn't so disconcerting. It does make him feel like he is here purely in his professional capacity. And he isn't. Because Gillian isn't a corpse. Though sometimes she acts like one: cold and indifferent.

'Well, I really can't say. Should we order a takeaway?'

'You've examined Abdikarim's body. Is there any way of telling if the overdose was accidental? Obviously, you found no signs of violence to indicate it was forced on him?' She puckers her lips to mull that over.

'No, none. He was a child, he probably didn't know how much was too much. If it had been genuinely prescribed to him, the medical practitioner would have assessed his general health, his medical condition, and his weight to give him an appropriate dose.'

'But it wasn't genuinely prescribed. Dr Collingsworth claims his prescription pads vanish on a regular basis. That could mean a whole stash of prescription confetti floating on the black market. That's the biggest pile of shite I've ever heard.'

'It does happen.'

'It's just too far-fetched. Too many coincidences. Too many links. Let the court decide his credibility on this one. The odds are against him.'

Michael runs his hand up her leg. It feels soft and warm; the higher his hand ventures the warmer it becomes. 'Or maybe we should forget the takeaway for now and go upstairs?' he suggests hopefully.

She doesn't seem to hear him, but the big Alsatian definitely does. It lifts its head from the floor, its ears prick, and it fixes him with a warning glare. What's wrong with that dog?

'What wouldn't I give to know how Rachel Snyder fits into this . . .' Gillian fantasises.

'Me too . . . Then I could tell you and I'd get what I want, like a night of passion.' Michael sighs.

The phone interrupts their respective fantasies. Gillian picks it up. 'Riley? Do you know what time it is? . . . Are you still in the office? . . . Are you sure? You don't say! You are my hero!'

She puts the phone down and grins at Michael. 'You won't believe it but it looks like Riley has just solved my puzzle.'

'Has he?' *Bastard!* Michael finds himself thrown from the saddle of his fantasies.

Chapter Forty-two

Jon Riley twists his lips, raises his brow and nods with mock appreciation, 'Have you moved on to the good doctor now, Gillian? You're a damn fast operator!'

She has dragged Almond with her. It didn't feel right to leave him behind in the house under Corky's watchful – and disapproving – eye. 'You're talking rubbish, as usual, Riley.' She pulls a face at him.

'How's Webber taking it?' Riley winks. He is like a dog with a bone! That's Jon Riley at his worst.

'Get off my case and focus. What have you got for me?'

Riley taps the side of his nose and smirks at Almond. 'It'll stay between us. I'll take this to my grave.'

'You may get there sooner than you think if you don't start talking sense,' Gillian warns him. She knows his games. It's all foreplay and no action, and certainly no ill will, but Michael doesn't know that. He is like a trapped animal. He doesn't know what to do with himself. He stands behind his moustache, looking embarrassed.

'So, I was sailing leisurely through all the high-security alert browsing history on that PC from Whalehurst, as you do on a Friday night when you have no life, unlike some people,' Riley winks at Michael Almond who pretends not to notice, 'and what do I find?'

'What do you find?'

'A website on the dark web called Knights Templar of The

Medieval Martial Arts Society of Whalehurst – open brackets – *Mass* – close brackets. Does it ring a bell? Why don't you have a look for yourself?' Riley heaves his bulk from his Maserati seat and offers it to Gillian. He points a plastic chair to Michael. 'Make yourself comfy, Michael. It's an interesting read.'

Gillian descends on Jon's computer. The website looks very professional, and very alarming. Against a stark black background, the Cross of St George is superimposed in the company of one of the most distinct neo-Nazi insignia: a swastika. In a column to the left are links to *Our Friends and Brothers in Arms*, and those feature some of the most virulent organisations Gillian has heard of, and some, probably even nastier, that she hasn't. Some of those she's heard of she knows from the *Prevent* training course. In the main they are alt-right and neo-Nazi groups selling their wares to the Millennials. A quick scan through the home page confirms the Knights Templars' of Whalehurst values and affiliations: aggressive racism, anti-Semitism, and Islamophobia. It is dressed in a pretentious and apocalyptic language with pseudo-scientific references to Nietzsche and his Über-mensch philosophy. Gillian's stomach turns, but her heart skips a beat. She has found her overarching motive: Rachel Snyder was Jewish, whilst Mohammed Abdikarim was black and Muslim. That's why they were targeted!

'So that's what they get up to, our smart-arse crusaders,' she mutters under her breath.

'That's not all. Take a look at their blog. It's that tab at the top.'

Gillian clicks on it. The latest entry is dated 1 March, the day before Watson's death. It is a pompous diatribe about the physical prowess of the Aryan race and the inferiority of all other races. The author, the *High Marshall of Whalehurst Order*, is making a solemn promise that *the drug-cheat negro will be exposed and sent away in shame; that there is no room for people like him at Whalehurst. Further updates to follow soon.* There are no updates on the website, but Gillian could write one herself: the death of Mohammed Abdikarim. This is more than they bargained for.

'This is better than a confession.' Riley rubs his hands with glee.

'Except that the *High Marshall of Whalehurst Order* isn't exactly a DNA match. We need more. Can we link the authorship of this website to any individuals at the school?'

'Hm . . . it was accessed a couple of times from the school PC, but it was set up on a different device . . . a device that is not connected to the school's network.'

'I'm going to have that school turned inside out. I'll get those damn bloody *Templars* one by one until one of them talks.' Gillian has had enough of pussy-footing around a bunch of teenage sociopaths and their rich daddies. She calls Webber and Macfadyen to meet her at the station. She is already heading for her office. The moment she gets there she will approach the duty magistrate for a search warrant, circumventing Detective Chief Superintendent Scarfe in case he tries to stop her. She has totally forgotten about Michael Almond abandoned on a plastic chair with Jon Riley for company.

Chapter Forty-three

Josh was lying in the dark with his eyes open. He could hear George's shallow breathing on the other side of their shared room; he wasn't asleep either. They had nothing to say to each other. What was there to say?

The cops had raided their headquarters and found the iPad behind the wall panel. Monty had sworn blind that one could not find an electronic device if it was switched off; Monty, the arsehole supreme, had been wrong. Their individual tablets had also been unearthed from their hidey-holes in their rooms, and confiscated. This time the police had gone through their dorms with a fine tooth comb. They had looked under mattresses and between floorboards; they had emptied their wardrobes and opened every box to inspect its contents. It looked like they knew precisely what they were looking for. The fact that they hadn't uncovered the camera in its resting place out on the sports field was of little consolation. The police had enough to go on.

That bitch detective, Marsh, was on heat, buzzing around with a mad look in her eye. She had even told her superior officer to remove himself from *her* crime scene when he turned up to demand an explanation after Featherlight had called him to complain about the damage to property. The big chief with a funny lip had listened meekly to DI Marsh and left with his tail between his legs. She had assumed full charge of the situation and wasn't taking any prisoners – or, more to the point, *not yet*!

She and her sidekick, a bloke with combed back, sleek hair and wearing a suit too smart for a copper, had set up stall in Featherlight's office, interviewing each of the Knights Templar separately. They didn't bother with anyone else in the school.

There was not a sliver of doubt in Josh's mind that the police were onto them. Now that they had got hold of the iPad it was only a matter of time before they stumbled across the website. Josh had never wanted that fucking website to go live, but Monty, the arsehole supreme, had insisted on having *a presence*. Contacts is what makes us stronger, he would waffle on and on. It's a secret society, no one will know about it – it is by invitation only. Yeah right, except now they had a gatecrasher at the door and every fucking secret was spilling out into the daylight. Dark web – secret society, bollocks to that!

A quick conference after the cops had left revealed that everyone in the group had been asked the same questions, and everyone pleaded blissful ignorance: the boys knew nothing of the existence of the iPad behind the panel in a locked room to which only they had the key; they had forgotten to mention their personal electronic devices the first time the school was searched, sorry it had slipped their collective mind to do so; none of them really knew Bradley Watson, or Mohammed Abdikarim, or Rachel Snyder sufficiently to be able to make any contributions to the police investigation . . . No, they didn't have a problem with Mo being black or Rachel being Jewish. Why would they? And as for the Knights Templar, it was just a little game they played, flirting with medieval weapons, as boys do. No, there was no particular philosophy behind it, no extreme doctrines, just a bit of fun. They had become interested in the Knights Templar after Dr Featherstone taught them about medieval history and the Crusades – an interesting period in history, was it not? Dr Featherstone was very passionate about it; it had rubbed off on them, blah, blah, blah . . . all total bullshit, of course, served neat, and the cops knew that too.

Josh was under no illusion that the two detectives bought into any of it. They had just listened. The detective sergeant had been taking notes: word by word. They would compare their statements at the station and they would find gaps and discrepancies. The Knights Templar would be as good as crucified. It would go hand in hand with their passion for the Crusades.

Joshua shuddered. A freezing-cold current travelled down his spine and made him shiver. This was a fucking catastrophe! A criminal record to his name, and his military career would go down the fucking drain; he would go back home to Mum and Dad and become an accountant, or an insurance broker, or a vicar. His life would be strapped inside a straitjacket.

With his personal links to Rachel, he had the most to fear. A number of Rachel's photos on his iPad had been photoshopped and used on Snapchat during the *Cyber Campaign*. He would have to be able to explain that; he would have to be believed. Someone would have to take the fall for this fiasco, and sure as fuck, it wouldn't be Josh.

He shifted in his bed, sat up and whispered in the dark, 'George, are you awake?'

'What do you think?' came the grudging response.

'They aren't going away.'

'I know.'

'We have to throw someone to the wolves.'

'I've been thinking that.'

'Monty's crossed the line.'

'But he'll drag all of us down with him. Plus, he has a good lawyer.'

'I know.' Josh turned on the lights. He was standing in the middle of their room, wearing only his shorts and a grim, determined expression. 'A dead man doesn't need a lawyer. And when he's dead he won't mind if he has to take the blame.'

George swallowed hard. He sat up, threw off his duvet. 'You serious?'

'Have you got any better ideas, other than we all go down?'

'In the end, Monty's fucked up and he'll have to take the flak.'

'It'll be neater this way.'

'How?'

'It has to be tonight, before the cops are back. We'll get together like we need to let our hair down, booze comes out, we'll get him drunk – It'll have to look like suicide. A guilty conscience, et cetera.'

'All of us?'

'Archie won't take any convincing. He's already pissed off with Monty big time.'

'But what about Eddie? He's Monty's lapdog.'

'Eddie will put the noose around his neck while we're all watching so he doesn't change his mind later on. We'll make sure he's up to his eyes in it.'

Chapter Forty-four

The body is dangling from one of the two sturdy hooks upon which the medieval lances used to rest. The lances are lying on the floor, alongside the swords and other weapons from the arsenal in the Knights' Templar HQ chamber. It appears that before dying Monty Collingsworth decided to make some sort of a peace offering by laying down his arms. He looks humble and defenceless hanging in place of the weapons, wearing just a white vest and a pair of boxers. Not quite the High Marshall.

He has been found after failing to turn up for the morning roll call. The whole school searched for him, not for long as they all knew where to start. They had to kick in the door to the room – apparently Monty was the only person with the key. The key was found on a leather-upholstered chair with carved wooden arms, an authentic artefact which once belonged to the Bishop of Bath and Wells and was gifted to Lord Whalehurst in the early sixteenth century. It was Monty's favourite chair, Joshua Tyler informs DI Marsh as they both stand and stare at the forensics team cutting down the body.

'You can't be here!' Only now does DI Marsh notice that a civilian is loitering unchallenged at the crime scene. 'Everybody out! Can we clear the scene, please.'

'He was my friend, he'd like me to be here,' Tyler objects tearfully, but is firmly escorted away.

Dr Featherstone breaks through the police line. He charges at Gillian, his eyes bulging with anger, foam in his mouth. He sticks his finger in Gillian's face. 'Look what you've done! This is on your conscience! You killed him! You murdering bitch!'

She recoils and makes a few unsteady steps backwards, her back hitting the wood-panelled wall.

'Take him away! Please take this man out of here!' she cries out. She can hear his threats and recriminations from the landing. An officer tells him to calm down, but that only provokes more rage.

Gillian feels a huge headache coming on. The pressure is building up in her temples and radiates towards her eyes. She sits down in the bishop's chair and squeezes the bridge of her nose, her eyes shut tight. Featherstone is right: it is her fault. She should have arrested Monty yesterday. She had sufficient circumstantial evidence to hold him in custody for further questioning. Only she had wavered. She wanted to avoid a confrontation with Scarfe – she was already in deep trouble with him for challenging his authority in public. In addition, she had expected William Jones to turn up instantly to get Monty out, tell him what to say and, effectively, undermine her investigation. She thought she could do with a bit more time and a bit more evidence. She had the iPad and it would go to Riley to check if indeed this was the device used to create and operate the Knights' Templar website. She didn't count on Monty's guilt – or fear – or shame, or all of them combined getting the better of him. She had misjudged him: she thought he had no shame or guilt, or fear. She thought he was a spoilt brat who would get away with murder unless she had crossed all her t's and dotted all her i's. So she had let him be, for now, alone with his conscience. He shouldn't have been left alone with it – he couldn't handle it. It was her fault, she had to agree with Featherstone.

Michael Almond is on the scene, giving the body a preliminary examination. He sees Gillian slumped in a chair, rubbing her forehead, her elbows sliding off its arms. 'Are you all right, Gillian?' he asks.

'Was it suicide?' She never answers questions, she only knows how to ask them. 'Has that boy killed himself? He has, hasn't he!'

236

Chapter Forty-five

Sarah sat in the front row of the gallery, arm in arm with Jonathan. He had grown a beard or more accurately let his facial hair take over his face; he hid his pain behind it. Mohammed Abdikarim's parents were here, and they too had not missed a single day of the trial. Mr Abdikarim – Abdul – had been wearing the same suit and a sequence of identical white shirts every day; he was clean shaven and particular about his appearance. And then there were the Watsons: he a gentle giant, she a small, genteel woman with a quivering voice. In adjournments of the hearing, the six of them – six bereaved parents – would gather together at the bottom of the stairs in the courtroom and look at each other, seeking a leader in their midst to take charge and tell them that there was somewhere else they had to be, something else they had to do, some purpose still left in their existence even though they had been brutally stripped of the title of parent. Sometimes, they would go for lunch together in a little independent café across the road. They had come to know each other. To fill the tortuous silences during which pain reared its ugly head and drew nails through their hearts, they would talk about their jobs and their lives, but not about their dead children. None of them could bring themselves to mention the children. It was too raw to even say their names out loud.

Sarah drew a perverse kind of comfort from knowing that the accused boys' parents were sharing the same gallery. She was acutely aware of their shell-shocked presence. They too, in a way, had lost their children and their innocence, and possibly their future had been snatched away by their vile acts. Still, their children had got to keep their lives. That's the fundamental difference between them and us, Sarah reminded herself. She blanked them out. That was the nearest she could get to forgiveness.

She and Jonathan would see DS Webber and DI Marsh every day, and nod silent greetings to them, but they didn't talk to them; there was nothing more to be said between them and the police. It was all down to the judge and the jury now.

Monty Collingsworth's father was also sitting in the gallery day in and out, but his wife could only take the first few hours of the first day before she stormed out of the courtroom, never to return. Sarah wondered if it was the shame or the pain that had sent her off. Running away and burying her head in the sand wouldn't give her peace. At least, Sarah hoped it wouldn't. She herself knew no peace and she would never know it. She didn't come to this court hoping to achieve the elusive closure – she was not naïve. She was here for two reasons: to learn the truth and to see justice done, and she would stay here to the bitter end.

Monty Collingsworth's suicide had been an escape from justice; hopefully the rest of them, Joshua Tyler, Archibald Holland, Edward Vincent, and George Cable-Rye – names she had burned into her brain with a red-hot branding tool – would pay for what they had done, for whatever their part had been in this crime. They were charged with being accessories after the fact to murder and hate-crime, the principal offender being Monty Collingsworth who, being dead, was not included in the indictment and was, regrettably, beyond the reach of law. They were facing years in prison.

All four of the accused had pleaded not guilty; three of them had already testified, singing from the same hymn sheet, claiming ignorance and pushing the entire blame onto the one who could no longer deny it. It was easy to push the blame onto the dead, put it all behind them and walk away unscathed to bask in their promising futures. But, Sarah mulled this over and over again, they had witnessed his crime, and they had stood by and done nothing to stop him.

All it takes is for one good man to do nothing for evil to triumph.

The accused young men had done exactly that. Letting it happen was a crime in Sarah's eyes. She hoped to God that the members of the jury would agree with her. Retribution had to take place for justice to be served.

Today, it was time for Joshua Tyler to give his version of events. Sarah and Jonathan had been waiting for this moment with bated breath. Jonathan had always blamed Tyler for Rachel's death and had come here 'to watch the boy swing'. He needed that for Rachel's sake, he'd told Sarah, even though Rachel would not get her day in court, her death having already been ruled upon by the Coroner. But she wouldn't have been near the river had she been tucked away in bed that night. Joshua Tyler had driven her to go to that bridge and into the river. Jonathan believed that with all his soul. Sarah didn't know what to believe. Both of them would watch the young man closely: his every gesture, every twitch of his muscles, every word that would leave his lips, and they would judge him for themselves.

Joshua Tyler took the witness box.

He'd had a haircut recently. His dark grey suit was immaculate but inexpensive to ensure that the jury did not take an instant dislike to him as a spoilt rich brat. He neither frowned nor smiled, but looked suitably overwhelmed – shocked to be here. His schoolboy's body language declared, *It's a mistake!* His gaze was steady but humble – the gaze of an innocent man. He swore on the Bible with assured conviction, his tone serious and thoughtful, his hand pressed firmly into the Good Book as he vowed to tell the truth, the whole truth and nothing but the truth. He was so young, Sarah marvelled, so young and beautiful that, surely, he was nothing but innocent.

'Mr Tyler,' his barrister began, 'you don't deny being a member of an organisation that called itself the Knights Templar or the Medieval Martial Arts Society of Whalehurst?'

'No, I don't. I joined as the captain of Falcon House, just like Eddie and George, and Archie. All the house captains and of course the Head Boy are expected to join the Mass. It's a tradition at Whalehurst.'

'So by joining, you just complied with the tradition, correct?'

'Yes.'

'Did you feel under pressure to join?'

'No. I liked the idea of training in martial arts and I liked the code of honour that went with membership of the group. It was a privilege, and a responsibility as well – responsibility for the wellbeing of all the students at Whalehurst. I liked that. I've been well looked after at Whalehurst all the years I have been there. I felt I ought to give something back to the school.' Tyler nodded towards the gallery where Dr Featherstone sat in the second row, wiping an unruly paternal tear from his cheek. The eyes of the jury were drawn to the headmaster who in his tweed jacket cut a respectable and trustworthy figure.

'That's very commendable, Mr Tyler.' Having paused to give the jury the chance to absorb Joshua's words, his barrister continued, 'But there was a darker side to Knights Templar, wasn't there? The website with neo-Nazi affiliations which the Crown has already explored in some detail with your co-accused, and will no doubt, wish to talk to you about.'

'I had no knowledge of that website. I didn't know Monty had set it up.'

'Surely you knew Monty had far-right leanings – racism, anti-Semitism! You were friends, you must've known!'

Joshua Tyler lowered his gaze in demonstration of shame. This was bound to be the point of divergence between his and the other boys' testimonies. He wouldn't be able to deny his relationship and abrupt break-up with Rachel, and he would have to – have to! – explain why.

Sarah Snyder leant forward, her whole body taut with expectation.

When he lifted his gaze, his eyes were glazed with welling-up tears. They were fixed on Sarah when he finally spoke in a shaky, feeble voice, 'I knew . . . I mean, I suspected. I'll never forgive myself for letting him play me for a fool . . .' He sniffled and drew in a wheezy breath. 'I really cared for Rachel –'

Jonathan squeezed Sarah's hand. Blood rushed into her finger-tips; they went purple-red.

'Rachel Snyder?'

'Yes. She was a beautiful person, great fun, clever and . . .'

Sarah knew Jonathan was crying. His fingers were clutching her hand. He was squeezing so hard that it hurt. She glanced at him, their eyes locked on each other, their pain shared.

'We had a fantastic thing going, she invited me to her house, I met her parents . . .' Tyler offered them another contrite look, acknowledging their presence and paying tokenistic respect. 'When I came back to the dorms, I couldn't stop talking about them. I was so excited . . . They made me feel so welcome, like I was at home with my own mum and dad. It was then that I mentioned to Monty that they were Jewish. I'd only just found out. Jonathan – um, that's Rachel's dad – told me that they were celebrating Hanukkah, the Jewish festival of lights. I was fascinated. I shared that with Monty, and it bothered him.'

'Did it bother you – that they were Jewish?'

'No, not at all! It didn't – doesn't – matter to me. It was just an . . . interesting thing about Rachel. Unique . . . So, I said it. Monty went sort of sanctimonious on me. He . . . how do I put it? . . . He told me off!'

'For what?'

'For mixing with the Jews. I could tell it wasn't a joke to him. He was laughing, but it wasn't funny, and he didn't mean for it to be funny. He was deriding me . . . And I am so, so very ashamed to admit it, but I caved in . . .' He stopped, wiped his nose with his thumb and forefinger. His puppy eyes welled up. 'I gave in to him . . . I realised Monty didn't approve of me and Rachel because of . . . of who she was . . . I didn't want to make an enemy out of Monty. He was . . . he didn't tolerate dissent gladly . . .'

'Dissent?' Jonathan hissed under his breath. Sarah blinked away tears. So, Joshua Tyler broke her daughter's heart in the name of *harmony* – to please his deranged friend? Such a small price . . . The tears broke out and burned her cheeks.

'The next day I . . . I told Rachel that . . . that . . . she and I, we just . . . that it was over.'

'Did you tell her why?'

'No, of course not. I came up with an excuse – I said I had to focus on my A levels. She was devastated. I'm so sorry.' He hung his head. Sniffled. Looked up towards the gallery. 'But I didn't know Monty would go as far as to start this whole hideous campaign against Rachel. Believe me, I didn't have a clue! I was as shocked as everyone else by all that weird stuff that was being posted. At first, I genuinely thought that it was Rachel, that she was . . . um . . . angry, that she'd lost it . . . If I had known Monty was behind it, I would've stopped him. It was disgusting, what he did . . .' He peeked at the jury. It was a sideways glance from under his eyelashes as if he was assessing their reactions. It didn't feel remorseful. It felt contrived.

It was at this point that Sarah became certain that this was an act. Joshua Tyler was a lying shit. She had to fight back an impulse to stand up and spit in his face.

The barrister walked towards the stand to face her client. 'Mr Tyler, I'll ask you this now because the Prosecution is bound to raise it anyway: can you explain how the photographs of you and Rachel, from your personal iPad, have come to be used in the Snapchat stream that was part of Monty's cyberbullying campaign? If you had no knowledge of the bullying that went on, how is it that your private photos were used?'

'I can only guess that Monty must've got hold of them from my iPad. He knew my password. He knew I had those photos.

We often shared media and music on each other's iPads. We had no secrets – that way ... I mean, I had no secrets from him, but Monty ...' He suspended his voice, let it quiver on that cliff-hanger note.

Yes, it was just theatrics. He had been well coached by the team of lawyers his diplomat father had employed and paid good money for. But he was too good at acting, too Shakespearean: all method and no room for the heart.

'I see.' The barrister sent a loaded glance towards the jury, playing her part as a support actress to perfection. Then she leant closer to her client. 'Mr Tyler, are you an anti-Semite?'

'No!' was followed by a horrified stare, followed by a dramatic pause, followed by: 'God, no!'

'Let's move on to the murder of Bradley Watson. We have heard the testimonies of your friends, but the jury wants to have the fullest possible picture of what happened there. Can you shed some light on the Friday night in question?'

'We were in the pavilion. It was late at night, we were drink-ing. It was against the rules, but it was Eddie's birthday, so ... we're just having fun. Brad turned up. I thought he had just gate-crashed, like he used to sometimes ... I saw him talking to Monty. Brad handed a camera to Monty. I didn't make much of it. I thought maybe Brad had sold it to him. Brad was a wheeler-dealer sort of person, always handy if you needed something from outside.'

'Did you know he was dealing drugs?'

'Not until that night.'

'How so?'

'An argument broke out between Monty and Brad. Monty was pushing Brad, and Brad wasn't having it. They were right in each other's faces. It looked like a scuffle, but not very serious, not at first. I don't know exactly what was being said. Then Brad shouted something and took off. Monty grabbed a bow and a handful of arrows, and went after him. We all followed to see what ... And then we saw it. It was unreal ...' Tyler shook his head and looked directly at the jury so that they could see the horror in his eyes, the horror of a man who was no more than a witness to a crime. Then his eyes shifted towards the gallery to find the Watsons. An expression of deep sympathy was stamped on his face. He had it all so well-rehearsed!

He gave his account breathlessly, 'I didn't see it coming. Brad was running. He must have realised that Monty was serious. Monty stopped, adopted position, aimed and . . . he shot him in the back, between his shoulder blades. I . . . I . . .' He brought a shaking hand to his forehead and rubbed it repeatedly.

'Do you need a break, Mr Tyler?'

He looked up, pale and droopy-eyed. 'No. I can . . . I will try. Let me . . . By the time we got to Brad, he was dead. I checked his pulse – he was dead. Monty caught up with us. He was standing over Brad, he didn't bend down or anything. He looked mad, really mad. Threatening, like he was prepared to kill again! At that moment I was scared for my life. He said . . . I remember his exact words. He said: "He's been dealing here, in our school, to our kids. Scum. I gave him a fair chance to stop."'

'So why didn't you report this to the police?'

'At first, I think it was the shock, then the fear . . . I'm sorry, I was weak and a coward. Stupid, I know, but I was worried that we would be found out for drinking alcohol on the school premises. There are strict rules about that at Whalehurst – we could've been expelled. But most of all I was afraid of Monty. He scared us all. I thought he had lost it. I didn't recognise him. He wasn't himself. Then he took a deep breath and was calmer. We talked – he talked, and he reminded us it was our duty to protect the pupils at Whalehurst. You know, we were the Knights Templar, the guardians of the school . . . And Brad was the scourge, a drug dealer who wouldn't stop!' He gulped and peered at the jury. Sarah was looking towards them too. A couple of them, a middle-aged man and an elderly woman were both nodding. Joshua Tyler had hit the right note with them. He was playing his cards masterfully. 'I regret that. I was misguided and naïve. I know I should've called the police, and I apologise to Brad's parents for failing him . . .'

His words trailed off – another emotional chord struck with mastery.

'Let's move to Mohammed Abdikarim.'

'He was a great athlete. And a nice boy with huge promise. I admired him . . .' Joshua Tyler was in full swing now, reciting his lines without a single stumble.

'He received a lethal dose of a performance-enhancing hormone. According to the blog on the Knights Templar website, your society's website, the plan was to discredit Mohammed as a drug cheat, all because of his skin colour.'

'I didn't know what Monty was up to. It is unbelievable. It's insane! I don't think I knew Monty at all. He was a monster.'

Monty's father jumped to his feet and nearly tumbled over the balustrade as he screamed, 'Liar! You're a fucking liar! All of you, liars!'

Sarah watched passively as he was removed from the courtroom. The proceedings were adjourned following his scuffle with the security officers.

Chapter Forty-six

The foreman of the jury was directed to stand up four times to declare the jury's verdict on the charges of being accessories to murder brought against Archibald Holland, George Cable-Rye, Edward Vincent, and Joshua Tyler.

One by one, each of the accused men stood up to hear the verdict, and each time they cried with relief when they heard the words: 'Not guilty.' By the time it came to Joshua Tyler, Sarah had little doubt that he too would be absolved of any wrongdoing.

He was standing upright, his jaw tight with enormous tension, his eyes fixed on the foreman, willing him to stick to his mantra.

And he did. 'Not guilty,' he announced loud and clear.

Briefly, on an impulse, Tyler lowered his guard of regret and humility. He thrust his chin forward and punched the air with his fist. It was more like a salute than a punch: brisk and self-congratulatory.

Behind her, Sarah could hear the four boys' parents laughing, shaking each other's hands and thanking God that all was well that ended well. Their children would come back home − safe and sound − and be once again on the straight and narrow route to their bright and happy futures. The noises those people were making hammered at the back of Sarah's head. Instinctively, she hunched her shoulders and shut her eyes.

She and the other bereaved parents were led out of the courthouse through a side door to escape the onslaught of the press waiting at the bottom of the stairs by the main entrance. From a distance, they watched the young men, their parents and their jubilant lawyers giving interviews and reading out official statements prepared earlier. They had always known they would get away with it. The court hearing had been a charade, a show put up for public entertainment.

'Bastard.' Jonathan's eyes drilled into the smiling ex-boyfriend of his dead daughter. Somehow, Joshua detected that glare and looked back at Jonathan and at Sarah. He kept smiling. Open derision stole into that smile. The regret, the tears, and his earlier dramatic contrition had all but vanished.

He was laughing at them.

Sarah touched Jonathan's shoulder. 'Let's go home.'

He jerked under her touch and looked at her as if he was trying to remember who she was. He inhaled the musky April air, heavy with the earlier rain. 'You go. I'll walk home. I want to be alone. Sorry.'

Sarah let him go. She walked slowly to her car and sat there for a while with her door closed. She had an overwhelming sense of Rachel sitting next to her, curled up in the passenger seat, playing with the radio buttons, looking for a music channel. Sarah peered at her stealthily, only pretending to have her eyes on the road. She was desperate to find reassurance in Rachel's face that she was happy wherever she was.

She started the engine; her foot slipping off the pedal, the engine giving out a shriek. She remembered what Rachel used to think of her driving – not much. She sobbed to the memories of their banter in the car, to and from school. She wanted it back. Back!

Joshua Tyler, flanked by his parents, was crossing the car park, heading for a burgundy Audi parked opposite Sarah. His father gave him a chummy pat on the back. It was a manly and playful gesture all in one. Tyler offered his father a mock soldier's salute. They laughed. His mother, an elegant if slightly overweight woman wearing a long leather coat, hugged him and planted a kiss on his cheek. Tyler seemed to wince and pulled back a bit. His mother did not notice his reticence to be kissed in public. She was blinded with happiness and motherly love.

They jumped into their car and started reversing from their parking bay, levelling for a split second with Sarah's car. From the back-seat window, Tyler glanced up, but appeared not to recognise her. He put headphones on and started nodding his head to the music.

Sarah was compelled to follow them – to deal with it once and for all. She was not going to let them get away with it. She would cling to them like a bad dream. She would be their voice of conscience.

She tailed them all the way on the motorway, waited for them at the petrol station where they refuelled and bought sandwiches and coffee for the road. She couldn't imagine how they could feel hungry, how they could just get on with their lives in such a care-free, ordinary way. Her throat was tight; she couldn't swallow her own bile.

She took the same turn-off as they had done and followed them along a dual carriageway, and then off onto a narrow country lane, winding its way through a wooded area. A deep ditch lined the road to the left, with trees and shrubs reaching towards the sky without a hope of ever touching it. The bends were sharp and well-signed as such. The Tylers were clearly familiar with this stretch of road. They gathered speed and Sarah nearly lost them over the next rise.

She could not lose them! She was the voice of their conscience! She sped up. Yes, she was a reckless driver, Rachel would testify to that. She didn't have to know the road to be able to negotiate it at the speed of light.

She caught up with the Tylers and she couldn't – wouldn't – step on the brake pedal when the bumper of her four-wheel drive hit the back of theirs. In fact, some excited, unrelenting voice compelled her to accelerate. She was now pushing the Tylers' Audi off the road and down the deep and steep slope. She could see Joshua's eyes as he turned in his seat at the back of the car to look at the maniac who was driving them off the road.

This time he recognised her, panic set in, his eyes round with fear and he hit the rear window with the palms of his hands, screaming an inaudible 'Noooo!'

She wouldn't listen to him. She could only hear the voice in her head. The engine of her car roared as she rammed one more time into the Audi, which nosedived into the ditch and summersaulted in the air to land on its roof.

Chapter Forty-seven

They were going through the motions as they had always done, as if nothing had happened to make them change anything in their daily routines. Jonathan put the TV on at exactly 6pm to watch the news – a BBC reporter stood in front of the court-house relaying the not-guilty verdict and expanding on the relief that the families of the accused must be feeling right now; there wasn't a mention of the families of the victims, but in view of the not-guilty verdict the reporter would be libellous if he so much as intimated the young men could in any way be accountable to the bereaved relatives.

Sarah cooked dinner while the news was on. It was nothing fancy, tagliatelle from frozen with tomato sauce from a tin. They sat at the table, peering at their plates, biding their time. Neither of them touched their food. Neither of them touched on the sub-ject of the concluded trial. They would not be able to digest it. Instead, they drank tea and sat down in the lounge to watch the rest of the News: the children of Aleppo about whom nobody really cared were staring back at them with their big, frightened eyes. *They are alive*, Sarah mused resentfully. She shouldn't have, but she was not in charge of her own mind. Jonathan tried to draw a comparison between those children and the case but lost his thread halfway through the sentence. *Because they are still alive and Rachel is not,* the stubborn thought returned to Sarah.

At half ten Jonathan asked her if she was coming to bed. She said no, not yet. She was sitting on the sofa from which she had not moved in the last few hours, still dressed in her courtroom smart trouser suit. She was waiting.

Jonathan stood in the doorway, uncertain if he should just give her some space and go to bed on his own. A blue flash of frantic lights dying on their driveway jolted him from his reverie. He looked out of the window to see DS Webber and DI Marsh get out of a police car.

'What do they want now?' he asked her. 'I don't think I can deal with them right now . . .'

Sarah got up, went to the hallway and started putting on her coat and shoes. 'Let them in. They're here for me.'

'What do you mean?' He watched her, puzzled and alarmed, but he opened the door.

'Mr Snyder,' DS Webber said, his expression strangely apologetic, 'I'm very sorry but we need to speak to your wife.'

'Yes, come in. I've been waiting for you.' She rose from tying up her shoelaces.

'What's going on?' Jonathan stood sandwiched in the narrow hallway between her and DS Webber.

'I'm so sorry,' the policeman repeated incomprehensibly.

DI Marsh stepped forward, 'Sarah Snyder, you are under arrest on suspicion of murder and attempted murder –'

'I know, I know,' she nodded. She fixed her eyes on her husband and said, 'I love you.'

She was glad it was over. She was glad she could finally get out of the straitjacket of her own family home. She was glad she did not have to come back here, not for a long, long time. She had no regrets.

Chapter Forty-eight

The inventory of his injuries was long, but nothing that would cause permanent disability: a broken collarbone and a few cracked ribs, minor concussion, and lots of superficial bruising. Joshua had been thrown out of the car before it rolled on its roof and caught fire, thus dispatching Mum and Dad to the high heavens in a puff of smoke.

Joshua would have loved to have seen it: the petrol dripping out of the broken gas tank, a rivulet of it snaking its way to the smoking engine until BANG!

Apparently, death had been instantaneous; they wouldn't have suffered, it would have been too quick for them to register pain. DI Marsh assured Josh of that the moment he opened his eyes and asked what had happened to him and why he was here, in a hospital bed. She had been sitting by his bedside all night, waiting for him to wake up.

The woman was a tenacious bitch, Josh had to give her that. *A pit bull bitch*, he smiled under his breath, thinking of her with a certain dose of admiration. She was on his wavelength – on some level . . . She had been quick and unfeeling when she had offered him her insincere condolences, and then promptly moved on to ask him what the last thing was that he could remember.

He had told her, of course. And not without a sense of satisfaction. He clearly remembered feeling the impact of his father's car being smashed from behind – he remembered looking back – he remembered seeing Rachel's mother, Mrs Snyder, at the wheel of a large four-wheel drive – he remembered her face: deadpan, cold – he remembered calling out to her to stop. And then he remembered nothing until the moment he woke up in hospital.

'Are you sure it was Mrs Snyder?' DI Marsh had asked.

'Yes,' he had replied firmly and definitively, and turned away from her. He wanted her to go and arrest the bloody woman.

She had taken him by surprise and he didn't like that. He had dismissed her as a silly airhead. Even Rachel used to say that her mum was a harmless nutter, harmless being the key word. Not so! She was mad as fuck, true, but she wasn't harmless. The vicious bitch had nearly killed him!

In his hospital bed, Josh was contemplating the effects of her unexpected attack. He had his own room with a TV set and a nurse in and out of the room like a yo-yo. That was the luxury of having private medical insurance – no expense was spared: the best doctors, the dishiest nurses. *Thank you, Dad! Wherever you are – thanks, pal!*

He had just watched the six o'clock news – all about him and the others, and their reportedly relieved families. So, the media had not yet caught up with the killing of his parents, courtesy of Mrs Snyder. That was bound to be another nationwide sensation. Slowly, he was gaining celebrity status. Josh smirked at his comforting musings. He had a few reasons to smile, frankly. He had got away with killing two people, and giving a third one a gentle nudge into the afterlife. Poor Rachel hadn't been made for this world. Pain in the arse! She had been too clingy for her own good and wouldn't take no for an answer. A pity she couldn't take a joke . . . Brad had been a fucking liability, too. And a moron! He just couldn't understand the basic concept of keeping his mouth shut. And Monty? A pompous twat with a brain of a five-year-old with a Spiderman complex. Josh didn't mind him playing his little games with Mo, for whatever bizarre reasons, but he did bloody well mind him not covering his tracks properly. Monty had become a loose cannon and had had to be reined in.

A pretty nurse with a small waist and a nice pair of tits entered his room to check on him and scribble something on his chart. She had replaced the other one, Jane or something. Jane, a Jamaican and in her mid-forties, she was old by Josh's standards and held no interest for him. This one was young and sweet. He read her nametag: Emily. *Sweet name, Emily . . .*

'How are you feeling, Joshua?' Emily asked as she puffed up his pillow, her well-endowed chest level with his eyes.

'Fabulous.' He could see no reason why he would need to lie to her.

She smiled awkwardly and left. Josh watched her perky little behind with pleasure. There certainly were some wonderful benefits to private hospitals, thank you Mum and thank you Dad. *Thanks for thinking of everything!*

Joshua expected he would have more to thank his parents for soon: he recalled vaguely that he was the sole beneficiary of his father's in-service death grant. A neat sum of money would soon be coming his way, which was a welcome development. As was the fact that from now on there would be nobody out there clinging onto him and smothering him with unrequited love. It was funny how things had a way of falling back into place for those who didn't lose their nerve. Fucking marvellous!

Chapter Forty-nine

'I felt rotten arresting Sarah Snyder.' Webber is staring at the bottom of his glass. They have gathered at The Bull's Eye for an informal debriefing. Gillian has dragged Michael Almond with her – they have become inseparable recently.

'I know. I feel the same way, but we had no choice, she killed two people in cold blood, and put a third in hospital,' Gillian reminds him in the unlikely case that he might have forgotten. It is her way of making him feel better.

'Cold blood?' Mark groans. 'You've no idea what that woman's been through. Cold blood doesn't come into it. Everything is always so black and white with you, it makes me sick.'

'Well, it isn't, actually.' Gillian too reflects on the bottom of her empty glass. She wrestles with her own guilt – that for Monty Collingsworth's suicide. She can't resurrect him in order to keep him safely in police custody, so she pushes the pesky guilt out of her mind and rounds on Erin, 'It's your shout now. I'll have the same.'

Erin rolls her eyes. 'I was going home, but all right. Everyone the same?'

'Not for me, I'm driving.' Michael is the only one to show some self-restraint.

'What do you mean by *it isn't*?' Webber stubbornly returns to the topic of Sarah Snyder whom he has come to idolise in recent days. He now grasps at the straws. If there is any possibility –

'OK, I've been having my doubts.'

'About Sarah Snyder?'

'No, no doubt about that – she killed the Tylers, and meant to do it. The case . . . it just fits together too neatly. One – conveniently dead – perpetrator . . . And going back to Monty Collingsworth – his suicide. Something niggles at the back of my mind. Things don't add up. One: the key. Featherstone claimed there were two keys to that room: one, he gave to Monty, the other one, he kept with all the spares in his office, in a drawer, but it was gone by the time of Monty's death. He couldn't tell when precisely it had been removed from the keyring. The boys all vowed that there was only one key and that the headmaster was confused. What could be easier than making that fool Featherstone look confused and incompetent, and this is exactly why I'm having my doubts. Those damn *Templars* were too vocal about it. How would they know whether the headmaster had another key or not? Why would they emphasise that point so forcefully? The whole show with breaking down the door and finding the key lying on that chair for all to see . . . I'll tell you why: they were creating a diversion, to lead us towards their pre-fabricated conclusions. A second key would undermine the suicide theory if the door could've been locked from outside and Monty's key planted on that damned throne . . . I don't know . . . It's just so contrived . . . Too neat . . .'

'Maybe, but finding the second key wouldn't *prove* that it wasn't suicide.' Erin lowers the tray with the drinks for everyone to grab their glass.

'But it would introduce reasonable doubt.' Gillian takes a sip of her red wine. She hasn't eaten so she knows she is going to wake up with a nasty headache tomorrow morning. That's what drinking on an empty stomach invariably does to her.

'Is that it?' Webber asks.

'No, there is one more thing: Monty's motive for killing himself is conspicuous by its absence. I remember, throughout the time I had spent with the little shit, the boy was an arrogant cock-sure little so-and-so. I wanted to wring his neck a few times. His and his lawyer's . . . Unless I really misread him, he thought he'd got away scot-free. William Jones, that pompous arse, had got him out on the stolen prescription angle, and that was Monty's weakest point. He was totally unfazed when we interviewed him about the website. Actually, he was even pushing his luck, making comments about everyone in the school being a computer geek *and* a master archer – were we planning to arrest all of them, and so on. I just didn't get the feeling that he was about to top himself.'

Erin and Mark nod in agreement.

Michael Almond speaks out of the blue, 'And it is possible that he didn't.'

Everybody's eyes are on him. Gillian demands, 'Explain that.'

'It's simple, really, and it's been there, staring you lot in the face. The level of alcohol in his bloodstream was so high that it is possible that he may have struggled to tie the knot on that rope, as professionally as it was done, and string himself up on that hook – at least, not without some help. Of course, he could've prepared everything in advance, before he got intoxicated, and the alcohol came in later for some Dutch courage, but . . .'

'But what?' Gillian's cheeks are burning. She can't believe what she is hearing. Even an outside chance of . . .

'Well, the rope was burned . . . Not all of it, only a stretch of a metre and a half. The rest of it was pristine, brand new. Have you not asked yourselves why? Because theoretically it may have been damaged by the weight of a body as it was being strung up. The rope would have been sliding against the hook and creating considerable friction, if we assume for the sake of argument that a weight of a body was already attached to it. Frankly, it is something I would've explored if I were in your shoes.'

'Why didn't you mention that before then? For crying out loud, this is a vital piece of information and you just let it slide! You should've highlighted it, for pity's sake, Almond!'

'I did – I referred to the state of the rope in my report, but during the Coroner's inquest nobody took it up. I think all the other evidence swayed the Corner towards the suicide verdict.'

'No, it's my fault.' Gillian grinds her teeth. She was so perturbed, so troubled by Monty's supposed suicide . . . she so blamed herself that she did not register Almond's remarks. She couldn't bring herself to read it properly. 'I . . . I should've read the autopsy report.'

'You haven't?'

'I . . . couldn't bring myself.' She bites her lip.

'On that note,' Webber rides in to the rescue, 'I attended the examination – I should've spotted it. I should've said something. You were in pieces . . . It was down to me. I mean, the lesions to his lips and the bruising . . . I should've . . .'

'Yes, there were clear indicators Collingsworth had been in a fist fight before he hanged himself – or was hanged . . .'

'That's it then, we're re-opening Monty Collingsworth's case tomorrow.' If Gillian was in pieces, she has now picked herself up. She has a murder investigation to conclude. 'Go home now and get some rest. It's full steam ahead tomorrow morning. Mark, you're on good terms with the Super – talk to him first thing in the morning, get his blessing to re-open the Collingsworth case. Say, new evidence came to light, the usual spiel. Almond,' she fixes Michael with a stern glare, oblivious to the fact that once again she is imperially addressing him by his surname. 'I want that report of yours on my desk by eight a.m. Add some meat to the bone on that wretched rope. Erin, you'll get the magistrate to authorise another search warrant for the room where Collingsworth was found. Fine tooth comb – nothing must get past us.'

Chapter Fifty

Gillian has had a good think about this. She has spent the whole night mulling it over, pacing the width and the length of her house, re-evaluating every finest detail of this case. She had to determine which one of the Knights Templar was the weakest link. It wouldn't be easy to break through their closed ranks. In her mind she went through all of the boys' testimonies at the trial and she found him: Edward Vincent.

Accompanied by his lawyer, Eddie is gaping at DI Marsh and DS Webber, ganged up against him on the opposite side of a narrow table in the interview room. He doesn't understand why he has been brought to the police station now that the case is closed and his name cleared. He is frightened. He is pale. He looks like he is cold. His head is wobbling slightly on his very long neck – a poppy head on a thin stem ruffled by a breeze. He definitely comes across as someone who has a lot to hide. Gillian is confident that she has chosen the right man. He is the wheel that will come off and derail the Knights' Templar wagon.

She now puts the exhibit bag 17/MC in front of him. 'Do you recognise this key?'

He stares. Shakes his wobbly head.

'Speak up for the tape, please.'

'I don't think I do.'

'Let me refresh your memory. This is the second key to the Knights' Templar HQ. You know, the key that doesn't exist . . . Remember?'

'No.'

'I can see why you can't remember it. It didn't exist until we found it. Did I mention? We searched your headquarters. Again. I know, a bit of overkill, but look what we've found!' DI Marsh dangles the bag with the key in front of Eddie. 'You know where we found it, don't you?'

'No.'

'In the same place where we'd found the iPad. Funny that, don't you think? A coincidence like that . . .'

'Was that a question?' Eddie's lawyer enquires.

'It will be,' she barks at him. 'Did you really think that we wouldn't look twice in the same place?'

'I . . . don't . . .' Eddie exhales his frustration.

'You didn't? You thought it was a stroke of genius to put it in the old hidey-hole, didn't you?'

'No. It wasn't me.'

'Who was it then?'

'I don't know.' Eddie is visibly trembling.

'Are you scared of someone, Eddie?'

'No.'

DS Webber speaks softly, 'You can talk to us, Eddie. We'll protect you if you tell us the truth.'

Eddie peers timidly at his lawyer. There is a hint of hesitation in his eyes, but the lawyer addresses DS Webber. 'That wasn't a question either. My client is happy to answer questions. You need to put questions to my client.'

DI Marsh groans. 'OK, here is a question for you, Edward: did you boys hang Monty Collingsworth? All of you together? Was it hard to string him up? Was his body heavy?'

Eddie's body is shaking uncontrollably, his face contorting into a grimace straight from Munch's *Scream*.

'You don't have to answer that, Edward.' The lawyer tries to sound calm and assertive, his tone telling Eddie to hold his nerve. He readjusts his black-rimmed glasses and fixes Gillian with a condemning look. 'Those are speculations, DI Marsh, and you know it. Unsubstantiated speculations. If there is nothing concrete you wish to produce for my client's comments, I insist you release him now.'

'The rope.' Gillian heaves onto the table exhibit bag 3/MC. She pulls out of it the rope and shows it to Eddie. 'Can you see, Eddie, how this rope is frayed here, all the way . . .' She uncoils the rope, running her fingers along the roughed-up edge of it. 'We had it re-examined for any foreign fibres, any DNA, any tiniest molecules . . . so if anyone other than Monty handled this rope, we will know! And we found blood traces in the carpet . . . Monty was in a fight before he died. It could be his blood, but it could also be the other person's blood. Is it yours?'

'No! No! No!' Eddie explodes. 'That was Archie . . . I swear . . . And I . . . I didn't want to . . . They made me! Josh said we were in it together. It was my turn . . . He made me do it!'

'Do what, Eddie? Do what?'

'Stop now! I need time to confer with my client. We want a break!' the lawyer squealed.

'Yes. You may need one. We'll wait outside.' DI Marsh smiled. She had them. She knew she had them!

With Edward Vincent turning Crown witness and the other two striking a plea bargain, all the fractured bits of the puzzle have fallen neatly into place. Gillian and the team are bagging all exhibits in the Regina v Joshua Tyler case for delivery to the CPS Office. Every item has been checked against the index. That includes a long-focus lens CoolPix camera with an SD card full of horrific images that has been uncovered in the sports field of Whalehurst School, under the stands. One of the sniffer dogs tried to lead them there at the start of this investigation, Gillian recalls. If only they had followed that damned dog, they would have had Joshua Tyler there and then. Only his and Bradley Watson's fingerprints were on it.

Gillian is sorting out the paperwork. She reads Eddie's statement for the hundredth time and the horrific events of the night of Friday, 2 March, unfold before her eyes all over again.

Bradley is making the last phone call he will ever make. He has spotted Rachel wading into the river. He panics. He can't swim. He rings Josh on his Pay-as-You-Go mobile.

'Josh? It's me. I don't know who to call, mate . . . She's gone nuts.'

'What you mean?'

'She's going into the water – the river . . . You know that bridge on Ascombe? Yeah? Shit, mate! Someone's got to get her out. She's up to her waist. I'm fuckin' callin' the cops!'

'No, wait! Wait for us. We're on our way. Just watch her.'

'Thanks, mate.'

By that time, the Knights Templar are high as kites. They've been celebrating Eddie's birthday and entertaining themselves online at Rachel Snyder's expense, using the photos they commissioned Brad to take of her and popping party pills that Brad supplied them with.

They arrive in full force fifteen minutes later: Monty, Josh, Archie, George, and the birthday boy, Eddie. They are in good spirits, chuckling amongst themselves. Brad is relieved. He has been watching Rachel with bated breath as she searched through reeds and shrubs, looking for something, probably that iPad which she dropped from the bridge minutes earlier. He can't see her anymore.

'Here . . . here,' he waves to them.

'She still there?' Monty asks.

'She must be . . . but I can't see her.'

It is Monty who first lights his mobile phone's torch and shines it at the river; the others follow suit. Josh sings away, 'Raaachel, Raaachel, where are youuuuuuu?'

'Josh?' It is her. She answers him and the beams of their torches criss-cross in the direction of her voice. 'Josh, you believed me . . . Oh, thank you for coming!'

Josh sniggers, and then shouts towards her, 'No problem, Rach!'

'I'm a bit stuck! My foot . . . Could you help me?'

'What? Get wet? Come on, Rach, what do you take me for?'

Josh can't contain his amusement. He bursts out in laughter. The others join in.

'Who's there with you?' Rachel is alarmed.

'All of us, Rach. We're all here,' Josh teases.

'Raaachel . . . Raaachel . . .' They are all echoing Josh. 'Where are thou, Raaachel . . .' They are playing with the beams from their torches which skid across the surface of the water, hitting the girl in the face, dazzling her.

'Stop it!'

'Awww . . . who's been a little piggy?' Monty chuckles. 'Little Miss Piggy!'

'Stop it! Please . . .'

Josh snatches the camera out of Brad's hands. 'Pose for another photo, Rach! You're so good at being bad!' The flash of the camera goes berserk as a series of clicks triggers it. Rachel's mortified face is captured seconds before she turns her face and pulls away, deeper into the river. It is a matter of less than a minute when they lose sight of her.

'She's gone? What the fuck?' Eddie sobers up.

They wait in complete silence, hoping for a splash, a crack, anything.

Silence.

'She fucking drowned,' Josh says.

'Seriously . . .'

'Seriously she fucking drowned!' He is laughing his head off. It has to be the drugs. 'Drowned! Plop! Plop!' He pinches his nose and acts like he's going under.

'Someone's got to get her out!' Brad is the only who doesn't find it funny.

'Be my guest,' Josh points towards the river.

'I can't swim . . .'

They are hooting with laughter. Brad swears at them, 'Fuck off. Just fuck off!'

'Let's go. It's nothing to do with us.' Monty leads the way back to the school. Archie and George follow. Eddie hesitates.

Josh puts his hand on his shoulder. 'You're not staying, are you?'

'No . . . no.'

'Brad, you're coming too.'

'I'm going home. I've had it.'

'No, you're not. You're coming with us.'

They walk down the riverside path in total silence. The twenty-minute walk clears their heads and by the time they are back at the pavilion, they stare at each other, morose and scared. Monty turns on the iPad to delete the Facebook posts and close Rachel's account, which they re-activated earlier. Brad insists on going home. He is muttering something about being in shit and refusing to go back inside.

'Shut the fuck up!' Josh orders him.

'She's dead, Josh, and I'm not going down for it. If anyone saw me there, if the cops get the scent of me . . .' Bradley is losing it. 'I'm not . . . my old man – he'd fucking die if I went back inside! We gonna call the cops, tell them it was an accident –'

'No, we're not.'

'They'll know I was there. They'll know, man!'

'Stop shitting yourself!'

'I'm off to call the cops. What if she's still alive? What if they can still save her?' Brad gets up and starts walking towards the door.

'Stay where you are,' Josh growls, but he ignores him.

'You can't stop me!'

They are following him. It may be Monty or perhaps George who picks up a bow, strings an arrow and shoots. For fun. That's how it all starts.

It's a joke. It is meant to hit the floor next to Brad to spook him. And it does. He picks up pace and runs out into the night, crossing the sports field towards Ogburn Park. They start shooting around him, expelling Apache war cries. Arrows fly. Brad looks over his shoulder, trips and falls. He gets up. Runs. They send another volley of arrows. It's fun. It's like a hunting party with Brad as the prey. It's harmless. They're using only practice heads. They laugh.

All but Josh.

'He's gonna rat on us,' he says, and asks, 'Who'll do it?' He is holding an arrow with a sharp black steel head.

They stop laughing.

'Where did you get that?' George asks and gets no answer.

'You're not serious?' Eddie is incredulous.

'OK, it's me then.' Josh has a strangely manic twinkle in his eye. He nocks the arrow onto the bowstring and fine-tunes it into place. With a steady hand he aligns the sharp point of the arrowhead with Brad's back. Brad is beginning to climb the fence, but he won't make it to the other side alive. Josh releases the arrow and it hits Brad, right between his shoulder blades.

'Fuck . . .' mutters George.

Eddie takes off after Brad, but Josh hauls him back. 'Leave him there. He's dead, I assure you. He won't talk.'

Eddie stumbles back and falls on his backside. He can't speak.

Monty says, 'We've got to pick up all those fucking arrows.'

'Yeah, you do that,' Josh agrees. 'I'll bury the incriminating evidence, and then off to bed, gentlemen, for a good night's sleep. It's gonna be the hell of a day tomorrow when they find poor Brad.'

Chapter Fifty-one

The razorblade hovers dangerously close to his Adam's apple. It glints in the light reflected in the mirror. His head is thrown backwards and he peers down his nose at the reflection of his mortified face. He clutches the arms of the chair and shuts his eyes.

'OK, get on with it before I change my mind,' he mutters through his chattering teeth.

She presses the blade to his throat and swipes it upwards, the two-day stubble falling off his skin like dry crumbs. All is well until she hits the moustache.

'Bloody hell, is this reinforced with concrete? I'll need shears to shift it!' Gillian puts away the razor. It looks like Michael's moustache has morphed into a thatch. She leaves him in the chair and starts fumbling through the kitchen drawers in search of industrial scissors. She finds a pair, and returns holding the scissors triumphantly and snipping with them at the air above her head. He gazes at her, his eyes blazing with alarm. It looks like he is having second thoughts about entrusting his moustache – and his face – to Gillian's hands.

'Sit still, don't move.' She picks the first strand and cuts it off. It works. The feeling is liberating as layers of Michael's moustache hit the floor – liberating for Gillian. He feels bereaved.

She is going to introduce him to her parents and her daughter. She is taking him there for dinner tonight and this is the price he has agreed to pay.

'They need to be able to see your face, Almond,' she has said, 'to know who they're dealing with. That moustache of yours is like a bloody balaclava – you'd give them a heart attack if you walked in there wearing it.'

At first, he was prepared to agree to a small trim, but she wasn't happy with that. 'You must go with the times. The way you are . . . really, it's like you travelled in time straight from the seventies!'

The last strand of his moustache lands on his lap. He is fighting back tears as he looks at himself in the mirror, his face pox-marked with the remaining stubble.

Gillian attacks it with the razor. The pain he is experiencing is physical. It is as if someone was sawing off his right arm.

'Wow! Hello, stranger!' she exclaims when she is finished. 'You're not bad-looking, you know!' She kisses him on the lips, presumably to make him feel better, and she does, but only temporarily because then she pours some aftershave all over her hands and slaps it at the raw wound of his clean-shaven face.

Michael screams in agony. Both the cat and the dog scamper out of the kitchen in sheer terror. This relationship, he thinks when he half-recovers his wits, is going to be painful. He wonders what the hell he has got himself into.

THE END